PRAISE FO

"In a timeless tale that i   ⌐   erness
story, a mysterious Being pens and carves the fate of several
remote island villagers, just as the author, Karen Holmberg,
deftly uses her poetic ability to craft a riveting coming-of-age
journey of 'closings and openings.' *The Collagist* will appeal to
readers of all ages, and Romilly's quest for independence and
answers to family secrets will resonate with many young people.
An absolutely stunning debut."

—Tara Lynn Masih, award-winning author of *My Real Name Is
Hanna*

"*The Collagist* takes us to a timeless place of sea, sky and all
the natural beauty in between. Karen Holmberg's poetic prose
deftly navigates the blurry line between reality and the super-
natural. Themes of forgiveness and self-discovery resonate,
and Romilly's journey to claim her true self is all our journeys."

—Betty Culley, author of *Three Things I Know Are True* and *The
Name She Gave Me*

"Had I encountered this book when I was a young, insatiable
reader, I'm certain it would have been one of my favorites, but
even now I find myself hopelessly in love with its indelible im-
agery and delectable characters. Holmberg's alchemy of words
invites you to get lost in this story and never want to leave.
'There are many Beyonds,' indeed, and you will not forget *The
Collagist* or its meaningful mysteries."

—Diane Wald, author of *My Famous Brain* and *The Bayrose Files*

THE COLLAGIST

KAREN HOLMBERG

Fitzroy Books

Published by Fitzroy Books
An imprint of
Regal House Publishing, LLC
Raleigh, NC 27605
All rights reserved

https://fitzroybooks.com
Printed in the United States of America

ISBN -13 (paperback): 9781646034369
ISBN -13 (epub): 9781646034376
Library of Congress Control Number: 2023934869

Cover images and design by © C. B. Royal
Illustration by John Digby, as appears in the Dedication and Acknowledgments, used with kind permission of Joan Digby

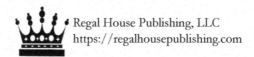
Regal House Publishing, LLC
https://regalhousepublishing.com

Printed in the United States of America

For my daughters, Ava and Lily

1

A Nick in the Sky

All afternoon Romilly had watched a fine, milk-pale line in the western sky, there and not there, oddly translucent like a mote in the eye. But unlike a mote, it didn't float or sink as she gazed. It was straight as a papercut, as if nicked in by the sharpest blade. Now and then Romilly's eye caught a slight dimming, as if something cast a shadow on the other side, then moved away. She watched her father anxiously—had he noticed? He kept his head bowed to his row. He rarely even glanced at her as she followed behind to rake the fallen wheat into bundles, braiding stems together swiftly to bind them into upright sheaves.

All the long workday, the nick grew gradually more visible as the sky's blue deepened, but it never changed in size or position. It wasn't disturbed when the day moon, resting on the horizon lightly as a bubble on milk, lifted off and away, grazing its left side. Swallows flew past it obliviously. Clouds drifted before it without the slightest hitch or snag.

Now the sun's fiery disk hung just above the horizon, and the dome of the sky was beginning to take on the dull lavender undertones of dusk. Romilly stood as tall as she could and stretched her arms overhead, arching her back to relieve the ache of stooping. Her hands felt enormous, fingers throbbing and thick from the chafing of coarse stems. As her eye sought the nick, she was startled to see a silvery point, like the very tip of a gigantic embroidery needle, emerge from it. At first, she thought it might be a shooting star, but she'd never heard of one in daylight, and it moved impossibly slowly. Deliberately, the point slowed to a pause as it reached the end of the slit; then it continued to cut horizonward at the same angle. When it touched the blue-tinged hills, the point shifted course and moved slowly left, following the horizon-line with precision. From the half-shorn field, Romilly followed the point of glinting silver as it neared the setting sun, until the white-hot blaze made her eyes water and her face wince. When the sun sank and her vision cleared of the molten afterimage, the silver point was gone.

Romilly followed her father home pensively, her heart thumping with dread, weighing whether to tell him what she'd seen. He'd swung his cradle scythe from dawn to sunset; his shoulders would ache, and his gaze would be full of falling stems. She had watched his limp linen shirt darken from abraded blue to almost black with sweat. At noon, he wouldn't eat the bread and cheese she brought him, but drank a pitcher of water at one pull, tipping it back in both trembling hands. As the sun neared the horizon, he had just finished a row. He stood a moment swaying lightly, then let go of the cradle scythe, which fell to the ground with a distant thud. He had stepped around it wearily, leaving it in the field—he who always carefully honed and oiled his blade each night. She would say nothing this evening, she decided. He had enough cares.

Two days ago, his brother had vanished, his sailboat seemingly swallowed by the sea on a tranquil, starlit night. In eighthmonth, her uncle always cast his nets far offshore where schools of sardine ran, pursued by mackerel and bluefish. When she'd met him that dawn on the wharf with a basket of muffins and a clay jar of tea, he had passed the backs of his fingers gently over her cheek in thanks, squinching his eyes like an affectionate cat, their private sign of love. It was her favorite time of day, the moments when sunrise still pinkened the crests of the swells and the dewdrops on the marsh grass beamed into the eye as bright as stars. He was the only uncle she had ever known, and childless. His partner had died of the sickness that took her mother ten years ago, making Romilly the closest thing to a daughter he was ever likely to have. In the evenings, she would sometimes visit him as he mended his nets before the fire. He would whistle the odd tune as his fingers sorted through netting, looking for torn places or untangling the dangling lead weights. When the tune stopped, he'd give her a smile and a slight bow from the waist, as if he were performing a concert. It was impossible not to smile back. Unlike her silent father, her uncle willingly scrolled out endless stories about the past—about village and family life in what seemed to Romilly like a golden era.

He and her father were from a large farming family that had raised market vegetables, apricots, and fields of strawberries on their rich acres. Her father was eldest, while her uncle was the youngest boy. The work was hard, he said—even the smallest children wiped dust off tomatoes and picked baskets of berries—but there were dances and midsummer feasts, and their father always paid them a little something for their work. A penny each twenty baskets of berries, he recalled. They were nine children (*Nine!* Romilly had gasped—when *two* were many now) and since they all had learned an instrument, they were in great demand for the village dances. What instruments? The accordion, the flute, the fiddle, the guitar, the mouth harp, the mandolin, the zither, and (here her uncle scratched the back of his head, pondered, counted on his fingers)—*ah yes, I'm forgetting my own instrument as a lad—I played alto recorder!* It was hard to imagine, but her father was famed for his skill growing tricky, delicate things, and had won fiddling competitions near and far, even across the Sound. This explained her discovery above a kitchen cupboard—a fragile violin, unstringed, the horsehair of the bow loosened and frayed—when she was looking for a place to hide her diary.

She had found the blank, vellum-covered journal on her mother's shelves. In it she collected all the memories and details she gleaned about the past—especially of her mother. In fact, in her mind she called it *the book of my mother*. She sometimes read through it from the beginning, wondering at how her handwriting had changed over the past few years from blocky printing to fluent cursive. She'd started it when she was nine, six years ago now, and it was nearly filled. It was her biggest secret, hidden because she knew her father would be disturbed by it. The niche above the cupboard was a place he would never think to look—finding the abandoned violin had convinced her of this. As deeply as she knew anything, she knew never to ask her father about the past, especially about her mother. Every time she had asked, there had been a tense, unpredictable silence, like the blank between a bolt of lightning and a clap of thunder. Her uncle, on the other hand, had guessed that she was writing down his family stories. When she shyly asked him to clarify a detail, he obliged with a fond, proud, approving smile. He sometimes called her *our young historian.*

That abandoned violin and an asparagus bed her father still tended faithfully with offerings of manure and straw were the only vestiges of a vibrant father she had one memory of: him tossing her in the air—the bliss of sudden weightlessness. She remembered grasping hold of his hair on either side of his laughing face, insisting *again.* That approachable father and that hopeful word had vanished when her mother died.

Now he raised only a few acres of wheat to sell and a field of oats and one of vegetables for their own use. Most of their land had gone back to briars and seedling pines. The orchard trees were wild knots of suckers and twigs, laced through with blackberry brambles. Each year the apricots were smaller, fewer, and harder, the flushed skin holding close to the pit. Except for her uncle, her father's sisters and brothers had left the village, moving inland or across the Sound where the winter weather was less harsh, or so her father said. But this made no sense: to live for generations prosperously, and then suddenly to leave? And the winter weather could be wild, but never bitter cold, and snow rarely lasted more than a day. Romilly and her father had always loved the lashing rain, or, rarer, the whirling snow of the winter storms. From her earliest years, she and her father would climb to the attic eaves to greet the arrival of the first gale, watching the rain walk off the sea in powerful bands that swept up the fields, finally dashing against the window. This was one of the few things that they still shared, but lately as she looked at his face, closed off and grim, she sensed they had different reasons for loving these tempests.

Her father and her uncle had been practically her only companions. She had no cousins in the village, no friends. They rarely heard from the older siblings who had moved away, making these aunts and uncles seem to her like vague legends. In school, she had somehow always been the eldest, far ahead of the others in reading and writing, but her teacher's approval was reserved, even begrudging. During Romilly's lessons, her teacher never leaned over her shoulder as she did with other students. Instead, she sat Romilly at the far end of the table, as if she still might transmit the sickness that had killed her mother, though there hadn't been another case these ten years. Her schoolmates were never openly cruel or mocking, but she knew their parents must have instructed them to stay away from her. Or perhaps these children just *knew*. Perhaps human beings had a way of detecting when someone is an outcast, the way animals seemed to know when one among them was sick.

The way she knew Micah. He was the only child in the village she felt connected to, though she had never even spoken a word to him. He didn't go to school, so she only saw him occasionally in the woods near her house, gathering firewood or trundling a load of nets in his barrow. When she met him on the path, he would always step off into the shadowy woods and wait for her to pass. Radiating from him like a signal whose code she knew—almost a shared language—was his loneliness and his outcast status. His left arm and the left side of his neck and jaw looked as if they had been dipped in melted wax, or as if seams of quartz ran up them. These scars didn't frighten her, and she couldn't think why they would make him an outcast. When she had asked her uncle about him, he told her the boy had been severely burned when his clothes caught fire, and his family had been unable to care for him. Or perhaps he himself did not care for his family. She thought this odd. Why would a child not care for his family? And besides, her uncle knew all the village business and never used the word 'perhaps' about anyone. At any rate, he explained, the boy had not been expected to live. But he *had* and resided in the harbormaster's attic. He did errands for the fishermen, gathered firewood to sell, and tended the small fleet of boats kept at the harbor for rent. The harbormaster was fond of him and had taught him to read and write and cipher so that he wouldn't have to attend the village school, where, unlike Romilly, he had been mocked and tormented. He knew the use of the compass and how to navigate by the stars and was already a passionate sailor. In fact, he was expected to go out to sea once he was seventeen.

Perhaps he had already gone; she'd not seen him all summer. As long as he appeared in the background of her daily life, she had not felt quite so alone. He gave her a standard of abandonment which she was far from reaching but could imagine. When their glances met, she knew there was someone who had an even smaller world.

Her world was her father, her uncle, and the healer Arra, their one close neighbor and an old family friend. Arra was the only person who regularly and unceremoniously gathered Romilly into her arms and kissed her cheeks, strong smacks of frank affection. Her uncle, who had an unreserved and joyful disposition, gave her a love as warm and nourishing as sunlight. Her father loved her deeply, she knew, but seemed afraid to express it. He seemed always to fear he'd lose her too.

Now her uncle had disappeared, *plucked off the face of the earth* she heard a fellow fisherman say, when she and her father had made their way to the wharf that dawn, hoping to see his sunny yellow boat.

2

THERE ARE MANY BEYONDS

Romilly awoke before sunrise and lay awhile listening to the silence of the house. The barred owls were sending their last low calls to each other from atop the trees, flute-like and mellow: *who-cooks-for-you, who-cooks-for-you-all*. On the table would be her bowl and spoon, the pot of oatmeal and the pitcher of cream. Her father would be in the barn by now, milking their two cows. Then she remembered the nick in the sky and the gleaming silver point travelling toward the horizon, and a chill spread through her belly. If she hurried, she could go out to the westernmost field before her father finished his chores. If her father saw her, she would claim she was checking the dryness of the wheat shocks. She yanked her dress off the chair and stepped into it, staggering slightly. In the kitchen, she spooned up three mouthfuls of oatmeal in rapid succession, chewing and forcing them down as she ran out of the house and along the path to the edge of the wheat field, the dew cooling her bare feet.

The line was unchanged. Where the silver point had seemed to be engulfed by the setting sun, the slit merely ended. The line in the sky now formed a sail-like shape as it traveled toward the horizon, then angled back, following the ripple of hills. All was motionless as a painting; even the leaves on the nearest trees hung with a glassy stillness. Then, just above the horizon at the sail's point, as if something was pressing from the other side, she observed a kind of bulge or stretching. A sharpness like a gigantic bird's beak burst through. The sky seemed to draw quite close, to be touchable, in fact, as the metallic beak pried at the point. The beak probed further, then lay flat like a silvery slat before the sky, drawing the point of sky with it toward—the *Beyond*. She felt freezing cold, as if all her world's heat had been sucked through that opening. The metal object was curved below, like a two-dimensional boat, rimmed in bright silver as if freshly honed—it was a blade, she realized, but of gargantuan size. As the blade lifted out and away the point of pale sky, a massive slab the dull rosy-tan of an apricot came into view, grasping the flap. With a shock she recognized that the paler plate at the end, ridged like wind-swept sand, was a gigantic thumbnail. It all seemed strangely close.

Something, someone was pulling open her world. Swift as a lightning flash the idea came into her mind that perhaps this was the Creator. Her neighbor Arra used to tell stories about a being who had created their world, but even Arra reported them skeptically. This, without question, was a Being. From beyond the flap, she heard a full, dull, and distant roaring like gusts of wind high in a tree canopy, and felt on her face a humid waft so powerful and sudden, it stopped her own breath short. When she could inhale again, she realized this wind smelled familiar and weirdly bodily—like tea when you lift the teapot's lid and a buffet of steam dampens your face, or like the balmy, fermented-barley exhalation of an enormous draft horse. For long moments Romilly squinted at the sky, her hair blown around her face, torn between the instinct to back up into the sheltering woods and the desire to walk out into the middle of the wheatfield—to give this Being a chance to see her. But then the flap slowly descended again; the thumbnail, at the last instant, slid out and away. She could hear a giant friction—like steady wind or distant crashing waves—from the other side and could see that the opening was now perfectly sealed again.

Her heart felt stretched open, larger than she had ever suspected it could be. She lay her hand over her chest and watched the beating of her heart lift her hand, the way a strong knock on a door shivers it visibly. But she was not terrified, she realized. She had a sense, in fact, that something had come to pass that she had always, somehow, expected. What she felt was an aching emptiness as the full measure of her loneliness broke upon her. She had seen something she couldn't share with *anyone*, ever, certainly not her father, not even with Arra. She couldn't risk disbelief, or the uproar of belief. Or even worse—being prevented from seeing this Being again.

When the day's work was done—the bowls and cups washed, wiped dry, and put away, her father dozing in his chair by the fire—Romilly picked up the oil lamp and walked noiselessly into the snug sitting room behind the fireplace. She shut the door behind her. The exposed brick of the chimney radiated the fire's warmth into the room. This had always been the coziest room in the house. It was where she had been born. It was also where her mother had been moved in her illness to isolate her, but Romilly refused to see it as a sickroom. It had always been her mother's special domain, where her stately secretary stood along one wall, the grain of the wood banded and inner-lit as a tiger's pelt. Behind the glass-paned doors were the only books in the house, some of them immensely old. Within the drawers were letters written in the finest crow-quill cursive in a language Romilly didn't understand, a language her mother had said was of the 'Old World.'

When her mother lay ill, Romilly's father had allowed her in the sickroom only once, when her mother insisted. To her chest she held four oval miniatures, sheltering them under her palm. One at a time, she held them out to Romilly. *These are portraits of my family's women, my mother, her mother, and my great-grandmother*, she had said, *all artists and scholars*. What is an artist? Romilly had asked. *An artist*, her mother had said, *is a healer. An artist makes whole. They will always be in my secretary, should you need them.* She was only five, but she remembered.

She set down the lamp on her mother's sewing table and raised the wick to brighten the room. Then she perched on the edge of her mother's chair, drew open the desk's surface with both hands, and pulled forth the miniatures. She had done this so often, she felt she'd memorized every detail. Sometimes she traveled backward in time, from her mother's face in the oval portrait on the wall, to her grandmother's, then her great-grandmother's, then her great-great-grandmother's face. It was strange how the portraits captured them all at about the same age— they had just entered womanhood yet were tinged with girlhood still. Sometimes she went forward in time, beginning with her great-great-grandmother, her neck cupped in a high ruffled collar like a jonquil's pale trumpet, ending with her own face in her mother's silver hand-mirror. These women had different features—her mother's hair had been a rich auburn like Romilly's own, whereas her grandmother had been quite fair haired. Whereas her mother, grandmother, and great-grandmother had gray eyes, her great-great-grandmother's eyes were so dark, you could not make out the pupils, and her hair was raven black. But all these women shared an expressiveness of mouth and lips, a glance in which a tender smile hid, and eyebrows finely arching as a moth's antennae. It seemed strange indeed that she could have inherited her great-great-grandmother's eyebrows.

Romilly looked at her mother's portrait and sleeked a finger along her own brow. Her mother's words—*an artist makes whole*—confused her more than ever, now that her world's wholeness had been ruptured by a Being. She felt a wave of dizziness as she imagined her life held, even now, in the hand that she glimpsed that morning. It was like the sensation of being on land after a day's sail, when everything still feels as if it's moving in all directions. And yet, nothing was changed. If that hand was holding her world, it must always have held it. Her mother's words—*an artist is a healer*—confused her too. No amount of nursing skill, none of Arra's healing arts, could save her mother. These were her mother's last words to her, a precious use of air. Romilly remembered standing outside her mother's door, forbidden to enter, hearing her cough and her ragged, shallow, throttled breathing. How was Romilly to see the wholeness of things? Her life felt plundered and faded, as if its truth had once been committed to paper, but some cos-

mic hand had taken up an eraser and rubbed at it—rubbed and
rubbed until all that was left were the pale traces on an abraded
surface. Her mother had died before she could give Romilly the
knowledge she needed now. She had no one to guide her, no
one to talk to about what she'd seen.

She stood and opened the glass doors of the bookcase, then
lifted the lamp to shed its light on the spines, looking for help
among the titles. Some were in the language of the Old World,
the lettering pointy and intricate. Because she couldn't read this
language, she had rarely opened these books. She tipped one
forward now, its body heavy as a brick, but cushioned and pliant
as a saddle. The leather spine was stamped in gold. The cover
was marbled paper that made her think of a pheasant's feathers,
scalloped with iridescent gold and royal blue and deep forest
green. Age and handling had varnished the cover and abraded
the corners so that thin wooden boards showed through. When
she opened the book, she was dismayed to find that the body
had separated from the cover entirely. The cords used to stitch
the folded pages together at the spine were exposed, smocked
like the breast of her nightdress. Reassembling the book, she
cradled it in one hand and strummed through the pages with
the other. From the midpoint, a faded red satin ribbon pro-
truded, notched into points like a young snake's tongue. When
she opened to this page, she saw a portrait under creased and
yellowed tissue. Lifting this, she found a young girl who might
have been her twin, a girl with the same loose, auburn-brown
curls and wideset, wave-gray eyes. She was pictured with a kestrel on her wrist, embroidered roses clustering the white cuff
of her gauntlet. Around her neck, on a cord, she wore a delicate
pair of scissors, very like the sharp silver pair her mother would
use for sewing. Under the portrait, in fine italic printing, was
the name *Yllimor*.

But that, she realized with a shock, was the mirror image of
her own name. And the girl was eerily familiar. She compared
the image in the book to the miniatures still laid out on the desk,
plumbing the faces for evidence of this girl. In her great-grand-

mother's face, she found this girl. Why had her mother named her, in a strange, mirrory way, after this ancestor? She studied the girl again. Had her mother inherited the scissors from her? Romilly knew where they were kept—in the drawer of her mother's sewing cabinet. She crossed the room with the open book pressed against her chest and pulled the drawer out. There were the scissors, identical to the ones in Yllimor's portrait, down to the black satin cord they were strung on.

3

THE INGRES

Romilly woke in the darkness, startled by a sudden sensation that she was lying in the hold of a ship that had drifted out into the open ocean, far from her own life. Then she remembered how her world had expanded the day before. She wondered if the great Being would open the sky again. As soon as she saw the first streaks of light in the east, she crept out of the house and ran down the path toward the wheat field, the hem of her nightdress growing limp with dew. The robins were already awake, calling to each other from the high canopy of trees, the quavering notes ringing in her ears with aching sweetness. In the middle of the field, she stopped abruptly. The horizon, so close as to seem touchable when the sail-like flap was lifted, now revealed its distance. The base of the hills was defended by a shadow-colored bristle of forest that refined into a sunlit, milky green fleece and then a blue-tinged gauze near the summits. She had never traveled even so far as those foothills and had no idea what was beyond them. There are so many Beyonds, she thought. Any place one hasn't been is a Beyond. The future is a Beyond. Even the past is a sort of backward Beyond. Suddenly she thought of her uncle and his unknown fate. He, too, had been engulfed in the Beyond, past everything but the imagination. For she could easily conjure multiple scenes of terror and disaster. She knew what death was—the ultimate Beyond.

But why should she think of him as dead, only the fourth day after his disappearance! There was a peculiar readiness in her village to accept the disappearance of things. Why had none of the fishing folk searched for him? Why had her father not rigged their own sailboat and set out to find his brother? All at once she wondered what would happen if *she* disappeared. Would her world let her go so easily? A churning emotion, compounded of frustration and determination and something unfamiliar, caught hold of her in a sudden propelling rush. It was anger, she thought, astonished. She took one last, scanning sweep of the sky. Its milky depths were beginning to darken, and she saw, or thought she saw, the faintest scar where the nick had been. But she couldn't tell if this was actual seeing or just vivid remembering.

Back home, she found her father crouching before the fireplace, blowing the coals alive and feeding them from a handful of curled wood shavings. He looked over his shoulder in surprise when she entered the door and stepped decisively forward, smoothing her nightdress down over her thighs with damp palms. She waited until he lay on the wood and hung the pot of water to heat over the fire, and then she spoke.

"I want us to search for Uncle."

His back and neck stiffened perceptibly as she continued.

"He could be sick. He could be adrift or have landed some-where—on one of the islands, for instance—and be unable to set out for home. We can't just wait for him to reappear on the wharf!"

Still, he was silent.

"We have our sailboat. We can rig it and set out this morning with the outgoing tide. I will pack a noon meal, and we can return with the tide before dark. Please, Father."

He stood and walked to the open door, where the scythe leaned against the frame, sharpened, oiled, and ready for the day. He grasped hold of the curve of the wooden cradle, worn pale by the friction of his hands.

"Please, Father! Let's not go out to the field."

"It could be what we find is *worse* than not knowing, daughter. I know what the sea can do to a body. I know what the sun can do."

"Father, to me there is *nothing* worse than not knowing."

He looked down at his hands, gripping and releasing the handle of the scythe. Then he looked up at Romilly under his brows. "I will search for my brother, but I must go alone."

Romilly thought of their boat, a milk-white, light-bodied sloop sleek as a gull, its only decoration the gilded script at its stern: *Ingres*, her mother's name. It had sat at its mooring since her mother's death. Her father tended her, touching up her paint, revarnishing the golden wood of the mast and tiller as needed, but he never sailed her.

"It will be far easier to manage the sails and tiller if I come with you, Father." She remembered, abruptly, what it felt like as a small child to be placed in the tense cup of the mainsail, feeling it vibrate with the captured power of a steady wind. She remembered the wild joy as the boat heeled under a sudden gust. But the last time she had sailed was when she and her father brought her mother's body back across the Sound to her people, to be buried in their family plot. Her uncle, the most experienced sailor in her father's family, had accompanied them on that voyage that seemed to go on forever, the wind muted and confused, constantly shifting direction. This is what her father couldn't bear to face, she realized.

Her father said nothing. But after they had eaten their oatmeal and had their tea, he disappeared into the attic, returning with a carefully scrolled and folded canvas in his arms. He spread the sails out on the kitchen's plank floor, examining on hands and knees for tears and mouse damage, and carefully coiling up the lines. Stored for ten years, the canvas and lines were stiff and musty with disuse, but intact. Gathering them in his arms, he moved toward the door and paused there, looking down at his feet a moment, then said, "We'll need water, bread, and cheese. And plenty of bandages. And spirits." He paused. "And something to make a splint, and an extra set of warm clothes and quilts for you, me—and him." And then he shifted the bundled sails to his shoulder and set off down the path toward the wharf.

❧

A half hour later, Romilly was wheeling a heaping barrow toward the docks. The sun was barely up, the first rays of light piercing the blue shadows between trees and lighting the edges of the trunks with a mist of gold. As she passed the healer's cottage, she paused. Someone should know where they are going, she realized. Arra was surely awake; she often set her decocting beakers bubbling in her giant fireplace during the cool of the early morning. But what if Arra tried to persuade her not to go? She thought of Arra's cornflower-blue gaze, a young gaze in a face weather-chapped and lightly seamed around the eyes from laughing, and from gathering herbs in the sun. No, she would be the last to talk Romilly out of searching for her uncle. Arra was fearless. Daily, Arra wandered miles through dense forest to gather herbs for medicines. She had set forth in a rare twelve-month blizzard to bring Romilly herself into the world, somehow sensing that the snow had brought on her mother's labor. This was one of Romilly's cherished stories, one Arra ritually retold on her birthdays. Romilly paused in front of the door, then knocked, the sound hollow and tentative. But Arra opened the door instantly, as if she'd been lying in wait behind it. She held a corked and wax-sealed bottle in her hand.

"For your journey," she said, holding the bottle toward her. "A tonic in case of sunstroke, but good for any kind of fever. And tell your father not to worry about your cows—I will milk them for you and turn them out to pasture."

"How did you know?" Romilly asked, wonderingly.

"I know things," Arra said with playful mysteriousness, a distant look in her eyes. She thrust out her chin and tugged a side lock of Romilly's hair gently. She set down the bottle on the window ledge and leaned back against the doorjamb, her arms crossed over her breast, scrutinizing Romilly's face and body.

"You are growing very like your mother. And I see you've

x

found her embroidery scissors." She pointed with her chin to Romilly's chest, where the silver scissors hung by the black satin cord.

"I thought we might need something to trim bandages," she said, startling herself with the determined, practical tone of her voice. She had decided to bring the scissors as she was about to leave her house, when a sense of an unknown, uncertain future made her want to hide like a small child in a closet or cupboard—some snug, safe place. Instead, she had gone to her mother's sitting room and stood before her portrait. Her mother held the embroidery scissors lightly against her lap, her gracefully tapering fingers through the eyeholes. She thought having something of her mother's would give her courage, so she opened the sewing chest and lifted them out, settling the cord around her neck.

"I...know...things," Arra said again, meditatively, parting her lips as if to tell Romilly a secret. Instead, she let out a sigh. "Actually, I saw your father pass by with his arms full of sails, so it was easy to guess. I'm glad to see him going after his brother. It was a good idea you had." She continued. "But you know, your uncle's not lost."

"He's not?" Romilly cried out. "How do you know? And how did you know it was my idea?"

"I told you; I know things." And then she explained how, gathering garlic mustard on the wet banks of the stream's mouth, she had looked across the flats and seen his boat pulled up on the shore of the closest island. The sails had been lowered and neatly rolled. He had not merely drifted there.

"Now, he might be sick," she added, "but he's definitely not lost."

"Why in the world didn't you say anything, Arra?" Romilly groaned.

"I was planning to say something today. I was hoping your father would bestir himself first. It's a soul sickness, this resignation to losing. How much must life take away from you before you fight to keep what you have," she said garrulously,

as if she spoke to him. "Of course," she continued more reasonably, "sometimes we must let go, sometimes we lose people.
But you, Romilly." And here she took the girl's face between her
hands, pressing her roughened thumbs against her cheekbones.
"You're more like your mother. You are what her people called
a 'worldwidener.' Such folks always expand horizons, but never
lose touch with themselves. Your father must keep good care
of you, while not protecting you overmuch. Tell him I said so."
She dropped her hands. "Now go!"

Romilly trotted down the path, hunching her back to force
the rickety barrow before her.

"You forgot the tonic," Arra cried after her, and Romilly
set down the legs of the barrow and dashed back, whisking
the bottle out of Arra's hand. A little of the fluid leaked out
onto her palm, and she felt a tingle grow there, probably due
to wintergreen or some other herb Arra had used. But she was
reminded of the cooling tingle she had felt along her skin when
she saw the sail of sky lift up. Could the Being she'd glimpsed
see her even now? Did they already know how the journey
would turn out?

At the wharf, she found her father readying the sloop. He
was hoisting the mainsail, which flapped and slithered loosely
around him in the rising wind. Before he noticed her, she set
down the barrow and tucked the cord and scissors under her
bodice. Then she brought the barrow alongside the dock and
handed down to him the jug of water, the handled basket con-
taining the loaves of bread and the wheel of cheese, the roll
of bandages she'd made from their store of plain cheesecloth,
and the bottle of spirits. Holding Arra's tonic to her chest, she
dropped down lightly into the boat, her knees bent to absorb
the shock. The boat rocked gently, the water kissing the sides
with a delicious crinkle.

"What's this," her father asked, as she held the bottle out to
him. He grasped it by the neck and turned it to the light. It was
the rusty brown of cedar bark, and murky.

"A tonic Arra gave to me—she said it was good in case of sunstroke and fever."

"Ah. Clever woman. How did you happen to see her?"

"Well, someone should know what we are about, you know, where we are going," Romilly blurted out, hoping he would have no more questions. Two days ago, she would never have described herself as a person who kept secrets from her father, but now, for some reason, she didn't want to disclose what she'd learned from Arra. Why raise hope, she thought. And what if Arra had mistaken another person's boat for her uncle's? But deep inside she knew Arra would never make such a mistake.

"She suggested," she volunteered awkwardly, "that we look around the backsides of the islands in case he took sick and landed there. Oh! And she said not to worry about our cows— she will milk them for us and let them out to pasture." As she spoke, she felt the blood rise into her face, but her father didn't seem to notice her discomfort. In fact, he didn't really seem to be listening to her at all. He almost cut off her last words with his own.

"Daughter, I want to make it clear that if we find his boat, on an island or anywhere else, you are to stay aboard, you are not to accompany me until I first find out how bad he—it—is. If he's sick—or worse—I'll not risk you. We will sail back for help, but I cannot afford—" He couldn't finish the sentence. "Promise me." Without waiting for her response, he strode toward the stern and began to unwind the rope from the wharf's massive iron cleat. She saw him blot the corner of his eye on his inner sleeve. Romilly crawled over the cabin toward the bow and, when he signaled her with a wave of his hand, uncleated the bow rope. Under tension and sun baked for many years, the rope was stiff and difficult to coil neatly. Her heart, both anxious and excited, heaved and squeezed simultaneously. She had not promised—she had not actually promised him anything! What was she coming to?

The passage out of the harbor was slow, the light wind loosely filling the sail which puckered and dimpled like a slack and overrisen bowl of dough. But as the sun rose the wind rose too and filled the sails taut. The sloop began to move through the water as steadily as if invisible horses were harnessed to it. The fishing boats had sailed out hours before under starlight; only one or two small skiffs moved toward open water in the distance, the rising sun glinting on pin-fine oars. The tide seemed suspended between drawing out and coming in, and Romilly felt the keel's centering strength cutting through the water with little resistance. Her father turned into the wind, and they came about to tack toward the lighthouse. Seated near the bow, she took up the slack in the foresail. The water made a satisfying crinkling and lapping sound as the hull pushed through, and Romilly was half-mesmerized, looking over the side as the water folded and stretched and broke into pennants of spray. Just then, a dolphin appeared portside and rode the bulge of wave forced up by the bow, its entire body gleaming with joy. When it arced out of the water it would look right into her eyes, the corners of its mouth turned up as if smiling.

As they passed between the lighthouse and the stone jetty, the currents intensified, strengthened by the depth of the channel and the draw of the open sea, and the swells gave way to shorter but more frequent waves that thudded dully against the hull. She looked behind her at the harbor, miniaturized by distance. She could see their farm, a golden handkerchief draped upon the drab hill. Buildings encrusted the edge of the harbor like a line of barnacles, white and silvery gray. The boats at mooring looked no larger than seagulls, except for the harbormaster's dark tug, which dozed alongside the seawall like a great-breasted loon with its head tucked under its wing.

She was looking at her past, she realized, a sealed-off time she couldn't return to. Something was about to happen, as big a watershed in her life as her mother's death. Startled, she thought how nothing, not even the tiniest event, not even her grasping of the foresail rope, could ever unhappen or ever be undone. When she turned back to face the open water, the lighthouse beacon, day-fire pale, beamed full into her eye. Soon they glided past it, and before them lay only the empurpled back of the sea, shrugging with great rolling swells. Romilly got to her knees and carefully crawled back to the cockpit of the boat to join her father, who had signaled he was ready to come about.

They tacked to port and followed the coastline north. Romilly could make out the three islands like a cluster of moles on the face of the water, their eastern sides fleeced with fire as the morning sun burned off the lingering mist. Romilly hadn't been to these islands since she was a small child, when, in midsummer, the farming folk would gather on the island nearest to shore. Some came by boat, while others hiked the five miles through the woods to pole across on large rafts, or, if the tide allowed, waded across the flats. Her mother was one of the women who, by tradition, swam the deep channel between the shore and the side of the island, emerging red, laughing, and shivering, her arms crossed in a hug over her contracted belly. At low tide, the revelers would gather on the flats to dig for clams, while others set gillnets for the striped bass that pursued the schools of bunker into the channel. She remembered her father and her uncle, their legs plastered in grayish mud up to the thighs, hauling a writhing sack of fish along the flats to the island's narrow beach, where they raked the bonfire out into a bed of coals. This was a holiday for the women; the men prepared the entire meal, and the women lay about sunning themselves or playing tag and mother-may-I with the children. Romilly and her mother would lie together on a sun-warmed raft, and her mother would sing her songs in the language of her birth, songs that sounded the way she thought mermaid song would sound. In fact, she had had a secret conviction that her mother was really a mermaid. She surfaced from this shimmering dream of the past to find her father's eyes upon her face.

"I am going to steer wide of the islands to see if there are any signs of disaster near the Hammock," he said. The Hammock, a bar of sand brought in by the ocean currents, was just below the water level at low tide. Many newcomers to their harbor who did not watch their maps had discovered it in an abrupt grounding which smashed keels and dashed sailors overboard. But her uncle knew the entrance to the harbor, indeed all the features of the bay surrounding them, as well as a parent's face, thought Romilly as she watched her father's face and noted a closed-off quality, a reservoir of speculation and—she sensed it—dread. For the first time she considered that he had his own theories of his brother's disappearance.

"If he had run aground, surely his boat would have been seen by one of the other fishermen," she ventured.

"Of course, daughter, but something might have washed up or caught upon the Hammock. That often happens when the tide turns." She noticed that he kept his eyes averted from the islands. Again, she felt his fear and knew as certainly as if she could touch it—he had some knowledge he was keeping from her.

"Father," she began tentatively, "when was the last time you saw Uncle?"

He glanced at her quickly, then looked back at the water. "Two days before he disappeared, I met him on the wharf at dawn. He was coming in from night fishing."

"And did he seem his usual self?"

"Maybe a bit more excited than usual—you know, he's always been a bit of a dreamer." Romilly knew exactly what her father meant; he called anyone who didn't keep their head strictly down to the work at hand a dreamer. If you had a habit of noticing the beauty of the clouds, or if you stopped your work to wonder at the identity of an unusual butterfly, you were a dreamer. Her father had called Romilly a dreamer many times. She knew he didn't mean it harshly, but simply as a way of pointing out a quality he claimed not to have time for, though her uncle had once told her that her father had used to draw and paint. Paint! She couldn't conceive of it. Like his music, this part of him seemed buried with her mother across the Sound.

"What was he excited about—did he say?"

Her father blew out his cheeks, then sucked them in and

seemed to be chewing gently at them. "No, nothing specific. He said he was out in the middle of the bay and the moon was rising out of the ocean, larger than he had ever seen, and he was all in ecstasy about the path of light on the water. I said he shouldn't allow himself to be distracted by such things, alone and all—that he needed his eyes to watch for tangling lines."

Romilly saw in her mind's eye the great golden spill of light as the moon pushed up through the mist in the far distance, the path of fresh twinkling silver upon the water as it rose. Like her uncle, she would want to follow and follow and follow it...

Was this what her father feared? That her uncle had allowed his attention to be distracted by beauty, and perished for it—a careless, avoidable death? She didn't think so. She wondered what else her uncle had said, what could have frightened her father so much that he seemed almost reluctant to find his brother. It couldn't just be a rhapsody about a beautiful moon. For the dozenth time she realized the sheer impossibility of telling her father what she had seen above their wheat field. The suppressed panic she'd always detected in him was even stronger since his brother disappeared. It had always frightened her, perhaps the more because he'd always attempted to cover it up. And she always pretended not to know it was there. She was weary of pretending.

"One more tack and we should be heading straight for the Hammock," her father said, interrupting her train of thought in which the unaccustomed spark of anger pulsed again. They came about, the sail luffing and folding over on itself until the wind filled it. As the boat surged forward in the steady wind, the scrubbing of water against the keel rose in pitch until it sounded like the lowest note of a violin. In the distance, Romilly could see the torsion of the water as it shallowed. The swells broke against the broad back of sand, then shoved over it in shallow, foamy streams. Already she could see that there was no debris or wreckage there. Her father allowed the boat to glide by the Hammock without comment, but once they had passed it, his lips tightened. For the first time, he looked toward the islands, nestling like velvet-covered buttons against the sloping coastline.

They came about and turned directly for the islands. The sun was now midway in the eastern sky. It's slanting rays lit up the black-green pines of the coastline with a silvery mist, behind which she could see bulges and creases, like the folds in a cow's neck when she reaches to lick her flank. Here and there she could see a glint of window and a shorn patch in the forest where someone had cleared a path to the water or created a breathing space around their cottage to plant a garden. That's how she thought of it—breathing space. Romilly loved the forest, but she was not a forest person, she realized. Her eyes were always drawn to wide open places; even now, her eyes sought out the quilt of paler green or golden fields beyond the forest. She even preferred the blindingly bright ocean horizon to the view of dense timber, each trunk so large that several people holding hands could barely encircle it, but glinting fine as needles in the distance. The forest was mysterious and stubborn, like a closed-off face, like a secret. She felt its power, and instinctively looked toward her father who was, she realized, scanning the forest too.

"Father," she asked, "among our family, did any live in the forest?"

She expected a curt *no*, so was surprised as he settled near the tiller and began a cautious reply.

"As a rule, no," he said, pausing. "We are farming people and crave open land. But your mother's aunt—your great aunt—partnered with a man from across the Sound who worked the woods. She rather disappeared from the family after that. It was said this forest man was a distant relative on my side."

"What do you mean, disappeared?"

"Well, she never came into the village after her marriage—we always had to go to *her*. Midsummers, when we had those festivities on the islands," and here he assumed the offhand manner with which he protected his dearest memories, "she was the one who cleared the trail through the woods, made ready the rafts, and ensured there was plenty of firewood gathered on the beach. She and her partner had a cottage on that island, in fact, and spent the summers there."

"What did they do for a living?" Romilly asked.

"Well, their house in the woods was on a wide stream, so her partner set up a sawmill. Our house was built of the lumber he milled," he added. "And that's about all I know." He motioned her to take the tiller so that he could snug in and re-cleat the mainsail lines, though the sails were perfectly filled. Her mind raced to get hold of a casual question that might induce him to continue. He had delivered to her, unexpectedly, the largest chunk of information about her family in recent memory. She fixed each detail in her memory so that on return she could ask Arra about this forest man. *What am I, your oracle?* Arra would say when Romilly brought her some dense nugget of history to explicate.

It occurred to Romilly that this cottage must still be on the island, though in her childhood she had never seen it.

"Was Uncle close to this aunt and the forest man?" she asked. "I mean, did he ever visit them aside from this summer gathering?"

"Yes," her father said brusquely, then seemed again to relent, settling back and feeling the smoothness of the tiller with his thumb. "He used to spend a month with your great aunt every summer, just after the festival. He'd stay on at their island cottage to take art lessons from her, and help her partner mill the wood that seasoned over the winter. That was, until their house burned."

"What? Their house burned down? How?"

"How would I know, child? I wasn't there. I heard from the townsfolk that it burned," he said. "And now, that's enough questions, daughter. I need to decide whether to come between the shore and the island or to go around the back." But Romilly could see that he was already heading for the shore.

"Is the tide high enough to enter the channel?" she asked.

"It should be, if we come on slow and careful—the Egg isn't

visible." The Egg was the name given to an immense boulder of granite that had somehow migrated from the shore to the end of the channel, as if to mark the beginning of the silt-filled cove between island and shore. At dead low tide, this boulder was completely exposed on the mudflats. A crack wide enough for a child to climb inside ran midway through the boulder, and Romilly remembered her mother laughing with excitement as she slid her slender body into the crevice, reaching down to help Romilly climb inside with her. At high tide, the boulder was covered by water and barely visible, glowing a greenish gold under the surface. So long as the boulder was submerged, a boat could safely be sailed into the cove between shore and island, though you still had to keep a sharp watch and steer clear of it, or the keel might be damaged.

Romilly scanned the unbroken, lightly brimming water in the island's shelter. And then her eyes focused beyond it, and she saw a marigold-yellow boat pulled up near shore. Her uncle's—she was sure it was his! He was the only fisherman who had painted his boat such cheerful color. But something was wrong—it lay on its side, resting on its keel. It ought to be anchored out in the channel where the water was deep at any tide.

Just as Romilly stepped onto the deck, grasping the mast and turning to shout to her father, their boat came to an abrupt and shuddering halt as if it had reached the end of a chain. Romilly pitched forward like an arrow from a bow. She felt the cleats gouge the front of her thighs as she slithered over the gunwales and plunged into the water. When she opened her eyes, all she could see was the filmy layers of her skirt swirling around her. She couldn't tell what was up or down, but as she turned about underwater, she saw a diffuse sphere of fire above her and swam for it clumsily, her skirt twisting around her legs.

When she reached the side of the boat, her father, knocked flat by the boom, was just staggering to his feet.

"Romilly, thank God," he said hoarsely. The boat was motionless, as if at anchor. Romilly let herself slip beneath the surface. Pressing her skirts to her thighs, she opened her eyes underwater and looked down to see the gold glow of a stony platform looming beneath her. She could just touch it with the tips of her toes.

Surfacing again, she wiped the water out of her eyes. "Father, it's the Egg—it has somehow fallen open in two parts and the keel is wedged between them." Her father reached overboard and grasped her under the arms. Blood from his head fell onto the neck of her dress. She kicked as he heaved her up until her waist hung over the side of the boat. Then she wriggled aboard.

"Daughter, are you hurt?"

Romilly peeled the skirt and underskirt off her thighs, where raised, white-edged red bars of bruises were already purpling. "I just have some bruising where I hit the cleats." Her father pressed a palm over one of the injuries and shook his head in despair.

"I should have suspected this—I should have known the tide was not near high!" he cried out in anguish.

"Father, how could you have known the Egg had fallen open? The important thing is—we've found Uncle." He wiped the blood out of his eyes with his sleeve and took a quick, apprehensive glance at the shore, then reached for the boat hook. Leaning far out, he probed the water, hoping to pry the boat off the rock. "Can't quite reach it," he muttered, dropping the boat hook with a clatter. He pivoted to uncleat the rope and haul the mainsail down, winding the rope about the loosely gathered canvas. As soon as the sail was secured, he scrambled out to the bow to throw out the anchor. He stood at the bow and tugged the line to make sure the anchor had engaged, then snubbed the line around the bow cleat. The stern of the boat began to swing around counterclockwise in the current, as if magnetically drawn to the island. He stood a moment to look at the shore where his brother's boat lay on its side like a great, wounded animal. He unclenched his hands and began to pull off his shirt.

"Wait, Father, we need to tend your head."

He came toward her reluctantly, almost sheepishly. "It's only that I can't see, daughter." The cut passed through the tail of his eyebrow; his browbone and forehead were badly bruised. As she touched the cut gingerly, the edges separated, but she saw that it wasn't quite so deep as she had feared. She knew from Arra that wounds such as this often needed to be stitched, but she hadn't thought to bring a needle and thread. All she had was the roll of gauze, which she fetched. Dipping an end in the seawater, she sponged the blood off the cut and bound his head round and round tightly to keep the wound's edges together. Tentatively, she reached under her bodice, then withdrew her mother's scissors on their cord, but as she prepared to snip the bandage her father held up his hand to stop her.

"You are wearing them now?" he asked.

"Is that wrong of me?" she asked, uncertainly.

"Nay, daughter, I am glad you have them at hand."

She snipped the gauze and tucked the end under, then surveyed his face. He looked shaken and waxy-pale, almost as pale as the gauze wound about his head, but with a tinge of sallow yellow. A few spots of bright-red blood were already seeping through the gauze. She was struck by how much he'd seemed to age just in the past week, how thin and almost translucent his face seemed.

"I've got to swim for shore, Romilly, and I meant what I said back home. You'll stay on board, make sure the anchor holds, make sure the boat isn't taking on water. I'm going to dive down to check the keel, and to see if the boat is sound enough to sail. If not, we'll walk back through the woods. Once I know the boat is stable, I'm going to swim to the island to find my brother. And if he is in any shape to be moved, we are going to take him home, one way or another."

Romilly looked at her uncle's boat, with its neatly furled sails and the anchor rope plainly visible, stretching from the bow to the upper edge of the beach where the sand was firm and stony. It seemed unlikely he was sick. If he wanted to return to the village, why wouldn't he simply sail back home? Was it possible, she thought, that he *wanted* to go away from us, wanted *not* to be found?

"Let me check the keel, Father. As much as you can, you should keep your head above water until your cut stops bleeding. Blood is coming through your bandage even now." Her father felt the gauze on his brow, then looked down at his red and sticky fingertips. She saw him consider.

And then she felt the coolness at her feet. A sheet of water was flowing forward toward the stern, eddying as more water joined it. The hull was nearly filled. Her father and she looked for a moment into each other eyes. Without a word, she packed the food, water, and medical supplies into a pitch-sealed basket, leaving behind the bulky clothes and quilts. She quickly stepped out of her dress, lay the dress over the supplies, and stepped off the edge of the boat, dropping into the water like a blade. Surfacing, she reached up to take the basket from her father and held it bobbing before her until he entered the water, then pushed it toward him so he could use it as a float to keep his head up. He began to kick, pushing the basket before him.

She swam ahead underwater like a fish. When she surfaced to take a breath, she saw that the *Ingres*'s gunwales were only inches above water. Her mother's boat was going to sink and settle down on the mudflats where it would be exposed at low tide, scummed and flagged with green sea lettuce as if abandoned. *I have not abandoned you,* she whispered to the boat as, burdened to the brim, she slowly rolled to the side. The mast pointed accusingly at her, and the sail and its captured air floated on the water like a great blister. Her father had not seen. He paddled steadily toward shore, kicking vigorously, pushing the basket on ahead. She resumed swimming with steady strokes, treading water at intervals to see if she could touch. When her toes grazed the sand, she turned to face her father. The *Ingres* had disappeared entirely.

He could see her gazing beyond him.

"Is she gone?" he asked.

"Yes, Father," she said, then bit the sides of her tongue hard so as not to cry.

"We'll recover her, daughter. Once the tide goes out, we

can see what the damage is. I'll have several hours to make the repair."

Yet with what? Romilly thought. A boat can't be bandaged like a head. At that thought, she looked to see if her father's bandage had gotten wet. There was an island the size and redness of a plum in the white cloth. But the bandage was dry and in place. As her father staggered past her, she plucked her dress from the basket, drying her face with it as she stepped out of the water. She stepped through the skirt, the cloth clinging to her wet skin, then wriggled and shimmied into it. It was a clear, hot day, and she knew the dress would dry quickly. When she looked for her father, she saw he had waded over to her uncle's boat where it lay on its side. Looking down on the craft, he shook his head, his hands clenched into fists.

"I've been a fool, daughter," he called over his shoulder. Romilly gathered her skirts and waded over to where he stood, following his gaze. Her uncle's boat was undamaged both above and below the waterline. She surveyed the vibrant golden hull with its carved garland of dark green ivy meeting at the bow, the veins and stems touched with gold paint. The lower hull's deeper green anti-fouling paint, which she had helped her uncle apply in early spring, was still fresh and new looking. The keel, curved and keen like a giant's skate blade, was perfect. It was clear the boat had simply come to rest on the sand like this when the tide receded. Even now, wavelets were licking along the stern and washing out the sand under the keel.

"Look at the high-water mark," he said. Romilly looked farther up the beach and saw a line of crisped eel grass about five yards from them. "I thought the tide was higher than it was because the Egg didn't show. It's still got a ways to climb." Romilly did some quick calculations.

"Father, then the tide should be dead low again around supper time. We should have light enough to assess the damage to our boat." She could see her father tense himself to bear the reality, the blow of having to stay some days in order to repair their boat. She could not imagine him being willing to abandon the *Ingres* even for a day. Her father gave a grim nod of his chin, then looked down at his feet as if composing a difficult sentence in his mind. She could see a muscle jumping in his cheek, and braced for an order to wait on shore, or walk back home on the woodland path come low tide. But when he looked up at her again, his eyes were remorseful.

"Romilly," he said, "I've been foolish on a second count. I *do* need you. You are far more capable than I've allowed. And brave. I was determined to send you home if we found my brother, but I'd be a fool to do so. You have far better judgement than I give you credit for. You are—" and here his voice grew husky, "very much like your mother, as fiercely stubborn, and just as strong."

Romilly reached out her hand and lay it on his forearm, her face shining in relief. He pressed her hand briefly, then turned to look toward the embankment. She followed his gaze, making out the merest thread of dry, pale-gold clay leading out of the stones and roots and disappearing between tree trunks. Stooping, he lifted the basket of supplies and handed it to Romilly, then scrambled up the bank and entered the woods, parting the branches so she could follow. The path was so narrow and overgrown that her father had to insert his body—thin as it was—sideways. Looking about, he found a stout stick with which to push aside the vines and branches so Romilly could follow, holding the basket carefully before her in both arms.

"Father, is this the path to the cottage?" she asked.

"Yes—I can't think where else my brother would be."

"Do you think it's still there?" Romilly asked anxiously.

"Well, it was stone-built, so I imagine it's fared well enough over the years. I haven't seen it since I was about your age, more than twenty years ago. When we had midsummer festival on the island, we never went near the cottage, but stayed along the beach. But I visited my brother there during the summers, on occasion. I didn't like it so much as he did. It was an odd place."

"How was it odd?"

"Well, first, it was full of creatures. Your aunt kept tamed birds that flew about the house—there was one barred owl who used to twist its neck to follow me with its eyes. And other creatures too. A fox cub she would feed morsels from the table. She had rescued these animals as young, or they found her in the forest, she claimed. They had no children," he added, in explanation. "And she had a room for her studio that was cluttered with books and papers, and lots of little pots simmering in the fireplace, full of mushrooms and bark. She gave me drawing lessons that summer," he noted meekly. "She said I had promise as a draughtsman, my ships and buildings were so detailed, all to scale. She said I had a good sense of perspective," he added, and laughed wryly. "But I didn't see much use for that—my future was in farming," he finished, "and that was that." Though Romilly thought she caught, in the set of his shoulders and his pinkened neck, a tinge of wistfulness.

"Brother loved those animals, though, and it was sometimes hard for him to come back to us. As I recall, he brought home with him once a crow he'd taught some words, but it flew back to the island. Your aunt had some sort of charm with animals."

As he spoke, they were picking their way up a steep and mossy hill. He'd fallen silent, and all she heard was the whack of his stick against branches and his ragged breathing. At the edge of a clearing, he stopped.

"There it is—the cottage," he panted, pointing the stick toward a house made of rounded beach stones. It had a steeply pitched, slate-shingled roof, and diamond-paned windows like deep-set eyes in the thick walls. Romilly made out the vestiges of a garden that must have surrounded the house—a wisteria vine on a collapsed wooden arbor, a massive rhododendron smothering the arched door, a pointed cypress draped in a veil of bittersweet vines. They seemed exotic as zoo animals among the mountain laurel and birch saplings that were trying to take over the yard. To the side of the house was a round well, built of the same beach stones, complete with a timber windlass and a staved wooden bucket. The roof over the well was padded with thick green moss.

"If he's not here, I can't think where he'd be," her father whispered, as if to himself. He motioned her to follow him through lank grass that struggled to grow amid the moss. As he reached for the latch in the door, Romilly heard a nasal *gaw, gaw*, then a clicking rattle, and a crow landed atop the rhododendron. Her father ducked and threw up one arm, startled, but the crow preened calmly, running a wing feather through a beak that gleamed with the sumptuous silvery sheen of charcoal. He cocked a reddish-brown eye, over which passed a pale inner lid like a quick curtain, and said, "*What'syourname?*" to Romilly's delight.

"Romilly," she replied.

"*Yllimor? Yllimor?*" he crooned to himself, questioningly. Romilly started—

"What did you call—"

"Ah, good, you've met Robbie," called a familiar voice. They spun around to see her uncle walking up the flagstone path toward them. "He found me when the sky split open and the moon fell. Good old Robbie. He must be almost a hundred years old now. That's how long it feels I've been away, yet still he knew me. Do you remember Robbie, my brother?" Robbie hopped onto her uncle's shoulder, gently twirling and preening the graying hair over his ear. Her uncle smiled peacefully, head tilted to the side, looking much like a prematurely aged boy. He pulled a raisin out of his bib pocket and handed it up to Robbie, who cocked his head and plucked it gently from between her uncle's fingers. "What interesting headwear, brother," he said, and then, with more concern, "Is that blood?"

4

THE UNABANDONED COTTAGE

Her father stood stock still, but Romilly sprang forward and flung her arms about her uncle's waist. Robbie *chuck-chuck*-ed his approval. Her uncle was unharmed. She suddenly realized how much she needed his whimsical conversation and stories. He had always been fond of exaggeration, a quality that had frustrated her father. And in addition to *dreaming*, he had been known to engage in what her father called *extravagances*, such as spending an entire winter of evenings carving ivy vines, painting them, picking out the detail in gold—just to decorate the bow of his sailboat; such as planting an entire field of sunflowers just for their beauty. She was inclined to laugh at his description of the moon falling as just his way of describing his predicament. But his next words caught her short.

"Go ahead, stare at me like I'm crazy, brother. You wouldn't be staring so, had *you* seen a great flap of the heavens pulled back. Something has us in its palm."

"If I'm staring, it's because the whole village thinks you're dead, but here you are, not dead but daft, playing with a bird as if you were a runaway boy."

"Why is everyone always so apt to suspect catastrophe? Besides, that's *exactly* what I am, brother—a runaway boy, and it's about time. Our village life is so thin you can just about see through it, like a piece of greased paper. There's something beyond all this," her uncle said, lifting one arm and flicking his wrist in a crisp flourish toward the sky, "and I'm going to find out what it is."

"Let be, brother," her father said, and reached to clasp his upper arm. "I'm just glad to find you in one piece and above water. Right now, I'd like to go inside and see if we can build a fire. It will be chilly come evening, and we haven't had breakfast nor our midday meal."

With that, her father turned and inspected the door. The paint hung in strips and the peelings crunched underfoot like cinders, but the knob turned, and the door swung easily on its hinges, as if they had just been greased. Inside, a low fire was already flickering on the hearth and casting its glow on soot-sheened cobbles. On the grate, Romilly saw a large bluefish, its body cavity stuffed with green bayberry leaves that smoked sweetly. As droplets of oil fell into the ash they sputtered and gave out soft hisses.

Romilly looked wonderingly around the room, which was the width of the entire cottage, with a smoothly sanded, wide-planked floor. A long table divided the space into a kitchen and a sitting area where she saw a sofa, embroidered with black-berry vines, under a diamond-paned bay window. A few of the upper panes were broken and admitted an actual bramble. The sofa looked surprisingly clean and bright after years of aban-donment. Vividly embroidered, lavender-white flowers delicate as single petaled roses seemed to reach to her across the room, while the blue-black berries gave off a satiny sheen. The long table had been scrubbed until it had a waxy, hand-worn polish. In a corner, she saw a small pile of leaves, pine needles, and debris that had been swept together, along with a ball of filthy rags, a tin bucket, and a few tools.

"I know," her uncle said, as if he had read her mind. "It looks like someone has been caretaking the place. I swept up the leaves blown through those broken panes, but the floor itself was quite clean. A piece of canvas was thrown over that sofa to protect it, and the table and mantelpiece seems to have been scrubbed and dusted recently. There was even a nice pile of kindling on the hearth. Some prudent person had once sealed the chimney with rags so creatures couldn't get in, but they had been removed and piled next to the kindling," he said, chuckling. "It almost seemed like an innkeeper had prepared for my visit."

While he was speaking, Romilly walked over to the mantelpiece to look at a woman's portrait in terracotta pencil. Her hair was drawn into a loose braid over one shoulder, and one forearm rested on a table. On her other shoulder was a kestrel, its creamy breast streaked with rust and flecked with black, like the seed-tipped down packed inside a milkweed pod. His breast looked so silky and plump she had the urge to touch it. Lined up on the mantel underneath this portrait were dozens of tiny clay animals: a badger, a sinuous mink, a bear rearing on hind legs, her twin cubs at her side; a camel, so haughty it almost seemed to be sneering; a tiger, belly to the ground, crouched to spring. Each animal had been carefully and precisely painted, down to the finest tufts of hair in the tiger's ears. The mink's round jet eye gleamed mischievously, lit up with the tiniest of white highlights, applied with just a single hair. She reached out a fingertip to touch it.

"Romilly, don't!" her father spoke sharply. "I don't like this at all, at all—this is raising the hair on my neck! What kind of house doesn't age or become derelict in over ten years' time? You can bet on it—someone's living here, someone's about to come back and—"

"Nonsense," said her uncle briskly. "I've been here almost four full days and seen no one. Whoever tended this cottage is not interested in sharing it with me. Maybe Robbie's the keeper, eh?" he said, reaching up to stroke the crow who leaned into his palm like a dog.

"Brother, this is not a joke—someone's lay claim here, someone's—"

"But all of life is jokes, see, with both rhyme and reason. We will find out in due time, I warrant, why this cottage seems to be inviting us back." While he spoke, her uncle was reaching with a spatula to maneuver the fish onto a large platter waiting on the floor. As he slid it off, she could see that only the crisped skin held the flesh against the bones, and her stomach gave a long, rolling rumble.

"Someone's hungry," her uncle announced cheerily, smiling up at her.

He didn't seem daft in the least. He looked determined, calm, and—free. Her uncle looked free, and also—whatever is the opposite of lonely.

After their lunch of fish and bread and cheese, after she had re-bandaged her father's wound, relieved to see the edges had sealed, her uncle helped her make up beds on the floor of an upstairs room. In a cupboard, her uncle had found several woolen blankets as well as thick velvet drapes, a deep wine color, that had been removed from all the windows and stored there. He showed her how he had made his own bed in the other room by folding these curtains in layers and padding them with the blankets. They made reasonably comfortable pallets, but they would have to sleep fully dressed until she could retrieve the quilts and spare clothes from the broken hull of the *Ingres*, where, she thought sadly, they were collecting silt and seaweed. But soon she would wash them and set them to dry on the tall, sweet grass.

Her father resisted her attempts to lead him to his pallet for a rest after his meal. No, he was planning to stay in that strange house as little as need be, he said. From the upper window she watched him wander outside, select a sunny patch in the long grass of the yard, and lie down there, his lips moving as if he were talking to himself. She was sure he was planning the afternoon and evening salvage missions and was relieved when she saw him draw his cap down over his face and interlace his fingers on his chest. This was her chance to have a private conversation with her uncle. She ran downstairs to find him kneeling before the fireplace, methodically banking the ashes from their cooking fire.

"Uncle," she said, "did Father tell you about the *Ingres*?"

"In about three words, aye. I mean this quite literally. Said *She ran aground*."

Romilly nodded, hesitated, then plunged on. "Uncle, I have so many questions."

"I'm sure you do," he laughed.

"First, where did Robbie come from? And what did you mean when you said Robbie was a hundred years old?"

At the mention of his name, Robbie flew from his perch on a coat rack to the wooden table, giving a low chuckling purr. Her uncle stood up and leaned a hip against the table.

"Ah, I just threw that in for exaggeration's sake," her uncle said, smiling as he stroked the bird. "Robbie is twenty, aren't you, Robbie? The first spring I came here Aunt had just found him fallen from a nest in that cypress tree at the edge of the yard. He looked full grown when I came, but he was still a baby, weren't you, Robbie? Now you're a dignified elderly gentleman, like me!" Robbie sidled up to him and tweaked her uncle's overall pocket. Her uncle reached in and pulled out a raisin, which Robbie tweezed with extreme delicacy from his fingers.

"Can I ask other things?" Romilly ventured tentatively.

"Of course, my niece," her uncle chortled. "Ask anything you like. I'm not like your father, who's practically a vault when it comes to relinquishing information."

"Can you tell me about that portrait? Is it my great aunt? Why has she a kestrel on her shoulder?"

"Yes, that's your aunt. She was not wont to display her image, but she was pleased with that self-portrait. But I drew the kestrel—she was teaching me how to draw and paint wild creatures. And I'm still somewhat proud of it, truth be told," he said. He drew himself up with a grave and self-satisfied air, but his eyes were twinkling.

Romilly smiled at him. "Yes, it's a beautiful drawing, Uncle. But why a *kestrel*," Romilly persisted, "because I've seen a similar portrait in my mother's old books, but of a girl. And the girl's name was Yllimor, the name Robbie called me when he met me," she continued, faltering as she blushed. "And that's my name, only backward."

"You don't know the story of your name?" her uncle asked, in mock bafflement. "Does your father tell you nothing?"

Romilly had that sensation she was growing used to, of having lived in a house her entire life, only to find a secret passageway that led to whole new wing of rooms.

"You know, I hope, that the aunt who lived here was not my aunt by blood, but by marriage? She was of your mother's people, actually—the younger sister of your maternal grandmother, that is, your mother's mother." Romilly nodded for him to go on.

"Well, this gets complicated, so pay close attention. When *my* father and mother—your paternal grandparents—died only a year apart, your father was able to take over the farm. He was practically born into steady middle age. But I was still very dependent on my mother. Her death devastated me. I was a bit younger than you are now, maybe a year or two, and I needed a mother figure. I found one in your great aunt." He paused, his eyes assuming an unaccustomed somberness as they came into focus on her face. He examined her silently for a moment. "You are actually very like this aunt in face and manner—to your mother too. Perhaps that's why I have always had a particular fondness for you," he said, his face relaxing into a smile that put the twinkle back in his eye. "But to go on. Your great aunt was very good to me. She convinced your father to let me visit as much as I liked, and to spend the summers. In a way, she was a foster mother. She had hoped to have children of her own, you see, but partnered late. She was my teacher too—almost everything I learned about natural history I learned from her. She was particularly knowledgeable about animals, and about plants and their medicinal uses. Arra was her pupil too—that's how Arra came to be the village healer, though Arra also studied across the Sound. Anyway, Arra used to spend a great deal of time here. She'd walk the five miles, collecting plants all the way, then spend a few days with my aunt decocting this or that, brewing medicines, trading knowledge. You may not remember, but this great aunt helped Arra care for your mother when she fell sick. They tried everything they knew to save her."

No, Romilly thought sadly. She had been kept away from all that concerned her mother's final illness.

"Anyway, the book you mention is, I believe, a book on medicines for treating wasting fevers. I remember it contained a portrait of Yllimor, your great-grandmother. She was a widely respected healer in the Old Country during the time of plague and had cured many sufferers of a disease that resembled the one which killed your mother. I remember your mother asking for this book to be brought out when she lay so ill. Your mother had chosen your name as a palindrome of Yllimor's—this is a custom in your mother's family going back many generations. For example," he added, "your mother's name, Ingres, was derived from Sigren, her mother's name. Though actually," he added with a thoughtful air, "that's more of an anagram than a palindrome." Romilly wondered at this mirroring. Her name gave her a way to understand what she had always felt: a compelling, almost magnetic connection to her mother's people.

"Unfortunately, even with the help of this book, your great aunt could not save your mother. The remedies in it proved ineffective against this new kind of illness."

Romilly reached out a finger and gently stroked Robbie's back. He chirruped hoarsely, half in pleasure, half, it seemed, sympathetically. Her uncle said, his voice also husky, "So you see, I know what it's like to lose a mother. I've lost my own mother. Then my foster mother moved away. I know all about loss, having lost my own partner, and my dear friend—your mother."

Romilly thought about this a moment. His losses were even greater than her own.

"But why did Aunt and Uncle leave their cottage? Father said their house in the forest burned down, but that doesn't explain why they would go away completely."

"You have probably noticed that many things disappear in our lives."

"Yes, Uncle. But not you, it turns out!"

"No, not I. Though I *do* want to stay on this island. I would have come back to the village to tell you this if you hadn't found me. We have much to figure out about our world, and I feel we will learn the truth shortly."

"But what does this have to do with a kestrel? If Yllimor was pictured with a kestrel, and your aunt had a kestrel, should I be expecting a kestrel to come into my life, as well?" she asked, attempting to joke.

"But one already has," her uncle said.

"How do you know?" Romilly asked, in wonderment.

"Because Romilly's kestrel will take a message to the Being who lives beyond our sky."

Romilly stared into his eyes, which had narrowed shrewdly. "How do you know I know?" she asked.

"Because when I told your father about a great flap in the sky opening, his jaw dropped and he gawped at me, whereas I could read on your face, clear as a page in a book, 'So Uncle has seen it too.'"

"I did see something like that, only it was over our fields at sunset, after the day's harvest work was done. But nothing since."

"This Being is trying to communicate with us, Romilly. Trust me, if we go out at night upon the flats, just where the Egg split, they will come again. It's been three nights now they've come."

"Father wants to repair the boat this evening, while the tide is out. But that's impossible! There's a great hole in the hull, most likely." She paused a moment, then rushed forward. "Uncle, you've never even asked how we came here!"

"But I know, my niece. You sailed here on the *Ingres* and ran aground on the Egg, which had split in two pieces and opened like a book. I was watching from the foot of the path when the collision happened. I had been checking on my boat."

"And yet you didn't help?"

"I was alarmed at first, but when I saw you two swimming

heartily for shore, I ceased worrying. I knew it'd be best if you came ashore yourselves. You see, I know your father: if I'd run down to help you, your father would have prevented you from ever seeing the cottage, and we wouldn't have had a moment alone. He would expect me to bring the tools and wood *to him* and would camp out on the shore rather than enjoy these charming accommodations. He might have insisted that I sail you home in my boat and leave him behind to make the repair. He took a dislike to this place after your mother died. But now that you have 'found' me here, I get to play host!" her uncle said, bowing low from the waist.

"But how are we to occupy Father tonight so that he doesn't come with us to the flats?"

"The last few nights, the Being has appeared where the Egg lies open, when the moon is a quarter risen. Moonrise will be shortly after sunset, and the moon should be in the right position about two hours later. We will have to hope he'll be sound asleep. He should be, after all this tumult."

Her uncle reached out his hand to Robbie, who sidled up his arm to perch on his shoulder. "In the meantime, I have a lot to show you. Come with me. I must introduce you to your kestrel."

5

The Kestrel

They left the cottage and walked around the side of it, through the ruined garden. Romilly noticed boxwoods, shaggy and immense, and roses pied crimson and white whose canes at the base were as large around as her wrist, their thorns in rows like shark's teeth. A sandy path led to a small stone outbuilding nearly overgrown with ivy. There Romilly saw a perch made of a piece of driftwood attached to a wooden post. Her uncle gave a sweet, piping whistle, which was answered by a faint peeping song. Then Romilly heard a flutter behind her, and a dove-sized hawk with a glossy chestnut back alighted on the thumb of his outstretched hand. Robbie gave a startled, throaty *gaw* and raised the feathers on his head and neck, making him look twice as big. Her uncle chuckled.

"Robbie is displeased we are making friends with this rival and raider of bird nests," he noted. As if sulking, Robbie flap-hopped from her uncle's shoulder to the ivy-smothered gutters of the hut, wallowing clumsily until he reached the peak, where he glared sullenly at the kestrel from a reddish eye. Romilly felt a bit disloyal to him as she took pleasure in the kestrel's delicate beauty. Two black bars on its face framed the enormous, slightly flattened sphere of black eye, depthless as a droplet of ink. Its beak was curved and keen as a rose thorn, and its talons, also jet black, dug her uncle's flesh like pincers as it settled itself. Her uncle winced slightly through his smile as he swiveled the bird around to the perch. The kestrel hopped weightlessly onto the branch.

"I have something for you," her uncle said, as he reached one hand into the bib of his overalls. "Close your eyes and reach out your arms." She felt him lay a flat weight across her palms, and opened her eyes to find a falconer's gauntlet, the thin white deerskin gray and stiff with age. When she turned it over wonderingly, she started: embroidered in still-vivid deep-red silks and silver thread, roses clustered the cuff.

"That must be my aunt's gauntlet, passed down through her family. I found it in the cupboard of an upstairs room while I was sweeping up and dusting."

"This is the gauntlet Yllimor is wearing in the portrait! But how is it, given the time passed, that this kestrel remembers its training? Is it the same kestrel my aunt kept?"

"Nay, they are not like crows—kestrels live quick and hot, and I have not heard of one surviving past ten years of age. I have no idea where this bird came from, or whose it is, but Robbie appears to know it. He shows all the symptoms of sibling rivalry. A few days ago, around the same time Robbie showed up, I saw the kestrel on that white cedar at the yard's edge and called to it on a whim, because I was remembering my aunt and the past. And 'lo the bird came and landed on my hand." He admired the bird, looking it over from the tip of its beak to the sickle shape of its minute talons. "Put on the gauntlet—let's see how you do!"

Romilly grasped the lip of the gauntlet with one hand and let it dangle downward. Slowly, she slid her palm between the lips of the cuff, then pushed her fingers inside, feeling the coarse texture of the raw inner surface. Suddenly her hand became a numbly armored thing. She curled her fingers into a stiff fist. The instant the glove was on, the kestrel hopped onto the back of her hand, bobbing its chestnut tail, feathers fanned. She could remember cutting roses that weighed more. It perched primly there, tilting its head to show the russet patch in the smoke blue feathers on its crest, and stretching out one wing in a leisurely way, as if it wanted her to admire the brilliant white dots in graduating size down the black-tipped, pewter flight feathers. Attached to one of its ankles was a slender jess of shiny leather, worn dark and limp; the other jess was missing.

Romilly gazed at the jess, formulating an idea. If she could write a note light enough, she could roll it into a scroll and tie it by means of the jess. Then the bird could fly it out of the sky's opening. But how would she tell it where to go?

"Uncle, how much do you know of falconry?" she asked.

"Well, when I was a boy, I handled my aunt's kestrel, and she'd begun to teach me how to cast it off my fist and whistle it back. When this kestrel appeared, it's as if she brought with her a wild idea about how to contact the Being. I know it's a bit of a longshot. The problem is, once you cast her off your fist, what if she flies elsewhere? What if she keeps flying through the flap and doesn't return? We need her to perch on the edge of the flap so that the Being will see her."

"And my note," Romilly added.

"Yes," her uncle chuckled, "now we are thinking alike! We need write a note on the finest paper we can find. It must be flexible and light, but sturdy enough to roll into a scroll and large enough for the Being to see it. Remember," he stressed, cocking his head toward her, "how small a kestrel from our world would look to a giant like that!"

Romilly gazed at the bird, remembering the size of the thumbnail she had seen through the flap in the sky, easily as large as the platter her uncle had served the fish on at lunch. From the Being's perspective, the kestrel would be about the size of a housefly. How would he notice a tiny scroll tied to the kestrel's foot? And even if he noticed it, how would the Being untie it or read such minute printing?

"Uncle, I've thought of an alternative. Couldn't we attach a cord to the kestrel's jess, like a kite string, before we send it up and out through the flap? If so, we could tie the note to the end of the cord, and the Being could pull the scroll up. It could be a large sheet, in fact, large enough for the Being to read without much difficulty."

Her uncle smacked his thighs in excitement. "Romilly, I think that might work! In fact, in training, a falcon is always attached to a lead—it's called a creance, and you spool up the extra cord on its spindle. I bet you anything we will find a creance among my aunt's falconry gear in this hut." At this, he crossed to the door, lifted the wood bar, and swung the door open. A waft of air smelling of damp stone, earth, and mildewed wood greeted Romilly's nose. A bar of daylight lit up shelves veiled in a gauze of cobweb, but behind this film she could see an orderly row of books.

"Well, we can be sure no one's looked in *here* for ten years or more," her uncle said. On the top shelf, just out of reach, she saw a willow basket, while on the wall to her right hung a tarnished brass whistle, slim as a pen.

Her uncle poked his forefinger through the cobwebs and reached for the basket.

"Ah, I remember—my aunt would keep all her training implements in a handled basket such as this."

They bent their heads to peer inside. Covered in a layer of gray dust was a bobbin wound in what looked like time-yellowed crocheting yarn, as well as a tiny, sewn leather pouch and some other tools that looked like metal nippers. Her uncle drew them out one by one.

"This here is her hood, which she would have worn when young or when she needed calming during her manning."

"What is 'manning,' uncle?"

"To man a falcon is simply to accustom the kestrel to human company—another word for taming."

"Well, in this case," Romilly said with a wry smile, "it's more apt to say 'womaning.'"

"Aye, niece, that it is! And that's not the only case in which our notions of who's in charge should be upset. You are of your mother's line through and through. All formidably strong women."

Romilly drew out the spindle of cord, wiping off the dust with the hem of her skirt. Unwinding a foot of the cord, she tested its strength. As hard as she yanked, she could not break it. Her uncle looked on approvingly.

"That's linen. There's nothing stronger or more resistant to time. Still, let's go out in the yard and play out this cord to see how much length we've got and make sure it's all one piece."

Just as he finished these words, her father appeared around the corner, his hair tousled and woven through with strands of dried grass. Romilly looked to his bandage and was relieved to see that the blood there was beginning to dry to a reddish brown. At his voice, Robbie, who had been biding his time on the roof peak, waded to the gutter and shivered his wings imploringly, as if hoping for sympathy and attention from the newcomer.

"Make sure what's 'all one piece'?"

"Father," Romilly said, converting her surprise to a smile. "How was your nap?"

"Too long," her father replied gruffly. "Should have gone down to the beach to see about the boats. The tide will be turning by now, brother. We've likely missed our chance to move your boat to the channel, so it doesn't rest on its keel that way. But we can look over the *Ingres* and make a provisional repair."

"We can move my boat if it pleases you, brother, but that keel's a solid chunk of lead. Resting like that for a day or two more won't do her any harm. I'll show you where the tools are. If we can patch the *Ingres* so as she floats again, I'll use the wood from those old rafts to build a cradle for her so I can make a proper repair. What's got you all flustered?" Romilly's father was surveying the basket and the tools with barely suppressed alarm. The kestrel—drawn up tall and still in the presence of a stranger—he didn't seem to have noticed yet.

"What's this all about—what are these tools for? They aren't for boat repair."

"True. I was telling Romilly about my boyhood here, while you slept."

As if at the mention of his boyhood, the kestrel stepped forward onto his shoulder and began to preen its breast feathers. A look of astonishment and dread passed over her father's face.

"Where on earth did *that* come from?" he cried out, taking a step back involuntarily.

"We don't know, Father," Romilly said, in her gentlest tones, reaching out to touch his arm.

"Yes, we don't know—" her uncle repeated, more stoutly. "And isn't that wonderful?"

6

THE KEY

Romilly's uncle mollified her father by taking him to the tool-
shed at the back of the cottage. There her father found several
boards of the right thickness, a chisel, and even a plane, but not
an awl, so he borrowed a knife from the kitchen to carve pegs
and holes. He would patch the boat sufficiently to float at high
tide, then anchor her in the channel until her uncle finished
building the cradle. For the *Ingres*, her uncle had pointed out,
was not going to be seaworthy until he could make a proper
repair. Her father agreed but insisted that he and Romilly would
walk home through the woods as soon as the first repair was
made, returning the following week to sail the *Ingres* home.

As they walked back down the path to the shore, her uncle
was explaining his plans for the cottage. How he would reclaim
the yard and garden from the forest and prepare a small veg-
etable plot by next spring, how he would build a dock off the
back of the island for his boat, and continue fishing just as he
had before, bringing his catch into the village. Maybe adding
some crabbing and lobstering to his trade. As he walked with
the boards under one arm, he kept looking over his shoulder
at them, often stumbling or being lashed by a brambly tendril,
or coming to a standstill as the boards wedged against a sapling
tree near the path. Romilly smothered a giggle as he groped at
the hair on the side of his head, where a spider, its web ruptured by his forward momentum, was scrambling to get free.
He captured the small being in his palm and released it onto a
hazelnut leaf, his stream of chatter unbroken.

"—and perhaps I'll even bring some dairy goats over—" he
was saying as they reached the bank overlooking the shore, but

he fell silent when he saw the *Ingres* lying on her side half buried in water, her once pristine white hull now scummed a yellow brown. He stood there gazing, mopping his forehead and the back of his neck with his handkerchief.

"What a pity," he murmured as he picked his way down the rocky bank, then strode out to the edge of the water. Seating himself in the sand, he set down the boards, unlaced and removed his boots, then rolled up his pant cuffs. Romilly came up behind him and waited, her eyes filled with tears. Her father, having insisted on carrying the heavy trug of tools, was puffing with exertion as he dropped onto the sand to free his foot from a boot. Her uncle looked at her briefly, all the laughter drained from his dark eyes, and they waded out together to the boat. A great gouge in the paint had exposed pale yellow wood, in the center of which stared a black and splintery chasm where the rock had punched through. Water washed in and flowed out again with each small wave. Her uncle put his hand to the craft's side, stroking her as if she were a suffering animal, then crouched down to feel the edges of the great black wound just in front of the keel, studying the planks to see which would need to be replaced and which were sound.

"Well," he said, "we're lucky in one thing." He pointed higher on the hull where the boards cupped sharply.

"Where she's injured, you see, is along the flatter bottom where there's not much curve to the planks at all, so we should be able to chisel out the mangled place and peg some new boards to the ribs." He reached into the wound and felt behind for the frames. "The ribs are sound. It's going to take some strength and patience to peg boards in without an awl to create the holes, but I think she'll hold water if we seal the joints and pegs well with pitch." Just then, her father came up behind her, catching her eye briefly before he turned his eyes to the damage. He seemed oddly relieved, as if, in his mind, the hole had assumed gargantuan, irreparable proportions.

"I'll bring out the tools," he said, turning to jog back to the beach, splashing through the shallows in relief and gladness.

Her uncle followed Romilly's father with his eyes. When he was out of earshot, her uncle reached up to grasp her sleeve.

"Romilly, your father and I have this well in hand. We may only have this one night to contact the Being. Why don't you fish out the quilts and clothes and such, then run back up to the cottage with them. Then you can lay out that cord on the grass, the way we talked about, and wind it back onto the bobbin nice and neat, so it'll play out easily. And you can get to know your kestrel, perhaps find it a name."

"Is it a female, Uncle? You were calling it a 'she.'"

"This one's a female. The male has slate-gray edges to his wings."

Romilly thought for a moment. "Mira, Uncle. I'll name her Mira."

Her uncle beamed at her.

"In the pantry, you'll find some tidbits of fresh rabbit you can give her. This will get her used to you."

Romilly ran back through the woods, the rolled bundle of quilts and clothes cooling her chest, her heart singing a high, giddy tune whose only word was *Mira*. She skipped to the edge of the clearing, paused to lay the quilts over some low-growing laurel shrubs, then walked with soft steps to the little hut. Her kestrel perched serenely, preening her breast and the crimped down of her underwings. When Romilly whispered *Mira, Mira* the kestrel tilted her head in attentive increments, her eye a fathomless, brimming well of blackness. Moving slowly, she leaned over to grasp the handle of the wicker basket, then backed away until her bare feet felt the path underfoot.

She dashed to the edge of the clearing. Setting the basket down, she withdrew the spool. In the path she had found a stone with which to weigh down the end of the cord, and now she backed slowly across the clearing, unspooling as she went. It was difficult to find a straight path; the clearing was dotted by tufts of birchlings as tall as her shins. Often, she had to weave

the cord between branches and push it down to the base. She
wondered that there was any clearing left at all. Undisturbed,
ten-year-old saplings would be big around as her wrist, at least,
and relatively unbranched. When they grew in thickets like this,
it was a sign they'd been lopped off at the ground, perhaps
repeatedly. Sometimes the sole of her bare foot was gouged
painfully by the sharp stub of a cut-down sapling. Yes, someone
had kept the forest back with pruners, and must have scythed
the grass at least once a year. It was one of the mysteries of the
place, that it could seem both abandoned and tended, vacant
and occupied. Lost in these thoughts, she reached the other
side of the clearing, relieved to find the cord whole and tangle
free. She stooped again, securing the loop of cord under a broken branch, then retraced her steps backward, laying the cord
parallel to the first length. She repeated this three times before
the spool was empty. Pacing the clearing, she had found it was
thirty large paces wide. Would one hundred and eighty paces of
cord be enough to reach the Being?

Romilly rewound the cord neatly, forcing herself to be patient and meticulous, imagining it unspooling without a hitch as
the kestrel flew upward. When all the cord was neatly wound,
she placed the spool in the basket and returned the basket to
the hut, crooning *Mira, Mira* soothingly as she slipped past the
kestrel. Now to feed her. As she was trotting back along the
path toward the cottage, she saw Robbie clear the trees and
land atop the rhododendron near the door. He must have been
visiting her uncle and father on the shore. She smiled as she
imagined her father scolding the bird to *stop meddling*, hollering
at her uncle to send the *nosy thing* back to the cottage so he
could get on with his work in peace. When she neared the door,
Robbie greeted her with a low, muffled *caw* and she saw he was
holding a small metallic object in his beak.

It was a bronze key, the size used to secure a cupboard or
cabinet. The head was cast in a butterfly shape. Robbie sat on
a branch, eyeing her askance for a moment, then positioned
himself with a series of hops, stretching out his back to offer

her the key. He held on to the shaft with his beak for a moment, like a dog with a stick, then slowly, almost reluctantly, let it go. Romilly held it in her open palm, gazing at it in wonderment. She knew that crows often collected metal and other shiny objects, but the way in which he had given her the key made her feel as if something had been entrusted to her. Slowly, she withdrew the cord with her mother's embroidery scissors from under her dress, picked open the knot, and threaded the key onto it. She reknotted the cord firmly.

Inside the pantry, she saw the saucer of meat atop a tall larder with two large doors. Curious, she swung the larder doors open, expecting them to be empty, but the shelves contained a small cloth bag of raisins, another, much larger sack of rye flour, and a similar one of fine cornmeal, enough for at least a week of baking. Her uncle must have brought these supplies with him. Evidently, when he left the wharf days before, he hadn't intended to come back, at least for a while. Perplexing questions filled her mind as she walked back to the hut with the saucer of meat. Why not let his family know? Why subject them to the agony of worry and uncertainty, or images of him drowned or injured? If only there were a key to such secrets, as tangible as the key she now wore around her neck. Although, she thought with a sense of irony, what use is a key when you have no earthly idea what lock it fits?

As soon as Mira's keen eyes spied the saucer of meat, she began to tremble at the edge of her perch. Romilly set the saucer down on the ground and withdrew the gauntlet from the wicker basket, sliding her left hand inside, admiring for a moment the embroidery. The silver threads, though smoky with age, still glistened in the sunlight. Mira could no longer wait. She hunched and sprang to Romilly's wrist with the gentlest tap. Romilly bent her knees and picked up a morsel of the rabbit meat in her fingers. Murmuring *Mira, Mira*, she offered the stringy meat to the kestrel, who tweezed it out of her fingers deftly with the point of her beak, cocked her head back, and with a series of rapid flicks, positioned and swallowed the tidbit. She gazed around, opening and closing her beak reflectively. She let out a series of high, cricket-like peeps, as if asking for more. Romilly obliged, offering Mira bits of meat until the bird began to refuse. Romilly felt herself relax, as she watched the kestrel's eye wincing and closing drowsily. For a moment she allowed her gaze to drift over the cuff of the gauntlet, losing herself in the embroidered field of intertwined roses, following their stems and noticing the detail of the thorns, where a silver highlight—the tiniest of stitches—suggested keen points.

Suddenly, her mind snapped into focus. Nestled amid the blooms, minute but perfect, was a key with a butterfly-shaped head, stitched in bronze metallic thread. She didn't need to draw the key from under her dress to know it was identical to the one Robbie had brought her. A tingle started at the back of her neck, passed across her back and chest, and trickled along the outstretched arm that held Mira. Something—or some-one—relentlessly pointed her toward clues. But what could the key be for? Gently, she moved Mira close to her perch and the bird, startled awake by the movement, hopped lightly onto the smooth branch.

She stepped stealthily along the path, a familiar feeling of guilt and longing swelling in her chest. But why guilt? A key had been given her. By a crow, it was true, but all the clues—Ylli-mor's portrait, Robbie calling her by that name, the kestrel, the gauntlet, and now the key—suggested that she had been cho-sen to find something, to connect pieces of a puzzle together. When she approached the house, Robbie was still perched on the rhododendron. He cawed obnoxiously when he saw her coming, hunching his back and walking to-and-fro on a slender branch that flexed under his weight; he kept losing his balance and flapping his wings comically to regain it. When she paused at the door, he nonchalantly stepped onto her shoulder and be-gan to fluff at the curls over her ear. His rattling chuckle, muf-fled considerately, was still loud enough to make her eardrum crackle in complaint. As she passed the pantry, he took hold of her collar with his beak and gave it a decisive yank. Romilly realized he wanted a reward. Remembering the way her uncle had presented him with a raisin, she walked into the pantry and withdrew from the cloth sack a handful of raisins to keep in her apron pocket. Robbie bobbed with excitement as she handed one up to him. But he took it gingerly from her fingers like a well-mannered dog.

She surveyed the pantry and found that the cabinets there were secured by a swiveling piece of smoothed wood. She moved to the living room and scanned the cabinets near the fireplace, then the walls. She hadn't noticed the floor to ceiling draperies opposite the fireplace, perhaps because their color perfectly matched the dusky red of the walls. She advanced and touched the cloth gently, then grasped a fold between her thumb and finger, fondling the deep velvet. She saw a divide in the curtain which, when parted, revealed a glimpse of polished wood. She tugged the cloth gently, feeling it glide back upon some invisible track. She was suddenly aware of the deep silence of the room. There were two doors behind the curtains, each carved elaborately with figures of animal families—a fox with her kits near her burrow, a deer with two fawns in a clearing, a swan upon the water with her nestlings cupped within her wings. Each scene was complete, yet interconnected though an elaborately branching tree, as if each limb had borne the fruit of these small worlds. The branches connected to a trunk where the doors touched, so that opening the doors would divide the trunk, while closing them again would heal it. This trunk led downward to an impressive knot of twisted roots.

"I see you've found my creatures," she heard her uncle say. Startled, she looked over her shoulder to find him standing in the front door, smiling broadly. "I didn't mean to sneak up on you—I came back up to look for some nails and other necessities your father sent me for." At his voice, Robbie launched from her shoulder in a dipping glide and landed on her uncle's head, sliding around on his slippery hair. He swatted Robbie down to his shoulder and strode forward. "My aunt commissioned me to carve these doors for her. It was sort of my graduation project. I worked an entire summer on them before I was satisfied." He paused to stroke a finger down the swan's arched neck. "I've always been proud of that swan," he said, reflectively. "It's bedeviling, trying to give a sense of three dimensions when working an essentially flat surface." Romilly looked more closely at the swan. Somehow, using a depth of less than half an inch, her uncle had been able to suggest the bowl-like curve of the swan's wing tips. As she gazed, her mind's eye saw the swan gently adrift like a leaf in a sunlit pool, the wind filling the cup of the curving wings as if they were sails. Her uncle's command broke her reverie.

"Go on, open them."

Romilly hesitated.

"Go ahead, Romilly," her uncle said, gently. "Nothing will harm you. I vouch for it."

Romilly grasped a brass doorknob in each hand and pulled the doors open. A diagonal shaft of afternoon sunlight divided the room and obscured everything behind it. She walked through light tangible as fog and saw as she emerged a large worktable upon which scraps of paper and books were spread out as if the artist's work had merely been interrupted. Clay vessels held implements: various sizes of scissors, a handled blade, tweezers, rulers, and pencils. Antique leather-covered tomes were piled up on the floor, their covers warped and split by moisture. Some were broken down completely to the bundled pages.

She circled the table and gazed down at an image whose nature confounded her. It was a butterfly the size of her palm, complete with delicate antennae, yet it was much more. The butterfly had been released from its pure shape, inside of which another world was going on: a man stooped to bundle a sheaf of corn, while a girl stood behind him with a kitten in her arms. In the background, a drowsing horse waited patiently, one back hoof cocked, harnessed to a wagon mounded with sheaves. Her eyes wandered back and forth between the two fused images. Immersing in the harvest scene, she became the girl, and felt the warmth of the living animal in her arms; then she became a giant on whose hand this delicate, improbable butterfly came to rest. A sensing of worlds within worlds—perhaps infinitely—made her head feel light, as if she were fainting into or awakening within a larger dimension of time and space.

Her uncle came around the table and gazed at the artwork over her shoulder.

"That girl looks more'n a bit like you," he said.

"Uncle, have you ever seen this before? Is this Aunt's work?"

"Nay, Romilly. I'm mystified. Your aunt worked in paints and clay. I never knew her to create such pictures. It must be some sort of collage. On the other hand, I wasn't with her in the weeks before she left, so I suppose they might be hers. I was taking over the farm chores while your father cared for your mother. And I've not been back inside the cottage since then. When we brought your mother back across the Sound to bury her among her people, my aunt and uncle left too, and resettled there."

"Uncle," Romilly began, tentatively, "did you ever prune back the seedling trees in the grass of the yard, or scythe it? When I was laying out the cord, it struck me that, untended, the yard should have filled in with young trees big around as my wrist or arm, by now. And when I stooped, I saw evidence of pruning back. And the grass must have been scythed back once a year at least."

"Nay, Romilly, I only made sure the roof was sound and that the shrubs didn't overgrow the house. What you say is true, though. The grounds show signs of caretaking."

"Also, Uncle," Romilly continued, lifting her eyes to look him full in the face, her eyes large and fearful, "I found the supplies in the pantry. You intended to stay here some time. Why couldn't you tell us your plans? You—you frightened us."

At her anxious expression, the impish twinkle faded from his eye. He looked at her long and solemnly and then said, "I don't know if I should tell you this. If I tell you, I can't *untell* you. But I'd been given a mission, a secret one, and it concerns you." Romilly looked at him apprehensively. She knew how burdensome it was to know things that you can't *unknow*.

"Shall I tell you?" her uncle murmured.

Romilly nodded her head, at first slowly and then vigorously. "Please tell me, Uncle. I don't like secrets. They create such huge spaces between people."

"Well, we can't have a gulf between us!" her uncle said, smiling. "But this is very powerful knowledge and something you weren't supposed to know until you attained majority." Romilly looked at him, her brows drawn in confusion.

"That's an old-fashioned way to say 'until you are considered an adult within the community.'"

"But I practically am, Uncle. I run the farm with father, and I'm finished school."

"Yes, but you've always been rather advanced for your age. You are—what?—fifteen and a half? Almost sixteen? You will reach legal majority at age seventeen. But I believe, Romilly, now more than ever, that you were born into the world an old soul, as my aunt would say. So, I'm going to tell you some news that I haven't shared even with your father. Which is that my aunt, who has been for some years a widow, is—I'm not even sure how to say this—passing along her worldly possessions."

"Whatever do you mean? She's dead?" Romilly gasped.

"No, most definitely not. She sent a letter, a statement of trust, to Arra. And in this letter, she says that she wants to retire from the world and wishes to bequeath this land and house and all it contains to you, for your possession when you achieve majority."

"This cottage will be mine," Romilly said, blankly. "Mine?" she repeated uncomprehendingly, as if this word came from a language she didn't know.

"Yes, niece, yes! *And* the land around it—in fact, the entire island belongs to you. And that's why I disappeared. When Arra put me in possession of the letter I immediately crossed the Sound to see if it had been registered with the magistrate there. And it had. And then I came straight here to see about the cottage, intending," and here he looked somewhat sheepish, "to put it in order and hoping to live here as the caretaker until you are ready to be on your own," he rushed along, then paused. "That is, of course, if you'll have me."

Romilly threw her arms around her uncle's shoulders and buried her face in his chest, holding her breath to suppress her tears. "Something of my own," she murmured, muffled. "Something that connects me to my mother?"

"Breathe, dear girl, and let those tears out. I guess you've stored them up for a good many years. You've had to be strong for your father—I know how that is. You must have been so lonely."

Romilly took in a shuddering breath and looked up into his face, the pooled tears tipping out onto her cheeks in a steady flow. Her uncle led her out to the sofa, plumped himself down, and gathered her into his arms like a little child, her back and shins firmly encircled by his sinewy arms. Strange that, at his touch, a curious feeling of hollowness, of starvation for sheer human touch, flared up vividly. Longing for her mother surged inside her, released from the reservoir where she had tried to seal it away. She had thought such longings would pull her into pieces if she allowed them out. Or worse: that expressing them would remind her father of his own grief. She was much like her father in this, for she knew he'd also constructed a brittle façade of strength he didn't truly feel. And a sense of guilt for accepting a comfort that her father—love him as she did—could not provide, also spread through her, as if she were betraying her father. But she needed affection too much to resist her uncle stroking her dampened hair off her forehead while she wept. Robbie paced along the curving back of the sofa. Finally, as if impatient to conclude the grieving, he hopped down onto the cushion and pecked at her apron pocket. Romilly sob-laughed.

"He wants a raisin." She gave him his treat.

"See, now, don't you feel better?" her uncle asked gently, lifting the corner of her apron to wipe her nose for her, as if she were a small child.

Romilly nodded and rested her head against her uncle's shoulder.

"My father will not like this at all, at *all*," she said, twisting her hands in her lap. "He can't stand this place. He would never leave our house to live here, never, ever, ever. I would have to go off alone—Oh, Uncle, how could I bear that?" Fresh tears fell upon her hands.

"No, we can be sure your father, spooked as he is by this place, will be adamantly opposed to this legacy. For the cause," he said, drawing himself up with dignity, "I plan a return to the senses he believes I've taken leave of. I will behave as protectively as a sheep dog. It's a sacrifice, it's true, but you are worth it, my niece. And when it comes out that you own this cottage, as it must, I can tell him I intend to stay on as caretaker—again, only if you'll have me. Not that this will reassure him. He will probably still think I'm daft, even if my acting's brilliant. But here's what's most important: you cannot, even for your father, curb your flourishing into the person you were born to be. That'd be like cutting back a beautiful rose to the ground the minute it put forth buds. Or like preventing Mira from ever flying. You can't cut your journey of growth and discovery short—for anyone. Remember that."

Romilly wondered at this man. Whimsy permeated him through and through, yet he'd always—at the same time—been a boulder of wise strength she could lean against. She cocked her head and smiled a wet, wan, wry smile.

"It's just—too much to be believed. And now this Being. Perhaps it's well enough to leave that alone, Uncle. I don't know that I can bear any more discoveries. What does the Being have to do with Aunt, with this place? Why does this Being keep appearing? Why to you and me, but not my father?"

"I don't have the answers, my niece. But I know that I've always suspected something was fading out of our world, that things were—I'm not even sure how to describe it—dwindling away. Not just townsfolk moving away. I mean life itself, things seeming less vigorous, becoming paler somehow and more limited. Here, on this island, I feel substantial, more myself. I feel a connection to a time in my life when there was joy and fullness, even though much has changed, even though we're alone here, without your aunt and uncle, without your mother and my partner."

Romilly thought this over. She didn't have her uncle's years and perspective, yet what he said rang true. It explained her hunger for a past that seemed more robust and colorful and joyous: what she described longingly as *the bygone days.* "You've never told me much about this uncle. Why is that?" She sat up straight, made alert by this awareness. "Was he an unpleasant man?"

"Not at all, Romilly. And anyway, even if he were, you can be sure I'd tell you all about it. The older I get, the more I talk. My—I mean your—uncle... Is it all right with you, Romilly, if I just call your aunt and uncle mine, too, for simplicity?" Romilly nodded. "Anyway, my uncle was a quiet, tenderhearted man. He ran a sawmill, as I believe you know, and I think he enjoyed sawing and planing the boards smooth, but the felling of trees seemed to make him melancholy. Then, too, he wasn't particularly robust. The labor weakened his body. By early summer, he was exhausted. That's why they'd spend the summers here—to rest his body. In the summer, he turned his skills to making paper for my aunt's paintings, and in fact developed a great obsession with molding new types of paper from plant materials, and with concocting inks and pigments from the oak galls, mushrooms, and berries in these woods. He even fashioned brushes for her from the fur of various animals, and quill pens from the feathers of the swans and geese that nested on the shore. This was partly a way to afford materials, but he enjoyed the magic of it quite a bit. The natural world was his particular love. And I know he loved my aunt deeply as well."

"My father said my aunt and uncle went to live across the Sound when their house in the forest burned," Romilly said. "Do you know why it burned? Did you ever see them again?"

"Eh, he told you about the burning? When?"

"Just as we were sailing here. I asked if any of his family had been forest people and he said his uncle was, and he told me a little about this cottage—a very little. And he told me Aunt and Uncle had moved across the Sound after their house burned down."

"Yes, my aunt and uncle did move across the Sound after your mother died. Shortly thereafter we were told our uncle had died too. Apparently, he was out in his boat—it was a clear day, no storms brewing, steady wind. At evening, his boat washed back with the tide up to the wharf, almost as if it had a homing instinct. We assumed he had fallen overboard."

"How long ago was that?"

"It was a year or so after you lost your mother."

"Aunt must have grieved terribly, both for my mother and for him," said Romilly, remembering her own father's pale face, pinched and seemingly bled of life, and the disappearance of his smile.

"After my uncle's disappearance, I sailed across the Sound to visit my aunt and see what I could do to help her. She seemed more excited and worried than grief-stricken at her partner's death now that I think of it. She was subdued in the days afterward. She became quieter, kept to herself, folks said. I had asked a cousin to keep an eye on her, and he sent odd and sometimes alarming reports. She would go out sailing for days at a time, he said, which worried me. I was afraid she was trying to cross the Sound to check on her cottage, so I begged her not to, and promised I would inspect her house a few times a season when I was out trolling for fish. Once she resolved to live across the Sound, I saw her but rarely. It's been a good six or so years since—" Her uncle broke off abruptly. As she looked at his profile, it seemed to her he was deliberating on something.

"Romilly, I might as well tell you all. Your aunt would not have met with a warm return, if she had tried to live here or in the village after your mother died. You see, your uncle always would go away on his own for days on end. I never knew where. I never asked. My aunt would simply say that he was *travelling*.

One day, when he returned, she realized he was burning up with fever. Arra and your mother came to tend him, and then my partner—we'd just had our partnering ceremony—came also. The two of them, your mother and my partner, fell ill. My uncle recovered, while Arra and my aunt escaped sickness. But the townspeople were so terrified that my uncle had brought plague to the village, and this disease was so unknown and so virulent—my aunt and uncle had no choice but to leave their home. Your father told you their house burned. But it didn't just burn down, as your father told you—the townspeople set fire to their house and mill to drive my aunt and uncle out. They lived on this island for a month or so afterward, but the sense of being outcast was too much for them. They had always kept to themselves, but in a strange way were also at the center of the community, because they hosted the midsummer festival. Shortly after they had moved across the Sound, my uncle disappeared—for good."

Romilly looked down at her hands, folded in her lap.

"Does my father know his uncle gave the fever to my mother?"

"Of course!" her uncle retorted. "Though he was not part of the mob that set fire to their house."

"He hid all this from me—all except that their house had burned," Romilly said, sadly.

"Now you know why he has had an aversion to this place. It represents to him the worst possible loss, and I am sure he invests it with the power to remove other beloved things from his life."

"When we were sailing here, I noticed he could hardly bear to look at the islands," Romilly reflected. "Now I know why."

"I think, dear niece, that it is always better to know even the worst, than to hide from it."

"Did you hate your uncle for giving the sickness to your partner?" she asked slowly, looking up with him with great, apprehensive eyes.

"Not a bit!" her uncle exclaimed stoutly. "Romilly, how can I blame him? He nearly died too. He didn't have some malicious plan to spread that deadly fever."

"I'm glad, Uncle! I'm relieved. Because I am not angry with him either, I feel sorry for him. He must have felt very—heavy." As she said this, she realized she was feeling lighter, as if even the secrets you were kept out of transferred their weight. She imagined herself shedding, bit by bit, some tough and obstructing shell, as if she were hatching from an egg.

She picked up the edge of her apron and began to roll the fabric up nervously, then smooth it out again.

"Uncle, I have a secret too."

"Romilly, I wouldn't be surprised if you had many secrets. You're a deep one, you are." His eyes crinkled affectionately. Romilly raised her eyes.

"My secret is not as complicated or complete as yours. Robbie's aware of it, for instance." At the mention of his name, Robbie hopped over to Romilly and peered over her shoulder into her face, then polished his black beak against the upholstery as if honing a knife. "While you were away at the beach with Father, repairing the boat, Robbie brought me this," she said, withdrawing the cord from around her neck to show him the small bronze key. "Do you have any idea what lock this key fits?"

"Eh, I wondered where he'd flown off to!" He cupped the key gently in his palm, his face breaking into a smile of delight and recognition.

"Of course! This is the key to the cabinet where my aunt stored her papers. It's right over there—" and her uncle pointed through the double doors at the dim back corner of the studio. He grabbed her hand and leapt up, pulling her up from her seat. "But—how very odd. That key always sat in the keyhole, in plain view. I thought it was just a pretty decoration—there was no sense in locking up *paper*. Come along, let's see what Robbie wants us to find."

Entering a second time, Romilly saw the studio differently. She was not merely gazing, she was studying each detail intently, as if memorizing the features of a face. The sheer curtains floated before a wall of tall, nearly floor-to-ceiling windows, before which perched a thin-legged easel, muddy gray with many years of use, reminding her oddly of a great blue heron. Against the back wall, palettes, empty picture frames, and other tools dangled from pegs, while on shelves beneath, Romilly noticed clay jars of brushes of various sizes, from those made of the tiniest pinch of sable hairs, to those with dense rounds of bristles and substantial handles of turned wood. Corked glass medicine bottles held pigments so concentrated, they appeared to all be black. Bolts of raw canvas were propped up in the corner. Behind the worktable, a large fireplace with a tiled surround of black-green holly and crimson berries, against a serene sea-green background, drew her eye. With her fingers she traced the smooth glaze of the tiles, the darker seams in the stamped design where glaze had pooled. She ran her hands over the honey-gold, oiled wood of the mantel, the peg-work sanded perfectly flush. The air still bore the vague but nostril-clearing odors of linseed oil and turpentine. She turned her head, finally, toward the armoire of inlaid wood. A design of compass points in deep red mahogany was laid into each door. On the right-hand door, she could see a bronze escutcheon surrounding a keyhole's dark pupil. Coming close, she realized the design was also of a butterfly, the keyhole forming the head and abdomen.

She withdrew the cord from under her dress, then slipped it over her head. Her mother's delicate scissors clinked against the key, and she closed her hand around them both for a moment, then separated the key from the scissor and gripped its head, warmed from her body, between her fingers. Her hand shook a little.

"Steady, Romilly. I've scrabbled around in this cabinet many a time. There's never been anything inside that could hurt a person."

Robbie flew to her uncle's shoulder and gave a gurgling rattle, deep in his throat, that sounded encouraging. Romilly inserted the key and found it turned easily, but noticed no difference in the door. Nor did the door have a handle or knob, she realized suddenly—there was no way to pull it open. Mystified, she stood there, unsure of herself.

"Try turning the key counterclockwise," prompted her uncle, whispering.

Romilly pressed the key in the other direction, feeling a subtle resistance. At half a turn, she heard a slight click and felt a springing give as the door opened an inch. She let go of the key again to wipe her sweating palms on the bodice of her apron. Slipping a finger in the crack, she swung the door outward, then drew open the left-hand side. The cabinet contained many shelves set close together and was unexpectedly deep, as if it continued past the back wall of the room. Robbie flapped to a middle shelf, ducking his head and hunching his back so he could walk back and forth in the narrow slot, brashly tweaking scraps of paper with his beak. Each shelf contained a different weight and color of paper, the partial sheets and scraps carefully organized and held together with string.

Romilly reached her fingers out to stroke a sheet of paper. It had a felt-like quality, even though it was extremely thin, and was the rose-tinted beige of Romilly's own cheek.

"Are these your uncle's papers?" Romilly asked.

"Yes! I remember him making this batch, I believe, from cattail heads."

Romilly's uncle was eagerly and unceremoniously thumbing up papers and rubbing them to determine their thickness and texture.

"You know what I'm thinking, Romilly?"

"Yes, Uncle—you are thinking that if there are any sheets here that are light yet strong, we can use them for our letter to the Being Beyond."

"Yes, Romilly, yes! It must be strong enough to withstand being hauled some distance without tearing, but light enough that the kestrel's cord can bear its weight without breaking."

They examined the shelves intently. The shelves were well

organized, the bottom ones holding the heaviest and coarsest papers, and the upper shelves holding the lightest and sheerest. Romilly reached above her head and felt about on the topmost shelf. A sensation of glassy smoothness greeted her fingers, yet as she pressed down, she detected the cushioning of many layers.

"Lift me up, Uncle! I feel something silky up here, something like stroking a feather," she cried.

Her uncle grasped her around the waist and hoisted her up. She peered into the shadowy shelf and glimpsed an icy, opaque surface. The paper was so thin, Romilly struggled to tease the top sheet up. As fine as a dragonfly wing, it had a similar crisp rigidity. When she pulled it forward it whistled lightly, like wind across a dune of sand, and she had a moment's vertigo: as she held on to the paper's edge, she pictured herself borne skyward, kite-like. It was the finest tissue, and yet, as Romilly tugged the edge between her thumbs and forefingers, she realized it had considerable strength. It did, in fact, seem like an insect's wing, resilient in the way of alive things. She turned her neck to smile into her uncle's beaming face.

"This will do, Uncle—set me down," she said, and he lowered her slowly. The sheet of tissue followed, draping like cloth. It was the length of her entire body, and she had to hold her arms overhead to keep the end from brushing the floor. Her uncle grasped hold of the lower edge to lift it and they backed up together slowly until they stood alongside the worktable, then lay the paper gently atop the butterfly collage. Underneath the butterfly glowed, dimly visible as if under cloudy ice. The paper was the color of bright moonlight and cooled the golden heat of the sun's rays, palpable through the window's curtains.

"Uncle, have you ever seen anything so full of light!" Romilly cried out in excitement. Her uncle smiled down into her hopeful face, in which not a trace of fear or loneliness or hidden grief was visible.

"Yes," he said, "as it happens, I have."

7

SUNSTROKE

When Romilly and her uncle closed the doors and drew the curtains to her aunt's studio, she felt as if she had met again a person she'd been close to before her memory started. Some-one into whose lap she used to climb. Lost in these thoughts, she watched her uncle blow on the coals of the fire and build up a pyramid of kindling.

"Uncle, I must have met this aunt when I was very small, but I don't remember her. Do you think my mother ever took me to this studio? It seems so familiar to me, as if perhaps I used to play here. I seem to remember the smell, and the holly pattern on the tiles around the fireplace."

"I don't recall you coming here, but perhaps you did. My aunt made the tiles when you were just a small child. Your mother especially loved the ancient holly tree outside your front door. She used to cut leaves and berries and make wreathes for all the family in wintertime. Aunt glazed these tiles for herself and for your mother, but your mother passed away before she made use of them. Likely they are still in the attic of your house."

"But, Uncle, there's no holly tree at my house, not near the door nor elsewhere."

Her uncle came to the end of the table and gripped the back of a chair. His eyes were somber.

"Romilly, I don't want you to judge your father. When your mother died, he was beside himself with grief. He couldn't bear anything that reminded him of her. So the first thing he did was take his axe and cut apart that poor holly tree and hack its roots from the ground. Every time a seedling sprouted near the door, he'd pull it up by the root. He only seemed content when the dooryard was hardpacked earth so ruthlessly swept, it grew polished. The first day after her death, I threw myself before your mother's portrait and desk and made him promise to save her things for you. You have noticed he never goes in her study. Everything that belonged to her seems to scald him. I was shocked you convinced him to bring the sails to the *Ingres* down from the attic, never mind sail after me. And when that boat was damaged, I expected it to unsettle his mind—to sort of plunge him back to your mother's illness. Though the fact that he knows how to fix this damage, that he can restore her, seems to have heartened him."

With each new detail of her father's grieving, Romilly felt her anxiety grow. He'd been left alone a long time—it was well past midafternoon. Knowing him, he hadn't stopped work even for a sip of water, and it was a sultry, cloudless day. And what if his wound reopened? She put away the information her uncle had shared, as if her own heart was a cabinet no one knew about. She could feel the pressure of his story there, but there was no time now to process it.

"Uncle, I'm worried we've left father alone too long—will you go and fetch him? I'll stay here and prepare the evening meal. We may have to force him to rest."

He gave the fire a couple of jabs with the poker to settle the coals, then lay on some split logs. "Aye, niece. I'll run down to the beach and bring him back with me by force if necessary. I brought up some clams from the shore and left them in the pantry. I was going to make a chowder but do what you will with them." He turned on his heel with his usual springy gait, scooping up Robbie from the cabinet where he had been dozing on one leg. As he strode off, the crow blinked and fluffed up his neck feathers, as if rearranging his suit after a nap, and Romilly smiled after them.

Romilly went to the pantry and fetched the burlap sack of clams. She would open them, mince them, and use the rye flour to make fritters, if only she could find something to fry them in. Noticing a lidded jar, she opened it to find a wax-pale paste which gave off the sweet smoke of bacon grease. Then she took the bucket her uncle had left near the front door and crossed the yard toward the well. As she hauled up water, she noticed the bucket's wooden staves were pale gold, while the stiff hempen rope gave off a grassy smell like a freshly woven basket. Had her uncle brought these too? Or had some other benefactor known they would need to draw water? Each new task seemed to reveal some invisible hand working behind the scenes to help them.

She had much to process, and so much more to plan. Judging by the sun, it was rounding on five in the afternoon. She now had the materials for writing a letter to this Being—if they could find a way to occupy her father. She would probably only have space for one question. But what should it be? And how could she expect this Being to know her language? Perhaps they knew all languages. The most urgent and tormenting question was whether her world was even—actual. What if everything that seemed so real to her was simply the creation of this Being? Yes, this was the fear that squeezed her heart: that her world and all things that seemed substantial and richly alive were just the pretendings and make-believe of some all-powerful being, a kind of amusement, like a play. Perhaps death was merely this creator's decision to change the actors. The gradual *diminishment* of her world haunted her. Her father's pallor and thinness; the fact, she realized now, that hardly a single child had been born in the village in the past few years; that her family had scattered so far, she scarcely knew who they were. She didn't, she recalled abruptly, have a single friend her own age. How had these realities become so normal? There was a resignation to loss in her father, and even, until the appearance of the Being, in *her*. This resignation had made her feel dead inside.

As she thought through all this, she was shucking a small, sweet cherrystone, and another surge of anger sent the knife skipping out of the groove. The point embedded itself in the center of her palm, making a neat, clean wound like a slit in thin paper. She dropped the clam and brought her palm toward her face to watch the cut, anxiety rising in her—what if she, too, were made of paper? But blood welled up, first cautiously as if surprised to be set free, then brimming and crimson. Odd to feel only relief at the sting, then the dull ache as she thrust her hand into the wooden bucket of cold water.

Just then, she heard her uncle's distant shout. She ran to the door in time to see him stagger out of the woods and into the clearing, her father's arm slung over his shoulder. Her father's shirt was loosely draped around his back and shoulders. When she ran forward and placed her hand on her father's chest, his skin scorched her.

"Sunstroke," her uncle was gasping. "And he's badly sunburned. We need well water, lots of it. Fetch the washtub." Romilly raced for the tin washtub in the pantry.

"Set it here by the sofa, and empty this bucket into it." Romilly did as he asked, while her uncle flung her father down on the sofa and began to strip off his shirt and trousers. "Now, take it, and the bucket in the yard, and draw more water." Heaving him up into a sitting position, he placed her father's feet and legs in the washtub and began to splash the cold water over his lap and legs with his cupped palms while Romilly ran with the buckets toward the well.

As Romilly returned to the house, staggering under the sloshing weight, she heard her uncle crying out to her, "And also rags, Romilly. I need towels and rags, as many as you can find." Romilly yanked the towels off the washbasin in the corner of the room and dashed back to the sofa, where she plunged them in the tub and wrung them out. While her uncle poured the cold water over her father, she draped the cold wet towels over his chest and head and packed them under his armpits.

"Uncle," she cried, remembering. "Arra gave me a draught before we left the village—she said it was good for sunstroke!"

"Bring it then, and quickly!"

Her father was beginning to moan and pull the towels away from his face.

Romilly fetched the bottle from the pantry, tore off the wax seal, and twisted out the cork. She gave it to her uncle, who supported her father's neck in one hand and brought the bottle to his lips. Her father grimaced and turned his face away.

"It's no use. I've caught the fever, the fever that took—"

"Nonsense," her uncle said crisply. "You have sunstroke brought on by your own fool carelessness, working shirtless and hatless in this sun, refusing to take a break or drink a mug of water. Drink, drink this, you stubborn man! We're trying to help you. Drink this, blast you, or—"

Romilly had never heard her uncle swear. Her father, also surprised by this outburst, seemed suddenly inclined to obey. He took three sips of the tonic, grimacing, then downed an entire mug of cold water. His face, normally pale and thin, was a uniform scarlet, as if he had been scalded in steam. As Romilly soaked and twisted out a rag and draped it over his forehead, his teeth began to chatter violently. She urged the bottle to his lips again.

"Nay," her uncle said, "slowly now. We don't want him to vomit. The man needs salt. Romilly, can you make a salty broth out of anything in the pantry?"

"The clams, Uncle—I've shucked them and saved the juice. I will make a broth with those!"

"That's perfect, niece. But first, will you please fetch more water?"

Romilly snatched up the bucket and ran with it to the well. She filled the bucket to the brim, then staggered with it back to her uncle, who began to pour the cold water over her father's lap and legs. Crossing to the fireplace, she unhooked the kettle, poured out half the water outside the door and added the clam juices. She forced herself to calm down, to move slowly and deliberately. Her head was spinning not just from the effort, but from the events of the morning. Aside from her mother's loss, nothing much had happened to her in her entire life, but now every moment seemed to bring new wonders or emergencies. When the broth began to steam, she returned to her uncle's side. He continued to pour mugs of water slowly over her father's legs and into his lap. Touching her father's chest, she realized he was already noticeably cooler, though the skin of his face and neck was scorched scarlet. He opened his eyes and gazed at her.

"She's healed, Romilly." He was smiling a sad, gentle smile in which was mingled a bit of quiet pride. Romilly was a little scared by the way he phrased this, as if the *Ingres* was a living being, a body. But didn't she also see the world this way?

"I'm glad, Father. I knew you could fix her. Now we just need to make *you* well again."

"I'll be all right. I just couldn't leave her alone to sink again, you see. Just as the incoming water began to shift her, I set the last peg. The tide will lift her soon."

He closed his eyes as Romilly stroked the back of his hand. He reached to stop her, gripping her wrist so tightly it hurt.

"She's beautiful, Romilly. I forgot how beautiful. But then, I have tried to forget everything, everything, haven't I."

Romilly looked up at her uncle anxiously, but he was smiling. Her father cupped the curl of her fingers gently in his palm and continued.

"I've kept much from you. Not just facts. But feelings. Knowledge of her. The past. I will try to do better, Romilly. I will try to be less afraid." He squeezed her hand, then reached weakly for the mug. She filled it again with cold well water, which he drank down in small, even sips.

"You'll need to move me. This water is ruining the sofa."

Romilly exchanged looks with her uncle, amusement mingling with concern. There was no way her father could make it up the stairs, where his bed had been made up on the floor. Convincing him to let her uncle carry him upstairs was even more unlikely. As if her father read their minds, he exclaimed, weakly, "Oh, for goodness' sake, just make a bed for me out of the way—over here by the fireplace. Or the studio—that will do. I'm tired." The studio! Romilly thought. She had relied on his aversion to the studio; they badly needed him out of the way if Romilly was to write the letter to the Being. Her uncle motioned to her to come near the fire, stirring at it with the poker to mask his whispering.

"Romilly, this is a wondrous transformation! Yesterday and this morning he was reluctant even to remain indoors. He hasn't been in the studio since well before he lost your mother."

"Uncle, relieved as I am by his change of heart, think how this affects our plans! How am I to write a letter to the Being with my father resting in there? What if he asks what I'm up to? What if he steals up behind me and reads the message? He will think I've lost my senses."

"Well, it seems he's also lost his senses, in the best possible way. It's likely, dearest niece, that he will sleep into the evening. Sunstroke is terribly exhausting. I will keep watch on him in the studio. Or, if you prefer, you can work at the kitchen table. I doubt he'll be on his feet before evening."

"What are you whispering about," her father said. They turned their heads to see him standing behind them, shaky but upright, wrapped in a large towel. He looked oddly like a little boy after a bath, the damp hair over his ears curling slightly. He held the mug out in one hand, the other gripping the edges of the towel to hold them together. "Can I have more of the tonic? It seems to have done me good." His face, she noticed, was a shining scarlet, but the redness was receding a bit from his arms and chest, whose thinness made it seem as if he were collapsing inward, like sand pouring down a hole.

"Uncle, is it safe?" she asked, as she reached for the bottle on the kitchen table. She went to her father, led him by the elbow to a chair, and sat him down.

"Yes, niece. Arra would put nothing in there that would harm a body."

She poured out the tonic into a mug and helped it to her father's lips. He drank steadily, tipping the mug back to ensure he consumed every drop. He ran his tongue over his upper lip slowly, reflecting. "Are you sure, daughter, that's the same tonic? Its bitterness is gone."

"Perhaps you are just used to it, Father." Romilly smiled at
him as he repressed a yawn, pretending to wipe his lips with the
back of his hand. "I'm going to make up a bed for you—will
the studio still suit you?"

Her father looked toward the curtains with a flicker of in-
quisitiveness. "Yes," he said slowly, "I think I should like to
sleep near the windows, if I might."

"That's a good idea, Father. We can open the windows and
let the breeze cool you. But first, let's see if we can find something for you to wear." Romilly fetched the basket of clothing
she had gathered that seemingly long-ago morning. She located
her father's soft linen shirt, a well-worn garment that had once
been indigo but now was faded to a frosty blue gray. He would
have to wear this over his drawers. At least his legs would stay
cool. She returned to her father's side and helped him thread
his arms through his sleeves, then buttoned the top few buttons
for him.

"You have the makings of a good mother," her uncle said,
as he strode to the studio curtains and drew them aside with
a sweep of his arms. Her father approached the doors and
touched, with his forefinger, a tiny, perfect replica of her aunt's
cottage. The building stones were engraved in precisely, the
windows with their diamonds of glass minutely rendered. She
had not even noticed it, hidden as it was at the edge of the
clearing in which a doe, alert, seemed to twitch her ears as she
stood over her fauns.

"I carved this cottage, here, when my aunt was teaching me
drawing. I once thought I might be an architect, or a builder.
I had forgotten all about it." His eyes traveled over the other
scenes. "Brother always had a gift for creatures."

He dropped his eyes to the doorknobs, then set his hands
slowly atop them and turned. When the doors swung open,
he stood for a moment perfectly still, then shuffled in. Romilly watched him anxiously. What memories would this place
evoke? Suddenly, she realized she had never *not* been apprehensive about his reactions to the past—images, reminders,

mentionings—as if she were the guardian of his pain. All her short life she had watched his face anxiously, calculating the cost to him of sharing the information she yearned for, afraid if she pushed him too far, he would close off the past entirely to her. She scarcely dared to breathe as he walked slowly up to the table, touched the paper lying there with his fingertips, then raised his eyes to the holly tiles surrounding the fireplace. He gazed at them a long time without speaking, then turned his head and called her name, softly. She stepped quietly to his side.

"When you were born, in deep midwinter," he murmured, "your mother cut holly sprigs and surrounded your cradle with them. She said their thorns would protect you." He seemed at peace with that memory and smiled gently down on her. "Think of that," he continued. "She loved you so." She slipped her fingers in the curl of his hand.

He took a careful, level glance around the room, then smiled faintly. "It's funny, I dreaded coming in here, but I remember the smell and the light and all I think of is the absorption of drawing, of getting the perspective of a building down proper. I forget what I was afraid of," he mused.

"I'm grateful for everything you tell me about my mother," Romilly cried out softly. She had a sudden, strange vista of her life, of being old and telling a lap-child everything she had gathered and gleaned about the past. What it would be like to have story upon story rather than the few images she possessed, so few they seemed to double and triple in number every time her father shared the briefest scene?

Her uncle, who had been arranging cushions and blankets near the window, approached them with gentled jocularity and said, making a low bow, "Your majesty's bedchamber is ready." Romilly turned to excuse herself, but her uncle grasped hold of her apron strings and gave a little jerk.

"This humble page will attend to the broth and the evening meal, milady. Your charge is to make sure this gentle knight doesn't fall asleep before he eats and drinks some more." Leading her father by the arm toward the bed, he continued. "And the gentle knight's charge is to tell his ministering daughter everything he remembers about his Fair Lady, her mother—or at least everything he remembers until supper is served."

After her father had finished the warm broth and had pushed away the second fritter she had urged on him, he turned his face to the window. For a few moments she watched his lashes slowly rise and fall as he watched the flickering light falling through the tree canopy onto the grass. Then his eyes closed, and his breathing slowed. She sat in stillness, wondering at the change that had come over him. He wasn't transformed, exactly. She could see that, even as he told her about her mother, he was beset by reluctance and fear. Sometimes he seemed to struggle onward, and sometimes he had let a long pause hang between them. He was like an injured person on a long foot journey who, to press on through the pain, must rest now and again. Yes, he was no longer completely avoiding the pain of remembering. The brittle, crystalline shell of false strength had begun to melt off him. Softly, Romilly rose and tiptoed out of the room. She fetched her journal from the basket and returned to the studio, sitting down in the chair at the worktable. She had two urgent tasks before her: first, to draft a message to the Being Beyond, and second, to capture the new images of her mother that her father had given her, this new hoard of treasures to pore over.

Her eyes came into focus on the paper before her, underneath which the collage gazed up, as if through sunlit water. Reaching under the paper she pulled out the collage to examine it again. She could see a faint glistening on the upper edge of the butterfly's wing, the sheerest film of paste. It occurred to her suddenly that a remembered person can be somewhat like a collage. You brought your own memories together with another person's memories, and somehow created the illusion of unity. But how had this collage been made? How could it hold such a volume of space and time, suggesting a whole world? Suddenly, a memory was returned to her, bursting like a star in her mind: her mother holding on her outstretched palm a cube of paper. It had been cleverly folded; one side contained a tiny peephole she could look in to. The cube rested, light as a dry leaf, on her palm—vacant, yet full too. She remembered her desire to enter its secret world, then finally giving in to the impulse, leaving her only the creased sheet, two dimensional and inert. As she recalled this moment, she was turning the collage over and over in her hands without really seeing it. But a roughness struck her, and suddenly she peered intently at the back side of the collage. It was a muslin-colored patchwork of papers, almost like a beloved garment that had been mended repeatedly. Penciled in a corner, surrounded in an enclosing flourish, was the single word *Digby*.

She carried the collage to her uncle who was banking the fire.

"What does Digby mean, Uncle?" she asked. He started.

"Where did you hear that name?" he asked, mystified.

"So, it's a name? Whose?"

"Why, it's aunt's partner, the papermaker. Where did you learn of that?"

"He's signed the back of the butterfly." Her uncle gave a prolonged, raspy whistle.

"Eh," he whispered. "That quiet, clever man was also an artist!"

8

THE MESSAGE

Her uncle was right—her father slept on until sunset, rousing once to take a long drink of water, murmuring a few times in sleep, but barely shifting position. Romilly sat at the worktable, her open journal before her. At first she thought she'd set down only what her father had told her about her mother in that golden half hour before her uncle brought their dinner, but on reflection, she decided to tell the entire story of the mission to find Uncle, since so much had been revealed and knit together of the bygone days. Every development—the collision with the split boulder, the discovery of the cottage, Uncle's reappearance, Robbie's *Yllimor! Yllimor!*, Mira and the gauntlet, being given the key, entering the studio, the discovery of the collage, then the paper—had contributed to opening the wellspring of the past. Whole individuals whose lives she had never suspected, others who were shadow figures flat as paper dolls, were now rounded and real in her imagination. She had discovered she had a living aunt—closest blood to her mother. Romilly wondered how the living could be kept at such a rigorous distance, so that they might as well not even exist. And why, she thought with some indignation, had her uncle never described his boyhood at his aunt's, when he had so freely shared his boyhood on the farm and those happy times. Then she remembered how he lost the people closest to him—his partner—and then, when the villagers burned them out, his aunt and uncle. And her father too, had changed, had darkened from that day. What agony that must have been, how ashamed her uncle and father must have been of their community. Shame, she concluded, was a great impediment to memory being passed on. It created walls around the painful moments of the past, like permanent blisters.

After her uncle withdrew, her father had admitted to his worst shames. Destroying the holly her mother had nurtured near the door. Destroying the holly tiles, too, smashing them into dust with his heaviest maul. After the uprooting, he confided, Romilly had searched and searched for the holly tree, as if she had hoped a tree could simply lift its roots and walk away—by the barn, in the orchard, along the path to Arra's cottage. Romilly had combed the dooryard for any stray seedling. When he'd found her digging with a teaspoon at a survivor, he had jerked her away by the arm, roughly—the only time he had ever laid a hand on her in anger. When he found a tiny, two-leaved seedling in a medicine bottle on her bedroom sill, hidden behind the curtain, he had removed it without a word to her. He had done everything in his power to eradicate her attachment to a past which had become for him an agony. But didn't he see, Romilly had asked, that by preventing her, he had merely made keener her longing to know? Yes, he saw this now. He still was not sure he could face his entire past, but he knew he had no right to prevent her from knowing all she could know about those from whom she came.

Where did that leave her? she wondered, as she listened to her father's steady breathing. Did his acknowledgment extend to her need to know the Being who had opened her world? It was strange how you could move so much closer to a person, yet still be so far from them. Softened as her father seemed toward the past, she knew her curiosity about the Beyond was a gulf between them. She felt uneasy. She had resented his nearly inviolable silence about the past because it made the past a secret, something she would never be privileged to know. Now she, too, had a secret. Several secrets, in fact—the first being what she witnessed in the wheat field, the second being her aunt's bequeathing of the island. She had judged her father for closing off truths. But in fact, she was no better, even as he opened up to her. But hers was a secret her village would find terrifying. If they had forced her aunt and uncle into exile over a disease unintentionally brought back from his travels, what would they do to her and her uncle for contacting an alien Being who seemed determined to open their world?

She fixed her eyes on the collage before her. She was like the Being, looking into the lives of these harvesters, into their enclosed and oblivious world. What should she ask? *Why do you keep opening my world? Where do you come from? What are you? Do you have a name?* To know a name was important; it meant a Being could be approached and addressed, that more could be asked. There was, it turned out, much history to her name. Just then, her uncle cracked open the door and peeked in.

"I went down to the shore to see if the *Ingres* was afloat in the high tide, and she was stable as a swan, so I towed her into the channel and anchored her out. Is he awake?" he whispered.

Romilly answered with a smile and a quick shake of her head. Her uncle beamed.

"Excellent," he pronounced. "Would you like your tea?"

"Yes, Uncle, I'm coming. I think I know the questions we must ask the Being." Romilly slipped the collage back under the paper, rose, and tiptoed over to her father to ensure his eyes were closed. Then she followed her uncle into the kitchen and joined him at the table, where he was lighting an oil lamp with a flaming twig. He poured hot water into mugs and set out bread and cheese. "It's a pity I forgot *actual* tea," he murmured mournfully. "But we can pretend, can't we!"

"Uncle," she said, smiling, "how come I always just call you Uncle. Don't you have a name?"

"Naturally, I have a name. But everyone calls me Uncle. I've always been called that, since I was a young man. Well," he reflected, "as a very young man, when there were so many of us, everyone called me Brother."

"Uncle, be serious. I've never heard your name. Don't you think that's strange?"

"Not for this family, Romilly. My name is Felix."

"Felix." Romilly tried out the name, squinting at him. "It

suits you. But Uncle Felix—I can't call you that. You will always be Uncle." She paused. "Uncle, I would like to know if this Being has a name," she continued.

"Very well. Proper introductions seem important." He chuckled.

"Uncle, you shouldn't tease! I've learned from my own name that names convey a lot of information. Even *having* a name," she cocked a brow at him, "is significant. Also," she continued, more confident, "I would like to ask why they are opening our world."

"Or why they *keep* doing it," her uncle added. "Are they trying to communicate with us? Are they even *aware* of us?"

"Yes, Uncle, but, unfortunately, we have two chances right now, a front side and a back side. And yes and no answers may not be so helpful."

"You are very clever, Romilly." Her uncle placed a finger on his temple gravely. "After tea, why don't you fetch the paper and lay it out on this table. I will check on your father in case he wakes, so you can write your questions. I will bring you a brush and ink for the purpose."

Romilly wiped down the table with a dampened cloth. Tiptoeing to the door of the studio, she listened to her father's even, almost purring breath, then beckoned her uncle in. He lifted the paper by one end and draped it over her outstretched arms. In the kitchen, she laid it down on the table as if it were a living, sleeping thing, then took a seat before it, smoothing it with her palms. Looking closely, she could see that it was poreless and smooth as the skin on her inner arm. Very rarely, she saw a short, fine, reddish fiber embedded into the paper. She knew paper was made from either cloth or plants but couldn't conceive of how you could liquify a plant's fibers to make a paper as glassy as this. She half-expected the ink to bead up on such a surface.

Her uncle had selected a brush and was busy at one end of

the table, uncorking bottles of ink and pouring out a drop or two into a cluster of saucers. He tested each one on a piece of scrap paper, squinting as he tilted the paper to the light to see how quickly it dried. Then he flipped the scrap over to make sure the ink hadn't bled through. Satisfied, he came over to her end of the table and sat beside her.

"Romilly, the ink is prepared. But I have no idea how it will react to this paper, whether it will bleed through, whether it will dry the same as on this scrap. If we fail, we can try again with another sheet, but when your father wakes, all this experimenting will be much more difficult, so let us hope the first time's the charm. Are you ready?"

Romilly nodded, swallowing with difficulty, and fighting the urge to wash her hands again. They were damp with nervousness. She picked the brush off the table and held it to her chest a moment with both hands, gathering her thoughts. Then she rolled the bristles in the ink, pressed the excess ink from each side, and formed a precise point. She leaned over the paper and sighted down the long handle of the hovering brush, hesitating.

"Romilly," her uncle whispered, "I am going to keep watch at the studio door. There's nothing to fear. If it comes out wrong, we'll simply try again."

She touched the point to the paper.

Afterward, it was as if she woke from sleep to find the letter materialized before her. In steady, clear print that spread almost to the margins, the blue-black of huckleberry juice, were the words:

WHY HAVE
YOU OPENED
OUR WORLD?

Her uncle was sprinkling the ink with fine sand and brushing it off with a turkey feather.

"Let's allow it to dry a few moments, Romilly, then we'll turn it over and you can write your second question." He looked at her more closely. "Romilly, your brows are drawn. What could be going through that mind of yours?"

"I was thinking how simple this question is, but how peculiar—that it's beautiful, somehow, perhaps like a line of a poem. My mother said, before she died, that I was from a long line of artists and poets, but I didn't even know what that meant. I have never written a poem or even thought about poetry."

"And do you think you know what it means now?"

"I think a poet must have the kind of mind that makes connections. That sees meaning as the magic that connects all things. And perhaps I have those tendencies after all. I am oddly unsurprised that there seems to be something or someone outside my world. I always felt there must be. I have always wondered where my mother went, for instance. After death," she added, softly.

Her uncle stopped in thought. He took up the turkey feather and twirled the quill between his fingers, making it spin. He looked thoughtful. "You think that, if this Being lives outside our world, then perhaps your mother is there also?"

Romilly nodded, her eyes large with tears.

"Are you hoping the Being might be your mother, child?"

Romilly nodded again, holding the tips of her fingers against her lips, which had wrenched in sorrow. Her uncle pulled her into his side with his free arm and she nestled her cheek into his ribs.

"Let's believe, then. Perhaps believing is braver than not believing. I will believe with you that my partner is there also. And if we are wrong—" Romilly lifted her head, and they gazed a long moment into each other's eyes. He shrugged, then hugged her to him more tightly. "If we are wrong, our belief still speaks to the depth and constancy of our love."

He let her go and tapped the table briskly with both hands.

"All right. Enough philosophizing. Let's see what's happened to the other side of this paper." Lifting an edge of the paper, he ducked his head to peer beneath.

"Aha! The ink *didn't* bleed through!" he exclaimed. "You can just see it, but if you write large, maybe even one giant word per line, I think it will work!" Gingerly, he touched the inked letters.

"Look at that, no smudging. It's already dry! Romilly, let's flip the paper over—you take the other corner." As they lifted the sheet, sand fell shushing to the table. They hoisted the paper until it stood on end, flexed, and draped down, revealing the blank side. Romilly could see the printing, reversed and blurry as if it had been finger-written into a frosted pane.

"Uncle, another color of ink would help distinguish the writing on this side."

"An excellent idea, Romilly." He picked up the various bottles and held them to the light. "The sun has set, Romilly—we must hurry. I can barely tell these colors apart."

"Judge by the cork, Uncle," Romilly said. "Here's one that looks more red than black."

"You're right, my girl!" He poured a few drops into a saucer. The ink was the color of a deep-red rose. Romilly swirled the brush in a glass of spirits, the brush tinkling against the sides. With a rag, she wiped the tip, then rolled the brush in the burgundy ink. Slowly, with more consciousness than before, she wrote four words in enormous capitals, one per line:

TELL

US

YOUR

NAME

9

THE BEING BEYOND

Romilly and her uncle sanded the writing, then carried the letter into the pantry and set it out of sight atop a cupboard. She felt wrung of thought, as if she had completed the hardest of examinations. She sat in the crook of the sofa, her arms around her drawn up knees, looking out at the evening. Through the fish-scale windows, she could see the faintest streak of greenish light through the western trees and the occasional flicker of a bat, pure black against shadowy gray. Her uncle was moving through the kitchen with a flaming bit of kindling, lighting the other lamps, when the studio doors swung open. Her father stood there uncertainly, blinking the sleep out of his eyes. Romilly rose and put her palm against his forehead. It was cool, but a single blister spread like a mask over his nose and cheeks.

"Daughter, how long have I been sleeping?" he asked.

"Almost four hours, altogether, Father. Uncle helped you to the house in the afternoon and it is just past sunset now. How do you feel?"

"I feel as if I've woken after a hundred-year sleep. Brother, when did you say the tide would be low again?"

"No need to fret, brother. While you were sleeping, I checked on your *Ingres* and she was afloat with but the tiniest of leaks. She'll be fine until morning. I was able to tow her along the shoreline and into the channel to anchor her out. She can stay there until I've built her a cradle and made the permanent repair. Can't have you springing a leak in open waters."

Romilly's father sighed and relaxed his shoulders, somewhat mollified.

"Romilly, do you think my trousers are dry? I feel foolish

walking about in just my drawers." Romilly fetched his trousers from a chair near the fireplace, where they had been set to dry. Her father sat at the table to pull them on, then ducked his head to look closely at the table's surface.

"Why, there's sand all over the table," he murmured.

"Yes, Father, it came out of your cuffs when I set your trousers there." Romilly flushed. Her uncle, who was banking up the fire, caught her eye and winked.

"I wish I could see her with my own eyes," her father said, wistfully.

"There's light enough for that. I warrant if you walk out between the trees to the flat spot, you can see her anchored in the channel. Romilly can take a lantern and go with you. Head toward the little hut and just beyond it you'll see the wide path opening out. Romilly, you can feed a late dinner to your kestrel on the way." Again, her uncle winked at her.

At the mention of the hut, her father's eyes took on an empty, haunted look, but his desire to see his boat prevailed. Holding the lantern in one hand and the crook of his arm with the other, Romilly guided him toward the door, ducking into the pantry to retrieve the saucer of minced meat. In the yard, fireflies were beginning to launch from the grass blades and up through the trees, disappearing, reappearing, sending cool, green-tinged signals to each other. Romilly steered her father around the side of the cottage and toward the dark form of the hut. She could palpably detect the tension in his body as they neared the building, so she released his arm.

"Stay here if you'd prefer, Father. I'm going to give the kestrel her evening feeding and I shan't be longer than a few minutes."

"Nay, Romilly, I'll come with you." Her father scrutinized the dark shape and followed Romilly over to it. Mira, at her approach, gave a high piping cry from her perch and quivered her wings at the sight of the meat. Romilly took up a strip of the purplish flesh and dangled it before the kestrel, who pinched it delicately, then, with the odd little toss of her head, ingested it. Busy with the feeding, Romilly didn't notice at first that her father was standing before the door of the hut, but hearing him lift the bar, she turned her head. He peered inside a moment, his hand braced against the doorframe, then disappeared into the dark tunnel with a determined rush. After a moment she thought she heard a dry, abrasive sound, as of a hand rubbing against stone or brick.

"Father?" she queried, stepping toward the door.

"It's all right, it's all right, I was just seeing if there was any hull paint or putty in there—it would be good to fill and paint those scratches where she scraped against the rock."

"I see. Well, we can look in the morning when there's light, but from earlier today I can tell you there seems to be nothing in that hut but some old books and falconry tools. Shall we walk to the flat spot?" She took her father's arm again and led him toward the gap in the tree line, where she could just barely see the crinkle of water in the last light. The path, soft, almost puffy with layers of dead and decaying leaves, led gently downhill where it gradually widened into a flat grassy spot overlooking the water. Shelf rock formed a bench at the end of the clearing, and Romilly led her father around to the front and gently sat him down. Beneath them, the *Ingres* floated like a ghostly curled leaf on the water, her bow rope fine as a spider's web. The silvery sheen in the western sky glazed her mast with a fine highlight. Hushed, crisp, the sound of the waves reached them, while in the tall grass on the edges of the clearing, crickets chirped sweetly.

"See, she's floating beautifully, Father. There's no need to worry."

They sat awhile in the pleasantly cool evening. A humid breeze rolled over them, smelling of birch leaves and soft water, and carrying the tinkling chime of pulleys knocking together on the mast rigging.

"Brother should have her fixed in two days, I should think. It will take a day to build the cradle, a day or two to repair her. So, three days at most," he mused. But he seemed unagitated by the delay. "I'm glad, Romilly, that you told Arra about our mission. The townsfolk might have worried." Romilly doubted, in fact, that anyone but Arra would notice a week-long disappearance. Aside from Arra and her uncle, she couldn't remember the last time anyone paid them a visit.

"Father," she began, then hesitated. He looked at her inquisitively but said nothing. She thought hard about her question, then decided to risk it.

"Father, today while you were sleeping, I found a piece of art with the name Digby on it and Uncle told me he was Aunt's partner and—the one who brought the fever here from his travels." Her father gazed at her, the expression of his eyes impossible to make out in the dim light. She held her breath, expecting anger, fear, exasperation, anything but what came next.

"Digby," he said slowly, as if tasting the word. "Digby was my friend and, it was said, my distant blood. But there were sides to him none knew about, not even I. He would never say, for example, where he traveled, or why. And none ever saw him leave or knew how he returned. I never pried. I accepted he must have his reasons. He was a frail man, so I assumed he was under the care of a doctor across the Sound."

"How did you become such friends with him, Father?"

"Well, because he had travelled widely, he had wonderful stories about distant parts of the world, their history and geography, their wars and struggles. As a young man I had hoped to go to university across the Sound. I thought, even—" here he looked almost ashamed—"of studying music. But I had to take over the farm after my parents died—I was the eldest."

"I found, once, a violin above a cupboard in the kitchen. The strings were broken, and it was very dusty, but quite beautiful. Uncle once told me it was yours. He told me you were the most talented violinist anyone had ever heard."

"Aye, that was true, though it seems vain to admit it. And Digby used to love to hear me play—so he encouraged me. Without him, I would have ceased music entirely. Digby *was* my university. In the few hours a week that I was free of labors, we would talk, or rather, he would talk, and I would listen, greedily. He is the one who brought me back that violin from his travels. He thought it would encourage me to play more if I had a truly exceptional instrument. But to work the farm took all the energy I had. When he fell ill, at first all I felt was alarm that I might lose him. No, it was stronger—it was panic. He was my connection to a larger world, he and—your mother. Somehow, it never occurred to me she'd fall ill tending him. When she grew so desperately ill, when she lay dying, while he recovered, why—Romilly, I'm ashamed to admit it—I saw his travels in a darker light and—I wanted him to suffer as I was suffering and to feel as destitute." Her father turned to face her squarely. "Romilly, I wanted him to know what it was to lose the dearest thing to him, as I had. In fact, I wanted him dead. And so, when the villagers took up torches and went through the woods to burn down his house, I did nothing to prevent them. And when he disappeared, when he was lost at sea, I felt—vindication. In my mind, he was responsible for separating me from your mother, my most cherished companion, my mate, and I wanted him to feel an equal devastation. I am ashamed, daughter, but it's true. I wanted to see him lose what was most precious—" and here he broke off, his breath rasping and heaving in his chest. Romilly stroked his arm with her palm until he calmed.

"You must think I am a terrible person," he said. Romilly shook her head, her own throat too tight for words. For a while, they sat in silence. The moon was beginning to rise over the far hills, seeming weightless, like a ruddy gold, rounded bud just leaving its sheath. Then it burst free of the horizon and hovered above it, enormous, mottled, visibly drawing away. Gradually, it grew silvery as if dewed. Romilly and her father watched, entranced.

"How beautiful," he murmured, grasping her hand. She gazed at his face, which the moonlight made wistful and child-like. Had she ever heard him remark at beauty before?

&

Romilly and her father walked slowly back to the cottage, the moonlight causing their long shadows to fall before them on the grassy path. When they reached the kitchen, her father dropped into a chair by the fire, leaned his head back and closed his eyes. He chuckled faintly.

"I can't believe I could still be tired, but I am. Must be growing old," he mused.

"Nay, Father, this has been the longest day of *my* life. And you've been through much more."

She brought him a mug of hot water, which he sipped gratefully. She shaved off a paring of cheese and placed it upon a slice of bread, which he waved aside, until a stern look caused him to reconsider. He bit into the bread and chewed pensively.

"Yes, I can scarcely believe we set out from home only this morning," he mused. "I feel like a different person than the one who pointed the *Ingres* out to sea. You're quiet, my daughter," he added.

"I have so much to think about," Romilly replied. "So many pieces of my life have come together in one day. My life suddenly seems expanded, like a piece of tightly crumpled paper that's been smoothed out." She faltered, then pressed on. "I always knew our family had a past, but events before my birth seemed like ancient and unrecorded history. Now I understand."

Her father smiled at her, tipping his head back in an exhaustion that was peaceful and against which he did not struggle.

"Romilly, I believe I'll go to bed now. Upstairs," he specified. "Under my own power," he added. He stood and gazed at her a moment, then ducked his head and kissed her on the forehead. When he turned away to climb the stairs, she touched the place of the kiss with her fingers, her eyes brimming.

Just then, her uncle opened the front door a crack. "Is he in bed?" he whispered.

"Yes, he just climbed the stairs." Her uncle padded in softly and approached the fire.

"Good! While you were out with him taking the night air,

I fetched the spool of cord and found a hook to use to attach the—why, Romilly, are there more tears?"

"Happy ones, Uncle. He kissed my forehead. He never does that!"

Her uncle's eyes grew large. "No limit to the miracles this place is performing on him! He finally appreciates what a treasure he has." He stared a moment into the fire, all the fun suddenly extinguished from his eyes.

Romilly looked at her uncle sadly. "You would have made an exceptional father, Uncle. You've been half a father to me."

"It has been my greatest pleasure to have part-fatherhood of you," he exclaimed, his hearty manner back. "Now, let's go prepare your Mira for her epic journey Beyond!" As if at the sound of this displeasing name, Robbie, who had been dozing on one leg on his perch in the corner near the door, ruffled himself up and emitted a garrulous croak.

"Yes, Robbie, we know you'll want to supervise the whole mission. Come along, old boy," her uncle called, reaching for him as if fetching up a hat. He plopped the bird on his shoulder briskly. Robbie teetered a moment, one stabilizing wing out, and Romilly giggled at him. He looked somewhat like a night watchman caught nodding off, catching his balance just before listing off his feet. He clacked his beak officiously, tossing his head, craning his neck to make sure Romilly was following.

"I've scrolled up our note and left it in the falconer's hut, attached to the cord and spool. Your gauntlet is all ready, and I left some encouraging tidbits of meat there too." They were crossing the yard toward the hut, whose leafy roof was silvered by moonlight.

"We'll take the path to the shore," her uncle continued. "The moon's high enough to light the way. I found a dory when I arrived, overturned and camouflaged with pine branches near the shore. We can row her out to the Egg, which is where the Being has appeared these last few nights. As far as I can guess," he said, peering at the moon between the trees, "if the Being appears, they'll do so in about an hour's time."

They were approaching the hut, and Romilly noticed Mira pull herself tall, then settle and fluff as she recognized them. In a slant of moonlight, her breast shone like a pearl. Romilly reached for the gauntlet leaning against the base of her perch and pulled it on. The silver threads ran streaming through the clustered roses, piled like a bank of storm clouds in the darkness. When she outstretched her gauntleted arm, Mira hopped onto it peaceably. Romilly took a piece of meat from her uncle's fingers and offered it to the kestrel, who took it delicately on the point of her beak and tossed it back, opening and closing her beak as if reflecting on its taste. Romilly fingered the jess on her right ankle.

"Uncle," she said, "are you concerned this jess might not hold the cord?"

"Nay, Romilly, if she were to pull the note too, I'd be concerned, but remember, we are only attaching the note once— *if*—the Being grasps hold of her line. I've tested the leather and I warrant it's strong enough. Besides that, where would we find leather at this point?" Romilly let out a deep exhale. The fact that there was nothing more to be done was oddly relieving.

"Shall we go?" her uncle queried, reaching his arm out in a gesture of gallant escort. "Actually, I will put gallantry aside, only for the purpose of going before my fine lady and tripping myself up on any roots that might otherwise detain or ruffle her ladyship." Romilly smiled at him and gave a slight curtsy as he passed ahead. They crossed the yard and entered the dark woods lapped by brief waves of moonlight as boughs shifted overhead in the slight breeze. As they descended the steep slope, her uncle reached back to help Romilly over the roots and stones embedded in the path. She suddenly felt as if, indeed, she was a character in some ancient or mythic tale. Reaching the shore, her uncle leapt nimbly down, then caught her by the waist and lowered her gently to the pebbly beach. The dory was pulled up at the waterline, tied to a stake driven deep into the sand. The brimming water seemed enchanted into stillness.

She waited next to the stern as her uncle untied the bow rope

and pushed the dory toward the water. Her heart was beginning
to pound and squeeze with something that would feel like dread
if it didn't have so much eagerness and longing mixed in. Wavelets swirled and withdrew around her bare ankles, whispering
take in, let go. She filled her chest completely as if about to dive
down through clear, deep water, then stepped lightly into the
boat and took a seat in the bow. Mira looked about alertly, but
seemed unalarmed, only dipping her tail to balance herself as
Romilly's uncle used an oar to push them off the sand. As the
boat gave small jerks forward, Romilly stroked her fingertips
down the kestrel's satiny back.

The moon hung before them, imperfectly full and yet somehow more beautiful for that. Their path lay in the broad swath
of glimmering moonlight. Her uncle set the oars in the oarlocks
and began to pull with strong strokes toward the middle of the
water, where she could dimly see the two halves of the great
boulder, conjoined islands in a sea of twinkling facets. When
they reached the stone platform, her uncle pulled in the oars
and held the lip of granite so that Romilly could step out. He
lunged onto the platform and stood there, one hand holding
the bow rope uncertainly and the other scratching the cowlick
at the back of his head, dislodging Robbie who flapped down
and began to pace along the stone.

"Romilly, I'm flummoxed. I never thought how we'd tie up
once we were landed—there's nothing to fix a rope to." Robbie,
who had hopped over to the crack where the halves once joined,
flapped back and grasped hold of her uncle's trouser cuff with
his beak, giving a sharp tweak. He strutted back officiously to
a place where two lips of stone still touched, hunching and
hopping up and down excitedly. "That's my Robbie!" her uncle
exclaimed gratefully. Fishing the end of the rope beneath the
kissing surfaces, he tied the boat up with a few half hitches,
then straightened his back to look full at the moon.

"Well, our vessel can't float away, our note is safely scrolled,
Mira is poised for flight on your arm, and it's a soft, beautiful
night. All we need is the appearance of one mysterious Being."

He dropped his voice to a whisper. "And now, look, the stars are coming out."

Romilly tilted her head to look up at the night sky. Near the moon, a star was beginning to glow with a steady, chilly light. One by one, smaller stars began to twinkle, mere pinpricks of light growing stronger and brighter as the last streaks faded in the east and the night sky revealed its inky endlessness.

"How will it happen, Uncle?" Romilly whispered, pulling her eyes away from the stars whose twinkling brilliance amid the fathomless darkness had made her head spin lightly. "I mean, where does it start," she whispered.

"Well, the last few nights it's begun as a star that starts to elongate, almost like a comet. The last three times, it's been a star just below and to the right of the moon." They stood in silence for a moment and then her uncle crouched down, reaching for the spool of cord that rested on the bow seat. Holding the spool under his arm, he licked his thumb and began to tie the end of the linen cord to the kestrel's leather jess. The moonlight lit the gauntlet white as snow.

"The night sky looks so much closer than the day sky, Uncle. It's easier to believe, looking at the stars, that there is someone or something Beyond. The stars almost look like the holes in some giant colander that's been lowered over us."

"For all we know, Romilly, there are many worlds, perhaps inside the very world we are in. Think of all that is going on beneath the water as we speak. Think of all that is happening in an average bucket of earth. Digby once returned with a microscope, and we looked together at the lives going on, the busy twirling and whirling and seeking in a droplet of water from the rain barrel. And to think we bathe in and amongst all those creatures!" he added, cheerily. He gave a tug to the knot joining the jess and cord, then gripped her free hand. His hand felt warm and comforting, and she realized her fingers were cold. "Have you caught a chill?" he asked, suddenly serious.

Romilly gave a shiver laugh. "No, I'm not cold at all, just nervous, I think. I don't know what I am. Excited, more. Afraid, in part, that the Being won't come again, and we'll never know."

"Well, even if they don't come, and we never know, think of all that's happened just today! Great changes! Transformations! Your father's let go of his rigid reserve and—"

"Uncle, look to the right of the moon!" Romilly cried. It was just as he described—a star was brightening, growing larger as if drawing near them. Her eyes smarted, but by squinting she could see the star had grown a tail. The star travelled swiftly upward and leftward above the moon, then paused and changed direction, moving downward at an angle, all the way to the black and rippling band of the horizon. Suddenly, something pushed from the other side and the triangular flap of the heavens bulged, the stars upon the surface warping and blurring as if suspended on a film of water. "It's falling forward!" Romilly exclaimed, feeling the hair stand along her arms as a prickling, pins-and-needles sensation traveled down her neck and spread along her back in a tingling wave.

The flap began to flex and ripple, and then, with exquisite slowness, to bow toward them, the moon in its radiance advancing as if to kiss their faces. For a moment the momentum slowed, and the flap seemed poised in that inclined position, but then it passed some tipping point and began to fall forward faster and faster, folding over with a sound like the scrubbing pulse of an enormous wing. Through the gigantic, triangular window, Romilly and her uncle stared at a distance-blurred, out-of-focus expanse of white and pale blue and green. Out of these depths, there suddenly loomed a forefinger, which hooked and warped the window's edge. Again, Romilly heard the gigantic intake and exhale, like the entry of a great wind into a grove of trees. Romilly's hair blew across her face. On her wrist, Mira hunched, the feathers of her breast separating and riffling in disorder.

"Are you ready, Romilly?" her uncle shouted. "Send Mira out!" And she tossed the little kestrel off her wrist. As Mira dove down, skimming the water, Romilly cried out in alarm, but the little falcon soon soared upward while Romilly frantically unspooled the cord. Too little cord, and the tension might cause the kestrel to stall, fall backward and flounder in the water; too much, and the cord might become entangled. Up, up Mira flew toward the opening in the sky, the cord spinning off the reel with a whizzing clatter, until, just feet before the edge, the cord went abruptly tight and the little kestrel began to hover like a moth, straining against her tether to reach the perch.

"The cord's played out!" Romilly cried in despair, as she watched the little bird sawing side to side like a kite.

"We'll have to break the cord, we'll have to cut it—ah, what a fool I am that I didn't consider this!" her uncle cried in anguish.

"If we break the cord, we can't attach the note," Romilly shouted. She reached under her dress to pull out her mother's scissors on their cord.

Just then, Romilly felt the line grow light. The leather jess had slipped off the kestrel's foot. For a split second, the cord hovered and then it began to slip back down through the air in a slack arc. Lifting off into the wind with three strong pumps of his wings, Robbie shot toward the jess, intercepting it just over the water, then climbed with it swiftly toward the opening in the sky, the strength of his wingbeats jerking the spool from Romilly's hand. Now it dangled and danced beyond their reach. Mira, meanwhile, was teetering on the perch created by the folded-over flap. Robbie landed on the lip and sidled a cautious distance from the kestrel, the cord and jess clamped under one foot. Romilly could see him tilt and toss his head, eying the kestrel with the disdain felt by an unsung hero.

"Well, this is an unfortunate turn!" her uncle cried, bewildered.

"Uncle, have you noticed—they don't appear any smaller in proportion to the opening! It's as if the distance has magnified them instead of making them appear smaller!"

"Very true, but right now my concern is how we will reach the spool to attach the note."

"Is there a grappling hook in the dory?"

"Yes! Romilly, you are a genius! But I'm still not sure how

we will be able to tie the note to the end of the spool. We need to extend the length of the cord somehow. We just need a few feet more."

Romilly reached under her dress and withdrew the satin cord on which the key and scissors hung.

"Uncle, if you and I pull the dory up on this stone and overturn it, you can climb up on it and reach the spool with the grappling hook. We can tie my necklace cord to the fishhook and the end of the cord to the note."

Her uncle was already dragging and heaving at the dory. Romilly joined him, and within moments they had upended the boat and her uncle was leaping atop it, fishing out over the water with the grappling hook for the spool that bounced lightly as the cord flexed.

"Got it!" he crowed. "Now, I'll hold it here. Romilly, you get the note and unroll it. As you'll see, I've attached the hook to the scroll itself, but now you will need to tie the note directly to your cord and the hook to the other end of it."

Romilly swiftly snipped the necklace cord with her mother's scissors, then slipped the key and scissors off and set them down on the stone. She withdrew the stout fishhook from the note and passed the end of the cord through the hole it had left, double knotting the cord it so it could not slip through. She passed the other end of the cord through the hook's eye and knotted it firmly.

"Here, Uncle, I'm finished," she panted, climbing up to him atop the dory, carefully pulling the note affixed to the cord up after her.

"I still won't be able to reach the spool myself. I am going to have to lift you on my shoulder," he said, carefully sinking to one knee while watching the grappling hook to make sure it still had hold of the spool. She stepped up on his knee and turned to sit upon his shoulder, and he gripped her legs with his free arm as he lifted her, the letter rising with her.

"Can you attach the hook?" he called, his voice muffled by the side of her skirt. "Mind the barb, it's quite sharp!"

"I've almost got it!" She lunged for the reel and the hook seemed to grip onto something. Tugging, she tested—yes, the hook had passed around the hemp cord, just above the spool. If only it held. There was no way to clamp or tighten it.

"Set me down, Uncle—we'll just have to pray the weight of the note is enough to hold the line taut." The note bounced gently at the end of the cord, then began to circle slowly, catching the steady breeze. Romilly and her uncle watched as, far above and silhouetted in brightness, Robbie bowed his neck toward his feet, grasped the cord in his beak, hunched a moment, then hopped out of sight. The note gave an abrupt bob as if it were a fishing line receiving a sharp nibble. Well, thought Romilly, they *were* fishing after all—fishing for the Being Beyond.

Mira, who had sidled away when Robbie leapt off the edge, lifted her wings and flapped out of sight. Romilly held her breath, her heart sinking within her, fully expecting the Being to start raising the flap. But instead the note began to rise, twirling with a weightless grandeur.

"They're taking up the line!" Romilly cried, in triumph. With excruciating slowness, the Being reeled up the note. In the moonless dark, the starlight glazed the note pale blue against the midnight sky. The note receded steadily, until it caught against the slight lip caused by the fold. Hard as it was to believe, the note was almost as wide as the opening, and Romilly understood why the Being had had to call the birds inside. She saw two sets of fingers—not at all enormous, of the same proportions as her own—reaching for the corners of the note. It must have been a trick of the atmosphere that made the Being seem a giant.

"They're pulling it inside," her uncle shouted, hoarse with excitement and triumph. But when tail of the note slid over the lip of the window, Romilly felt bereft. What if the Being closed the flap now, with Mira and Robbie and the note sealed inside this other world? For long moments, the opening remained as it had been at first—bright, with a diffuse green background and blur of pale blue—motionless and strangely vacant. Water

from the rising tide began to lap the edges of the stone platform. When the sheet of water wet Romilly's feet, she stooped
to knot her skirt above her knees. If the Being didn't respond
soon, she and her uncle would be forced to row for shore. She
was just about to speak of this to her uncle when he held up
his hand.

"Look—they're sending something down," he whispered,
pointing toward the bright triangle. A silvery tube, the cord
lashed slightly off center so one end dipped, slowly descended
until it was ten feet above them. Romilly thought she could
make out her lettering. Her uncle leapt atop the dory and went
down on one knee again.

"Climb aboard, Romilly!" Again, she took a seat on his
shoulder, but could not quite grasp the scroll. She was batting
at it, trying to swing the lower end around within reach, when
suddenly the Being released the end of the cord. The scroll fell
right into her hands, and the slack cord fell in coils and loops
upon the water.

"I've got it," she gasped. "Set me down, Uncle!"

Water lapped their ankles. They would need to launch the
dory, and quickly. Her uncle heaved the boat back over, threw
the oars into it, unfastened the bow rope, and pushed the dory
off the edge of the stone. Taking Romilly's arm, he steadied
her as she stepped into the boat, clutching the scroll against her
chest as she clambered toward the stern. He jumped lightly in
and seized hold of the oars. In the dark, jostled by waves, he
had some trouble setting the oars into the oar locks, but soon
he was rowing steadily for the shore. Low waves curled over
on themselves, then tumbled toward the sand with greenish
phosphorescence. Under the starlight, Romilly looked pale and
still as a figurehead. Gazing up at the window in the sky, she
watched as a palm that seemed as large as their boat pulled
the flap inside, then smoothed it upward with pillar-like fingers,
almost as one would paste down a sheet of paper, so the edges
matched. She heard the great shushing friction, just as she had
above the fields of home, of the palm rubbing and smoothing.

It sounded as if a strong wind had come up and was sweeping through the forested hills behind them. When her uncle heard it, he turned on his seat for a moment, then bowed his head.

"They took Mira. And Robbie," Romilly said dully.

"That they did," her uncle replied.

"Do you think they will send them back if they open our world again?"

"I had not yet considered a next time, but I suppose it's possible." He paused as the dory nudged the shore, grinding quietly on the sand. Romilly was looking down at her hands which held the scroll against her lap, biting her lower lip. He passed his hand along her cheek, then gave her chin a gentle chuck.

"Let's read the note before we jump to conclusions or let our hearts break," he said. He gathered up the armful of damp cord and placed it in Romilly's lap, then leapt out of the boat. Taking hold of the transom in both hands, he tugged the dory out of the reach of the waves, tying the rope off on the stake. Romilly climbed out and walked further up the beach where the sand was dry and still faintly warm. Kneeling, she reached under the collar of her dress automatically, then let out a wail of anguish.

"Uncle, my mother's scissors—and my key! I set them down on the stone platform!" Turning at the same moment, they looked out at the expanse of water, unbroken now save for the low waves, regular as a pulse, that marked the incoming tide.

"Romilly, I'm afraid the platform's under water now. And you know how strong the currents are when the tide comes full on. I'm not even sure we could find the platform in the darkness."

As her eyes sought the platform, Romilly noticed a tiny figure across the flats. The small, heron-white shape lit up by moonlight was a boy—she was sure of it—in a white shirt! As the boy waded slowly into the water, she lifted her arm to point.

"Do you see him too, Uncle?"

Her uncle followed the line of her arm. The boy stood motionless, and they watched him silently, conscious of the leisurely break of waves on the shore. Then he slowly turned around and waded back to shore. They watched his pale back ascend the bank and disappear among the trees.

"Uncle," Romilly said under her breath, "do you think he saw the sky opening, and the note pulled up and—all of it?"

"No way to tell, Romilly. I had too many distractions and crises to deal with to be thinking about spectators," he said, anxiously. "Should we have been more vigilant?" He rubbed his hands over his hair and drew his palms over his cheeks, pressing his fingertips together before his lips. "Let's reason this out calmly. First of all, what kind of boy could be out in the woods at this time of the night, alone? Why, if he were spying on us, would he step out into the water in full view? He stood there as if he wanted to show himself to us."

"Do you think he will go back to the village and tell folks what he's seen?"

"I rather doubt it, Romilly. I think I know who it is—I recognized his general attitude. There's only one boy it could be."

"Who, Uncle?" Romilly asked, but instantly the truth burst into her mind and she answered her own question. "Micah!" Her uncle nodded gravely.

For some reason the boy—her fellow outcast, the boy who lived in the harbormaster's attic—was watching them. He had disappeared from the village but had not gone to sea.

"Do you think, Uncle, that Micah's been watching all our activities these past days?

"Can't know for sure. Maybe he'd been living in the cottage until I showed up—remember, I found the place well-stocked with kindling, and oddly tidy. As if someone expected us."

"But, Uncle, surely Micah had no way to know you were coming. You must have simply caught him by surprise. Maybe he was checking to see if we'd gone away again."

"Something about that's not right. That lad and I are on good terms, after all. He could have just made himself known to me, Romilly. 'Twould be no harm if he'd stayed on a few days. You two could have gotten to know each other. He's a good-hearted lad, just a bit reserved."

Romilly looked back across the flats at the blank spot where the platform had been.

"I've lost four irreplaceable things," she said, thinking of Robbie's strident *Yllimor* just that morning and Mira's fathomless eye. Without her mother's scissors, she felt like a bead rattled loose from a broken string, disconnected from her past.

"We don't know you'll never see Mira and Robbie again. And after all, we have no idea why they turned up here in the first place, or from whence. And your key and your mother's scissors—though they are lost now, just think how well they've served you. They aren't gone out of the world. You may well find them in the morn. But you have this note, now, don't you? You have answers. Don't you want to see what this Being has to say?" At his words, Romilly wiped her eyes on her apron. He was right, she needed to have more hope and more resolve. She attempted to smile.

"That's all true, Uncle. I am ready to learn the answers."

The scroll was wound round and round with the cord and tied with a limp bow. Romilly pulled this open carefully. Her uncle kneeled on the tail of the note while she unrolled it onto the sand. Between her words, someone had written shaky, penciled capitals. They were difficult to discern, even in bright moonlight. Romilly sounded them out slowly, following the line with her finger.

I WISH
TO COME
HOME

Romilly gazed at her uncle in uncertainty.

"Home?" she murmured.

"Go on, Romilly," her uncle urged. "You wanted to know the Being's name."

Rising to her feet, she carefully lifted the note and draped it back down, revealing the other side. She smoothed it with her hand. The writing on this side was even fainter. Just then, the moon, which has been obscured by a bank of cloud, emerged to light up the paper like mother of pearl.

"'My name'," she read, then paused a long moment, blankly. "'My name'—" she broke off and gave a cry of wonder. "Of course, of course, Uncle—it all makes so much sense!"

"Of course *what*, Romilly? Child, read it out!"

"'My name is Digby'!"

10

THE PASSAGE

Romilly lay on her pallet a long time thinking about her mother's scissors, picturing them skidding along the stone in the currents, then tumbling off. In her mind's eye, she watched them fall silently, then land with a muffled clink on the firm mud of the bottom, where they were probably already invisible, furred over with silt. Tomorrow morning, when the tide receded and exposed the flats, she would wade out to see if she could find them, but she knew better than to hope. Remembering her uncle's words, she tallied the losses and gains of the last few days. She had lost precious heirlooms, but had gained an uncle safe and sound, a trove of memories of her mother, and a father she could approach. And an island and cottage were now hers. A second uncle, presumed lost at sea, was trying to find his way back home to them. Her father's peaceful breathing reminded her of the difficult choice she and her uncle must make. Her father and Digby had parted in anguish and rage. How could they reveal to her father that Digby, somehow trapped outside their world, was trying to come home? How were she and her uncle to help Digby return? For, clearly, he was soliciting their help.

She pictured telling her father about the note. He'd insist that they leave the island immediately, even if they had to abandon the *Ingres*. Yet, in a single day, this island had become her true home. She felt an attachment to the cottage that her childhood home could not evoke. For, as much as she loved it, the house she'd been born in now repelled her. The very timbers of the house vibrated with sadness, solitude, suppressed anger, and regret. She had always detected these—energies—but now she knew where they came from. Her father, now that he'd begun to open his heart to the past, might let light and air into the house, but for her the house would always be linked to her mother's absence. Yes, when she turned her thoughts to their house in the village, a devastating loneliness seemed to suffocate her again. What a strange weight loss can have, she thought, shuddering at a vision of her life trickling away in isolation and uneventfulness. She wanted her life to be eventful and meaningful and intense. Full and vivid, the way her life had been on the island.

She would tell her father the truth—that she was not leaving the island—even if that meant this was the last night of peace between them. She listened to his steady breathing and the occasional soft snore that she had always found oddly comforting. She felt glad to be awake and aware of this peace, and found herself matching her breathing to his, until, somehow, she was sitting on a swing hung from a gigantic tree and her father was pushing her higher and higher, so that she sailed forward and backward in delightful arcs through the air.

When she woke, she looked to the window and could tell by the sky's rich blue that she had slept until midmorning. Her father's bedding was neatly folded atop his pallet. Distantly, she heard the ring of a hammer: her uncle must be building the cradle on the beach. Romilly sat up, stretched, and reached for her dress, which she pulled over her head and buttoned. As she descended the stairs, she ran her fingers through her hair, detangling her curls the best she could. The kitchen was empty, but a place at the table had been set for her and on her plate was a johnnycake topped with a handful of wineberries. Her uncle had left a note on a curl of white birch bark: *Berries ripe on the overlook. Go pick!* Next to the door he had set a closely woven, handled basket. Romilly picked up the johnnycake, grabbed the basket by the handle, and trotted out the door.

She was glad to be given a practical, mindless task. While she picked the berries, she'd keep her eyes open for other edible plants to add variety to their diet of fish, clams, and unleavened breads. Pacing the yard just yesterday, she had noticed a lush growth of dandelions, whose young leaves would make an excellent addition to fish stew, or a bitter but healthy salad. She would look for cattails near the shore; the starchy, tender stem nearest the root was a good substitute for potatoes. Burdock, too, must grow here. She decided she would devote this entire day to foraging along the shore, putting off the difficult conversation that awaited. For they would be on the island for at least three more days, she thought joyfully.

But her first task must be to look for the key and scissors. The tide would be coming up again. She would take her basket first to the mudflats. Perhaps she'd even collect some sea lettuce there, which was also good in soups. She took a bite of her johnnycake, the edges crisp and almost transparent from being fried in bacon grease, and set off down the shore path.

"Well, what's my fine girl up to, this sunny day?" her uncle called out cheerily when he saw her coming toward him, but as she drew close, she noted the circles under his eyes and suspected he had had a sleepless night.

"Foraging," Romilly replied. "I am devoting this entire day to adding some variety to our rather limited diet. And distracting myself from my problems." She ran her eyes over the beach. "Speaking of problems, where's my father?"

"He says he's gone up to the white pine grove to gather pitch to seal the joints and pegs in the repair. He walked off with a jar and a spackling knife just a moment or two ago."

"That's odd. I should have met him on the path, then."

"Nay, Romilly. The white pine grows on the other side of the overlook, near where I anchored the *Ingres* last night. Truth be told, I think he wants to assure himself I know how to anchor out a boat," he said, his eyes crinkling with mischief. "The easiest way to get there at low tide is to walk along the shore. That's where, by the way, the wineberries and huckleberries are. They like those sunny slopes."

"Well, I was just going to look for my key and scissors while the tide is low, so I'm glad my father's not about. I've lied enough to him these last few days. I wouldn't want to lie about what I'm looking for."

Her uncle smiled at her, then turned back to the piece of lumber he was sawing.

"I think you're a bit harsh, calling yourself a liar. I prefer to think you are simply keeping your thoughts to yourself. And about our witness," he said, grunting softly as he pushed the saw through the tight knots of the wood. "When I crossed the flats this morning to look for your key, I saw footprints around the platform. Micah had a look around this early morning." As the end of the board fell to the sand with a thump, her uncle straightened a moment to stretch his back, then thumped his palm down on the plank.

"It's hard to be a human and always feel divided about our inside and outside lives. This here piece of lumber"—he brushed the sawdust off the angled cut—"it's critical for bracing, though it won't really show. Hiding, showing off; it does neither. It's just going about its business, being what it is. All humans, similarly, have a purpose. Your purpose is becoming clear on this island. Your aunt realized your potential, or she would never have given you this island, and Digby would never have shown himself to you. Your purpose is to shoulder open your world, even if you must contradict the way your father has lived since your mother died. It's that simple. You can't go against your nature. You can only decide, at every moment, at each crossroad, how you will honor your truth. In a strange way, though your father should be your teacher, you may end up being his."

"All morning, Uncle, I've been wrestling with the question of whether to tell my father where we were last night and what we learned. My father has admitted his rage at Digby, that he blames him for my mother's death. So, I'm afraid if I tell him that Digby wishes to come home, I know he'll make us leave the island immediately—and I am not willing to leave. I am happier here, I am less—alone, somehow."

"Romilly, it could be your father's anger at Digby that's kept his grief for your mother from healing in the first place. I know from my own life experience that a wounded heart cannot heal when it is infected with rage. Only he can decide to let his anger go. But you can choose to give him that opportunity."

"Then you think I should tell him about Digby?"

"I would do nothing yet. Be solid and still, like this support-ive timber. We are progressing toward something, I am sure of it. If Micah is lurking about, perhaps even he has a role to play." He crinkled his eyes at her affectionately. "As for your mother's scissors and the key, I looked all around the split rock and found nothing. But you should look too. Things tend to turn up on this island exactly when they are needed. And only for the person intended."

Romilly waded out to the split rock, wondering how such an enduring feature of the landscape could transform so abruptly and completely. What would future generations call this land-mark now? Would anyone remember it had once been known as the Egg? As she waded carefully around the granite platform, each footfall raised a tiny plume of silt. The snails, creating looping trails that crossed and tangled with each other, were uniformly covered in a velvety algae the color of the mud. A hermit crab, catching sight of the enormity of her foot, instant-ly withdrew into its shell. Its home adorned with barnacles and tiny anemones now looked like an unremarkable, stolid pebble. Setting her hands atop the stone platform, she put her eye to its hinge-crack, but saw only a slit of sky and her hanging curls reflected in the water.

She waded along the shore toward the channel. The bot-tom was firm yet cushioned, with an almost furry softness. In the shallows, the water was warm as bathwater, but she could already feel cool currents of the incoming tide braiding through the warmth. In the deepest part of the channel, the water became a dense, glassy green, milky with light-reflecting microscopic life. Atop a rounded boulder, an osprey sat drying its feathers, opening and tilting its wings so the breeze caught the pearly undersides. A silvery perch quaked under the talons of one foot. Near the shore, she saw a great blue heron poised watchfully, lifting one leg as it stretched its snake-like neck toward the water. At her approach, the heron lifted off with great pumps of his wings and wheeled away, releasing a coarse *awk* of displeasure. As she rounded the island, she noticed fewer oaks and red maples and more white pine and cedar trees, those near the water gracefully contorted from winter winds whistling through the channel. The bright green bristle tips were reflected in the water beneath. Between silvery boulders wrapped by tree roots, Romilly saw a kingfisher emerge from its tunnel to skim the water, its black-crested, disproportionately large head trailing a trilling squeal.

When the water became too deep for wading, Romilly leapt from boulder to boulder along the shore until the *Ingres* came into view. Her bow line was wrapped around an enormous, upright driftwood stump and secured with a stout knot. A second line anchored her stern out in the channel. As she gazed at the boat, her father's head and arm emerged from the cabin, and a silvery arc of water flew out of the bailer in his hand. She waved to catch his attention and he climbed out, stretching his back, his face broadly smiling as he called out to her.

"She's taken a little water overnight, but my patch has held!"

She could see that his sunburn was already turning to a deep tan on his lean chest and shoulders. He dove off the boat's edge and began to swim for shore.

She followed his progress with concern, but he emerged from the water smiling and pressing the water from his eyes with his fingers. The cut on his forehead was still sealed, as if it had already begun to knit together, and the fluid had drained from the blisters on his face. But the skin over his nose and cheeks was mahogany red, as if seared by an iron. He heaved himself up on a flat rock below her.

"At high tide, we'll tow her back around to the beach and winch her up on the cradle with a block and tackle. We were lucky to find one in the tool shed." He turned to gaze at the *Ingres*, proudly. "She's a lovely boat, Romilly. What do you say we take her out for a sail now and again once we're home?"

Once we're home, Romilly thought anxiously. She changed the subject by chastising him—he should be wearing his hat and shirt until his sunburned healed, not leaving them in a pile on shore—but as he continued to look at her with a joyful face, she faltered and fell silent. He was happy, actually *happy*. She smiled down at him.

"I'm glad she pleases you again. I'd love to sail with you."

Her father beamed. He reached for his shirt, using it to mop his chest and arms, then threading his hands through the sleeves. He plopped his hat atop his head and tapped it in place, then stood abruptly, as if intending to dash up the path.

"Oh! As I was collecting pitch from the pines, I saw that my brother's right—the wineberries and huckleberries are ripe and especially thick just around the shore a bit. Shall I show you?"

"No need, Father. I shall follow the berries I find here until I reach the best picking." His cheerfulness had opposing effects—it was an encouraging sign, but caused her own courage to flag. She couldn't tell him *now* that she intended to stay on the island, not while he gazed at her with such delight. If she told him at lunch, she'd have her uncle with her for support. She followed him up the narrow path that squiggled up the embankment, nearly closed over by the cushiony growth of huckleberry bushes. The huckleberries, such a deep blue they seemed a radiant black, clustered at the branch tips. They were the exact color, she realized, of the night sky.

"You'll stay and pick berries until lunch?"

"Yes, Father. I just saw Uncle and told him so. He's pretty far along in his work. By late this afternoon, you should be able to move the *Ingres*."

"I'm going up to the house, then." He picked up the clay jar in which the drippings of fragrant pitch glowed, pale gold as beeswax. "I have to melt this pitch and take out the sticks and needles. If you follow this path, it'll come up at the side of the stone bench we sat on together last night. You'll see the broad path leading past the falconer's hut. You won't get lost, will you?" he said anxiously.

"It's an island, Father," she said, smiling. "All I'd have to do is head back down hill, follow the shoreline either way, and I'd meet up with Uncle again."

"It's true. An island is a safe place for a child. Or a young woman," he corrected himself, smiling at her again, this time ruefully. "I've missed your growing up, being so much stuck in my own head."

"Well, so far as I know, I'll always be your child," Romilly said and kissed his cheek. "No matter how grown up I am." Her father lifted her hand off his shoulder, kissed her curled fingers, and set off up the path. Touched by his unusual affection, Romilly followed him with her eyes until his angular back ducked under an overhanging bough and disappeared, her heart aching and conflicted.

The shoreline was banded by a belt of huckleberry bushes. The wineberries grew higher up, nearer to the clearing, and she decided to pick these first. The canes were furred in sticky, flexible briar, and the fruit, smaller and rounder than a raspberry, was equally sticky. Her mouth had tasted nothing sweet for days and watered as she picked a handful of the tender fruits to pop in her mouth all at once. The juice washed over her tongue with a crisp, sweet purity. Within the hour, she had picked her basket half full and reached the top of the path. Through the gap in the trees, she could see the cottage and the falconer's hut to the right. She remembered Mira stepping off the rim of the flap and into the unknown. But what if she'd returned? What if Mira was waiting on her perch, just as she was yesterday?

Romilly hung the basket handle over her arm and walked swiftly toward the hut. Approaching from this angle, she noticed that the hut was built into a hummock of earth, so that part of the side wall disappeared into earth. That explained the sealed off, cool stillness the other day, as if they had entered a cellar. As she neared the hut, she looked eagerly toward the driftwood perch, but there was no elegant, coppery-breasted kestrel there. But she was surprised to find that the door to the hut was open. As she approached the shadowy opening, she heard a muffled noise as if someone was tinkering inside. She approached slowly, setting down her basket.

"Uncle?" she called, uncertainly. "Is that you?" Drawing near the door, she heard the harsh sound of a metal tool scraping the side of a bucket.

"Uncle?" she called again. She was standing in the doorway when her father strode out of the gloom toward her. In his hand, he held a bucket of mortar and a pointing trowel.

"Father!" she exclaimed, in wonder. "What are you doing here? What is that mortar for?"

Her father glanced at her and then quickly away, both nervous and abashed. "I noticed some loose stones yesterday, as if the cement had fallen out, so I just thought I'd point up the stones a bit."

"How could you have noticed anything in there—it's entirely dark."

"Oh, I felt about with my hands is all. I could feel the crumbling mortar." Under his attempted nonchalance, Romilly could detect something unspoken, the same fear and anxiety she had noticed in him when she caught him in the hut the day before. They gazed at each other for a moment, perturbed.

"My kestrel has—" She was going to say 'disappeared,' but stopped short. "My kestrel has flown off," she corrected, reflecting that this was, at least, not untrue.

"I noticed that, Romilly. Well, he probably had a handler somewhere else, after all, eh? Sometimes birds go off course."

"It's a 'she,' Father. Her name is Mira."

"Well, maybe she'll be back. If not, you can be sure someone, somewhere, is glad of her return. Are you coming to the house?"

"No, Father, I was just looking to see if Mira had returned. I've picked all the wineberries on the path and now I'll work for an hour or so in the huckleberries. I think I may be able to gather enough for a tart."

"It certainly will be tart, with no sugar about!" her father exclaimed. "I'll see you at the house, then, in about an hour." Romilly watched him as he walked toward the cottage, noticing the stiffness of his back, so at odds with his attempt at ease and heartiness.

Tentatively, she stepped inside the hut. She had thought that shelves lined the entire back wall, but to the far left she could see a narrow, pitch-black corridor. Groping her way along a rough stone wall, she reached a narrow room pungent with the mineral scent of moist cement. Feeling her way along the back wall, she realized that some of the stones used to form it were large and rounded—not shelf rock, but stones that had been tumbled in waves, evidently brought up from the shore. Parts of this rear wall were constructed later than the side walls. What could it mean?

Cautiously, she turned about and followed the side wall again, confirming with her hands the roughness and square-shaped faces of those stones in the corridor, which had likely been split off the shelf rock at the head of the path. Someone had blocked off a passage, she was sure of it. But a passage to what? And why?

Romilly's tart was a success. Her uncle kissed his hand to her.

"Tart indeed, yet the raisins add a bit of sweetness. Sweet, but with a smoky, bacony savor! Romilly, you are a genius!"

Romilly had picked huckleberries until her forearms were scrawled with fine red welts from reaching into the twiggy branches, collecting enough for the tart and a compote besides, which she planned to serve with their morning johnnycakes. At this rate, she thought, she'd have to forage several hours a day just to provide some variety to their meals. But the meditative focus of berry picking had been a welcome change from the human tensions of the past few days, allowing her to put off the dreaded discussion about staying on the island. But abruptly, at dinner, her father brought up the subject himself.

"Brother," her father said, tipping his chair back in front of the fire, "Do you think our aunt is likely ever to return to the island? To stay in this cottage again?"

"Why do you ask?" her uncle enquired with a studious neutrality.

"Well, I can see the place makes Romilly happy, and I wondered if our aunt would mind her spending some time here in the summers, as you did. If she were accompanied, of course."

"And would you be willing to accompany her?" her uncle asked.

"Nay, not I. I've made some peace with the place, but my own home is where I need to be. I built that house with my own hands and though it has been darkened by sadness, it's my sadness after all. I'm too old to change my life. I was thinking of you. You said, on our first day here, that you didn't intend to return to the village. And I thought perhaps, if you intended to stay, you could take care of Romilly for a few weeks in the summers, the way our aunt did for you." At these last words, her uncle pivoted his gaze. Looking at Romilly, he jerked his chin upward as if to say, *Now's the time, girl! Get on with it!*

"Father," Romilly began, hesitantly. "I *am* happy here. I feel strangely at home. And there's much to be done in this place— to look after it. I would like to have the summer festivals again, as Aunt and Uncle did in the olden days, and bring the garden alive again. I know how to—"

"Child, what can you possibly mean by that?" her father interjected, his face stricken. A red flush spread down his neck. "Are you thinking of *living* here, with Uncle? Leaving me, your father, and moving to a place you can't begin to understand, a place that I am struggling to put behind me? Do you know how much of my strength it's taken? Nay, Romilly, nay. I can part with you for a few weeks or even a month in the summer, but, child, you are all I have left, you are my most precious—" He broke off, shaking his head *no* with vehemence. He turned on Romilly's uncle. "This must be your influence, brother. You must have put this scheme in Romilly's head. Why would you do that to me? Why would you try to draw my child away from me? Why, after all I've lost—" He put his head in his hands and pulled at his hair, choking back a sob. Romilly, stricken, stood up from her chair to soothe him, but her uncle held up his hand, gesturing to her to wait.

"Brother, it's not as you think. But my conscience, at the same time, is not entirely clear. So just listen to me and try to be calm. Do you remember when I went across the Sound, because I had a letter from our aunt telling me she intended to retreat from her worldly affairs? Brother, do you remember that?" Romilly's father, his head supported on his hands, stiffened, listening intently. "Well, there *is* something I didn't share with you. The letter also contained a directive that concerns Romilly. Our aunt has deeded this island and cottage over to Romilly. Your daughter is now its rightful owner. I have verified everything."

Romilly's father picked his head up off his arms and wiped his palms over his cheeks, pressing his eyes until his fingers whitened. "You are either deluded or outright lying. Why would she do such a thing?"

Romilly saw her uncle catch his breath at this accusation. But he paused a moment, tilting his head to the side forbearingly. "I would *never* lie to you, brother." He paused again, giving her father time to absorb this. "I think," her uncle said, with extreme gentleness, "our aunt knows that *only* Romilly can bring life to this place again. She knows—she must—that Romilly has been living in a house of sadness. I think she wants to help Romilly—and perhaps you as well."

"How does this help me, brother? She wants to take away my best thing, my—my treasure!"

"Brother, Romilly is no one's treasure. Her life is her own. She must decide for herself. How long do you plan to shelter her? And what, aside from simply keeping her with you, are you accomplishing by isolating her from the past, from others, even from yourself!" Despite his best intentions, her uncle was growing exasperated. Both men breathed heavily for a moment. But rather than retorting, her father dropped his hands in his lap and looked down at his upturned palms for a long moment.

"This is too much. Too much…change. Too much all at

once." He slowly clenched his fingers into fists, then opened them again and smoothed his palms along his thighs. "I am trying, can't you see? I am trying…I am doing the best I can," her father said, at last, wearily, turning to Romilly. "I offered to do without you for several weeks in the summers—that counts for something, doesn't it? Now you are putting me in a very difficult place. It is…hard for me, it will be hard for me to visit you here. I can't expect you to know why, to understand, even if you knew."

"But what if I *could* understand, Father? What if you tried to explain? Don't forbid me, I beg of you. I don't want to go against you. But when I'm seventeen, I will have the full right to live as and where I please. And I wish to live here. I can't go back to the village; I can't, Father. I can't go back." She felt the tears coming and bit her cheeks hard to hold them back. "Father, I beg of you," she said, more softly. "If you can't visit me, I will come to you."

Her father looked at her mutely, the whites of his eyes stark in the mask of burned skin. And then he picked up his hat and rushed out of the cottage, leaving the door open behind him.

That night, lying on her pallet and fruitlessly willing herself to sleep, Romilly wondered at the way a perfectly delightful evening could collapse into dismay and confusion. The way, with no warning but the sudden quieting of the birds, a storm could come in from the sea, the wind suddenly lashing the tree canopy, turning all living green things to a paste. Romilly had lived through two such storms, one of which had blown in the glass on the upper windows of their house, leaving vacant eyes and a swath of shards. The cottage was quiet, now, but she feared the damage she'd find in the morning. Her father had not come in for the night, her father, who had always double locked their front door and banked the ashes of the kitchen fire, bringing her a hot brick wrapped in flannel for her feet. Where could he be? What must he be thinking? Romilly finally fell asleep to restless dreams of rising winds, of a sea that rose to flood their fields and surround their home, stranding it like an island.

She woke to the ordinary sounds of the morning. Her uncle was whistling softly as he poked at the ashes in the fireplace. She heard the *thunk thunk* and crisp ripping noise of the hatchet splitting small kindling off a log, and then the gasp of the bellows as her uncle brought the sleeping fire to life. She looked toward the window and was relieved to see that her father had come indoors in the night, crept upstairs, and gone to sleep. He was still asleep, his head pillowed on one arm like an exhausted castaway washed up on a beach, his lips turned down mournfully.

Romilly reached for her dress and crept out of bed, padding silently down the stairs. Midway, she drew on her dress, smoothing out the wrinkles as best she could and tucking her tangled hair behind her ears. Her uncle was still crouched before the fire, but when he heard her step he turned and smiled, pointing with his chin to the basin and pitcher. While she splashed her face with cool water and rubbed it briskly with the towel, she heard the creak of the kettle on its arm and his low whistle that meant he was pleased with himself. When she sat down at the table, he set a mug before her.

"Sassafras root tea," he announced with a beam of pride, tapping the side of his head with a finger. "Steeped it this morning and kept it warm for you. See, I can forage too."

She sniffed it appreciatively. "It smells delicious, Uncle," Romilly said. He smiled and turned back around to the fire to pour johnny cake batter from a dipper into the skillet. He picked up the spatula, tossing it in the air and catching it with a flourish to amuse her.

"Shouldn't we wait to eat until Father wakes?" she asked.

"Well," her uncle said, tilting his head and wincing as he gave the back of his head a thorough scratch, "it seems your father only came in to sleep just before sunrise, so I very much doubt he'll be aware of us partaking of breakfast. Or much else, before noon."

Romilly sipped her tea in silence for a moment. Though she was dreading her first interaction with her father, she felt aggrieved, as if, by coming to bed so late, he was informing her that he wished to avoid her. It was a kind of silent treatment.

"Uncle, what now?"

"What do you mean, dear niece?"

"I mean, Father is dead against my plan to live on the island. I am going to have to defy him to live here now or wait until I turn seventeen. Either way, I will break his heart."

"I wouldn't rush to any conclusions. I was in the kitchen when he came in at first light. He looked rather wild, hair on end and his eyes shadowed, but he was calm. He said he'd been sitting aboard the *Ingres*, asking your mother's spirit what she would want for you. He said, too, that there were grievances and old wounds that he would need to mend if you were to live here. I asked if I could help. He said perhaps but would say no more. Romilly, I think the main reason he's frightened of you living on the island is that he fears your aunt's return. And something else—it's almost as if he fears Digby, as if he knows Digby is still alive. And we know, *we know*," he stressed, "that Digby is striving to return. We just don't know how." With his spatula, he stacked the johnnycakes one atop another and set the platter in the center of the table.

Romilly considered her uncle's words. It was certainly possible that her father knew more than she and her uncle did. Until last night, her uncle had believed Digby to be dead. Perhaps her father had long suspected Digby was still alive; that he wanted to return. Perhaps he even thought the *Ingres* had run aground because Digby had planned it so, had wanted to keep them here. His behavior in the falconer's hut the day before was strange too. He'd shown an aversion to the hut ever since they had arrived, and yet she'd found him inside with pointing tools, making repairs. What could it all mean?

After breakfast, Romilly made her way to the falconer's hut, carrying a saucer of meat. She was haunted by the possibility that Mira might return and might be perishing for want of food. She knew that trained birds were often dependent on their handlers. But as she approached the hut, she saw that the perch was bare. Anxiety squeezed her heart—for Robbie, too, whose brazenness had endeared him to her. At least if he were with Digby, he'd be cared for by someone who had known him as a hatchling. This was a comforting thought. She rested her hand on the smooth driftwood of the perch. The door to the hut was closed and barred today; her father must have seen to that.

Just then, her ear caught a distant, muffled *caw*. Baffled, she looked at the sky in all directions. She tilted her head and listened intensely, trying to tune out all else—the bird twitter, the breeze in the tree canopy. There it was again, a muted *caw*. No matter how hard she focused her attention, she couldn't tell from which direction it came. It sounded almost underground, as if it came from beneath her.

"How strange," she murmured, her heart torn between bewilderment and hope that Robbie would suddenly appear, wheeling over the trees and dropping down at her feet or onto the ivy-covered roof of the hut, as he had before. For long moments she held her breath, but no call came.

I must have imagined it, she thought to herself, struck by how apt the saying *wishful thinking* often turned out to be. Then she heard a new sound, dull but with a slightly metallic tinge to it, like the ringing of a low-pitched bell. The regular, repeated notes seemed to vibrate the ground under her feet. They seemed, somehow, to be collecting in the hut, as if it were a reservoir. She put her ear to the door. Just then, she heard another distant *caw*, seeming to come from inside and behind the hut. She lifted the bar of the door, opened it a crack and called out, tentatively at first, then more firmly. "Robbie? Robbie!"

The thudding stopped for a moment, then started up with new urgency. Romilly pulled the door fully open. "Robbie!" she cried, her voice echoing in the dim, close interior.

Inside the hut, the sound of the blows was more resonant,

as if the end of a stout pole was striking the stone wall from the other side. She looked toward the dark and narrow corridor that led to the back wall, the wall that was made of the rounded beach stones. Romilly advanced down the dim channel, brushing the side wall with her fingertips, holding her right hand out before her to feel for the back wall, which finally greeted her hand, cool, smooth, and lightly gritty. She put her mouth close to the stones. "Robbie!" she called.

There was a pause in the pounding and then she thought she heard a voice, made faint by the density of stone. She couldn't make out the words. She placed her ear to the stone and covered the other ear with her palm. Whoever was on the other side was calling out a word she could not discern, only that it had two parts, two syllables. Her pulse, scrubbing in her ears, drowned everything out. But she had heard what she needed to hear. All the events and discoveries of the last few days came together into a powerful conviction.

"It's Digby," she said to herself, with sudden intuition. "It must be! How can I answer him?" She beat the stone with the heel of her open palm, but even striking hard enough to make her bones ache produced little sound. Romilly darted back to the front of the hut to search the shelves for any tool that she might use to knock against the stone. There were a variety of jars, books, baskets—all either breakable or too soft. Then, out the open door, she saw Mira's perch, a length of smoothed driftwood four feet long and two inches in diameter. She rushed over to it and began to wrench at it, just as her uncle came round the corner.

"Romilly!" he cried. "Why on earth are you breaking apart Mira's perch?"

He rushed up and took hold of her upper arms. She was panting hard. "Uncle, there's no time. Trust me—help me remove the branch. Quickly. I need it!" He took hold of the branch, twisting and jerking until the nails pulled out with a squeal.

"Now what?"

Romilly grasped hold of the branch with both hands and gasped at him to follow. She ran into the hut, swerved left sharply, and followed the corridor to the back wall, which was barely discernable in the gloom. She listened intently for five full seconds: utter silence, except for the sound of her uncle breathing near her shoulder. Backing up a few feet, she grasped the branch by one end, one fist atop another, raised it to her shoulder and began to pound the wall with all her strength. The wood struck the stone with a mellow, hollow ring. She paused to listen as the last reverberations faded away. Again, she lifted the staff and beat the wall until her shoulder ached and her hands grew tingly. She let the base of the staff fall and leaned upon it to get her breath back.

"Wait, Romilly. I think I hear something!" her uncle whispered. She held her breath a moment and in the silence heard again the distant, almost smothered *caw!* In the dark, she couldn't see her uncle's face, but heard his breath quicken. He groped about until he found her hand. "Could it be?" he whispered.

Caw! Caw! they heard, much nearer now and then a sudden, rapid, resonant thudding against the stone.

The thudding had ceased abruptly. Though Romilly strained her ears, she heard only the aftermath—a high-pitched ringing, as after a thunderclap.

Exiting the hut, they circled it slowly, looking for clues. Having fetched a shovel from the tool shed, her uncle climbed the embankment, digging two feet into the earth, but his shovel encountered nothing but tree roots and soil. Romilly led him back inside to show him the square-cornered stones of the side passage, urging him to feel how different the back wall's cobbles felt. Groping around in the dark, they determined that a patch of beach stones, some quite large, had been used to seal a shoulder-width opening. There was nothing more to discover. The hut was as still and close and silent as before.

Romilly and her uncle walked to the overlook and sat awhile

on the stone bench, discussing various strategies. They could begin dismantling the wall straight away, themselves. Or perhaps they should they take her father into their confidence? Romilly described to her uncle the several odd interactions she'd had with her father.

"He seemed to have an aversion to the place, yet just yesterday, as I was returning from picking berries, I heard someone tinkering and scraping in the hut and he came out carrying a pail of mortar and some pointing tools. He explained that he was repairing some loose stones. I found it odd, because earlier, he seemed reluctant to even approach the hut. And, also, as you know, it's nearly pitch black near the back wall." Romilly said.

"Do you think he's the one who lugged those big stones up from the shore?" her uncle asked.

"My mind's awhirl, Uncle. You said that Digby often would travel, but no one ever saw him leave or return."

"That's true, but not remarkable. They lived here completely alone, after all."

"Still, what if the hut contained a tunnel that connected to another world entirely? I know it sounds strange, but wouldn't that explain why no one had ever encountered the sickness he brought back? If Father realized Digby traveled back and forth through a passage, it makes sense he would wish to seal it forever—to seal Digby beyond it. Perhaps—" She broke off.

"Go on, niece."

"I wonder if my father, not you or I, was the first to know Digby wants to return. Perhaps when you disappeared, he even thought *you* had discovered the tunnel. That would explain why he didn't want to go after you at first."

"These are compelling thoughts, Romilly. Perhaps we shouldn't tell your father what we've found. After all, you caught him reinforcing the passage. Therefore, he must know—"

"So, we agree—"

"Oh, I'm quite persuaded," he interjected firmly. "In the note, Digby said he wanted to come home. And this *is* his home.

He's showed himself on purpose to *us*, because he knows *we* have no fear of the past—or the Beyond."

"But why wouldn't Digby, given the power he has to open the sky, simply open the wall himself? For us, it will take days, even weeks to break through—and heavy tools, like pickaxes and mauls, which I doubt we have here. But even if we did have the tools, there's no way we could hide the process from Father. For one, smashing that wall will be loud. Also, you'd have to cease working on the *Ingres*, when he's counting on her being ready to sail in just a day or two. We were going to walk home through the woods tomorrow," she continued broodingly, "and return for her shortly." Romilly looked out over the water at the *Ingres*, lying at anchor, her reflection resting on the calm water clear as a painting.

"Well," her uncle mused, "you and your father could go back to the village, and I could spend the week opening the wall instead of fixing the boat."

"No!" Romilly burst out, then flushed in confusion. "I didn't mean to shout. I'm not angry with you, Uncle. It's just that I *can't* go back right now, not even for a week. I don't know why—but the longer I'm away, the less I can bear the thought of returning!"

She thought a moment, then her emotions burst forth.

"But how will I stay here, Uncle? It will tear a hole in his life. What if I break his heart?"

At this moment Romilly stood abruptly, having heard a strangely human sound. She held a finger to her ear, signaling her uncle to listen. She heard it again, a high, hooting "halloo" coming from across the channel. Scanning the shoreline, she found its source: a small figure in a sky-blue dress, waving a white kerchief over her head. Distantly, the three syllables of Romilly's name floated over the water. It was Arra! Romilly sat up straight and grabbed hold of her uncle's arm.

"It's Arra, Uncle, look! How good it is to see her! I had almost forgotten there were any other human beings in the world." They stood to wave back, then watched as Arra picked her way along the stony waterline, then skipped toward the flats, lifting her skirts to splash through the deeper pools. Near the split rock, she paused, considering it, setting a hand atop it as if listening with her palm.

"Let's go down to meet her, Uncle," Romilly said.

"Nay, Romilly, let her come up the path to us. We should check on your father. If he wakes and no one's in the cottage, he may assume there's been a catastrophe. Arra has always had a good effect on him. He listens to her, even if he thinks she's odd. If she comes up to the house, all natural, as if it's the most normal thing in the world to visit us, perhaps it will calm him."

11

ARRA

Romilly crept upstairs and pushed the bedroom door ajar without sound. Her father slept on, curled on his side, his face bearing the mournful look that caused her heart to squeeze. His fear of losing her had grown into her like a vine around a young tree; his words *I'll not risk you* were like the hum of blood in her ears, almost part of her body. Yet she also knew that to grow independent of her father was a natural thing; and, like all natural things, it involved loss and change. Somehow for him, this loss was total, as if the loss of her mother had permanently warped his perspective. As if all partings meant death. She strained against these fine but infinitely strong cords binding her in place.

Suddenly, she sensed a bustle and energy downstairs, then heard Arra's clear voice greeting her uncle with a rollicking laugh. Her father stirred and gave a writhing stretch, and before she could turn and slip away, his eyes opened on her face. He looked searchingly at her a moment, as if memorizing her features. From the kitchen came the bump and scraping clatter of chairs being rearranged and the muffled tones of hearty folks trying, but failing, to whisper. His face changed, swiftly stiffening into suspicion, then dread.

"I hear voices," he said, as he pushed himself up to a crouch. "Who's here? Who's speaking with my brother?"

Just then they heard a decisive tread on the stairs, and in an instant, Arra was hugging Romilly from behind, peering over her shoulder at the bewildered man crouching on his pallet. Romilly smelled the minty fragrance that always accompanied

Arra, who dried large quantities of mint in the rafters of her house.

"Hello, dears," Arra said with frank pleasure. "I'm here in the capacity of laundress." She spun Romilly around and clucked, surveying her dingy and wrinkled dress. "It looks like they've been using you to mop the floors," she added, kissing her cheek with a smack.

Her father, speechless, staggered to his feet.

"What are you talking about, Arra?" he said, when he finally could speak. "How on earth did you know where to find us?"

"Well, it doesn't take a genius to figure out, when you didn't return yesterday, that you must have pulled your boat up somewhere either along the coast, or on the shore of one of these islands. And as the islands are visible from my collecting routes, I've been watching out for signs of you. And the smoke from the fireplace," she continued reasonably, "was a fair clue. Especially as I had blocked the chimney last year to make sure the bats and swifts didn't nest there. I figured one or both of you brothers must have landed here for a bit of a holiday. I could use one too. Oh! And as if *that* wasn't enough, I met Micah on the path and he said he had seen Romilly and her uncle on the tide flats recently, and that both seemed in one piece. Don't worry—I turned your cows out into the pasture before I set out to join you. Their milk was scant anyway. And Micah is bringing in your wheat, so it won't get ruined by rain. Not that we've had any rain lately." She smiled broadly, enjoying the baffled expression on her friend's face, especially as it turned pink with indignation.

"We are *hardly* resting here—" he spluttered.

"No? Sleeping until midmorning counts as rest to me!"

"We have had a *grave* accident. We're striving with all our strength to repair our boat so we can leave this—this—" and here her father struggled for an adequate word, "—calamitous spot as soon as possible!"

At this outburst, Arra's eyes, which had been sparkling with mischief like sunlit water, grew clouded and somber.

"I know you find this place deeply unsettling, friend, because it brings back memories of your terrible loss, but remember, too, that for a far longer time it was a place of creative contentment for your family, including Ingres. She loved it here. She *loved* her aunt, and her uncle too, which by-the-by was *your* blood. She wouldn't want you to darken this island with your dread and anger."

"Angry? I'm not angry! What do I have to be angry about?"

"Now you are just not being honest with yourself—or us."

Romilly watched this exchange uncertainly. Arra was opening the door to a room, shut up and locked since her mother's death, to air it out. In fact, she was prying off the lock and latches, right in front of the person who had installed them. She looked at Arra's face, firm but gentle, weathered yet girlish. Her graying hair, which she wore in two braids crossed and pinned over the crown of her head, must have been bright gold in childhood, but now had the multi-hued, metallic iridescence of a mussel shell's inner surface. Her whole being radiated honesty.

At these last words, her father bowed his head. But then he looked up at Arra from under his brows with the grim intensity, almost fierceness, that Romilly knew well. It was the look with which he protected his dark pool of grief. Yes, she was sure he'd built the stone wall preventing Digby's return. It was the perfect emblem for a man who walled up his anger and his pain. Who, she realized, loved his pain even more than he loved her. How could you ever truly feel safe with such a person? She felt her heart constrict.

Yet Arra was gently smiling.

"Come down and get your breakfast, man," she said, with coaxing reasonableness. "And then, I should like to hear all about your plans." Romilly's father swallowed visibly, then stood and passed by Arra and Romilly without a word. As he descended the stairs, Romilly heard her uncle greet him breezily, then continue sweeping the hearth and banking up the fire. He whistled a low, casual tune, as if Arra's visit was the most normal thing in the world, as if, for the life of him, he had overheard nothing, absorbed as he was in his puttering.

Arra looked shrewdly into Romilly's face.

"Look at that. You're suddenly as tall as I am," she noted, placing her hands on Romilly's shoulders and pressing downward. "Unacceptable." She cocked a brow. "I hear your uncle informed you about your inheritance, more than a year too soon. He's always been a terrible blabbermouth. Always desperately poor at keeping secrets."

"I wish more folks were terrible at that. I *hate* secrets," Romilly said with vehemence.

"My girl, keep the word *hate* in reserve. You may only need to use it once in your life, if that," Arra said, then smoothed the hair at the sides of Romilly's head. "You need a good hair-brushing," she noted, examining her face. "With our hypothetical hairbrush." Then she touched Romilly's neck, where the cord hung forlorn and empty.

"Where are your mother's embroidery scissors, child?"

"I lost them near the split rock," Romilly replied. She clenched her teeth and held her breath, but still, her eyes brimmed.

"Well, that's another story I need to hear."

"Uncle said things sometimes lose themselves when they have fulfilled their purpose," Romilly continued.

"But it feels to you as if you still need them, doesn't it?" Arra asked.

Romilly nodded her head silently, pressing her lips together.

"Some things *refuse* to be lost," Arra said.

"What do you mean?" Romilly asked, her eyes roaming over Arra's face uncertainly.

Arra reached into her apron pocket. "I mean, they are always wandering back into our lives," she replied as she held the delicate silver scissors toward Romilly on her open palm.

Breakfast was strained, at least for Romilly and her father. Her uncle chatted with Arra unselfconsciously, effusing about Romilly's attempts to vary their diet with fruity delicacies, boasting of how he had ventured into foraging himself, gathering sassafras root for tea. Arra had brought them a small cloth sack of genuine black tea and Uncle made a mock ritual of brewing it, pouring water from the kettle from a dramatic height, whispering a spell over the teapot "to speed the steeping." When he gave the first cup to Romilly for her approval, she breathed in the grassy, comforting fragrance gratefully. Her father sat uneasily, his eyes moving from one to another of their faces. She could tell that he could hardly bear to sit there, that every particle of him longed to leave the island. Her uncle was telling the story of her father's sunstroke, embellishing it with humor—

"—he seemed half-dead, but then, after a draught of your magical tonic, he was complaining about how cooling his legs with water would ruin the sofa! What was in that tonic, by the by?" Arra smiled but didn't answer, instead turning to Romilly's father with concern.

"I see you have a cut above your eye too. But it seems to be healing well. Did that happen during your sunstroke, or when the *Ingres* ran aground?"

Her father responded thickly, as if unused to speaking. "I had no knowledge of the Egg splitting like that, and because it no longer showed above water, I misjudged the tide. So, I suppose I've brought this on myself." He wearily indicated with a wave of his hand the cottage and the small group of breakfasters.

"Poor man," Arra murmured. "To be afflicted by the three people in the world who care most for you."

"Arra," her uncle interjected, "did you know about the Egg splitting in half? You said you'd been out to the island several times recently."

"I was last here a few weeks ago, in fact. The cottage looked tidy, everything draped neatly with canvas and recently dusted. I was planning to come out again around this time, but then you disappeared off the face of the earth and I decided to give

these two," and she gestured at Romilly and her father, "the glo-
ry of rescuing you." She looked at Romilly and her father with
affectionate pride. "And they have exceeded my expectations!
But to return to the Egg. A few weeks ago, when I crossed the
flats at low tide, I noticed the crack had widened significantly. I
figured the storm surge of the last nor'easter must have washed
out the sediments holding the Egg in place. You must remember that, when we were children, the crack was only about a
hand's-width wide. How I would have loved to have been here
when the halves fell apart. That must have been dramatic!" Arra
exclaimed, her eyes sparkling. "All things change," she mused.
"There are periods when the ways of life seem so stable that we
forget past upheavals. In my experience, about every ten years
there is a major upheaval, as with your mother's death, Romilly.
That was a very bad time for the village. And we seem to be in
another such period of intense change. It's rather invigorating."

"How," her father burst forth, "can you characterize Ingres's
death as anything other than a catastrophe?"

"It was a catastrophe, friend. But no catastrophe can go on
forever, even a death, or else no one would survive it. Romilly,"
she turned calmly, "do you remember climbing with your mother inside the crevice of the Egg?"

"Oh yes, Arra! It's one of my favorite memories."

"And now, children for hundreds of years might remember
playing with their mothers atop what they'll now call Split Rock,
dancing and frolicking upon the two platforms. How delightful
that would be. If mothers and children were ever to come here
again." She paused, scrutinizing Romilly's father's face, bowed
over his plate but red with suppressed fury.

"All things change," Arra said pointedly as she rose to clear
the breakfast dishes.

Romilly's uncle rejected Arra's offer of washing up.

"What? To have our esteemed guest, our *first* at that, lugging
buckets and handling rags? Fie! Go for a walk with Romilly. I'm

sure she has many questions about her new demesne." Seeing Romilly's questioning look, he continued, "That's just a fancy word for queenly realm." Romilly continued to sit at the table. From the front windows, she could see her father's brittle, receding back heading down the overlook path. Doubtless he was going to comfort himself by checking on the *Ingres*. Arra came up behind her and physically heaved Romilly's chair out from the table. Tilting the chair forward, she dumped her out of its seat unceremoniously, as if she were a wheelbarrow load of dirt. Romilly smiled, despite her worry. A waft of mint tingled her nose.

"So. Let's shift to the fascinating topic of laundry. Where are the garments you are not wearing at the moment?" Together, they gathered up the grimy trousers, shirts, underclothes, and Romilly's other dress. Arra bundled them into the center of the largest linen towel, tying the corners, then deposited the sack in the washtub.

"Now. We are going to scrub these clothes until not a trace of filth remains. That's always a wondrous aid to problem-solving. And you can tell me all your adventures."

"Arra, I don't know where to start. The last few days have been both eventful and—problem-ful."

"Why don't you tell me first about your father's change of heart. Your uncle said he's seen signs of real softening in him, that he has begun to share stories of the past and of your mother. Though, to *me*, he seems to have regressed."

"It was a short-lived openness, I'm afraid. He's sealed up even more tightly than before, thanks to me," Romilly remarked sadly. She looked up at Arra with a mixture of anxiety and determination. "I told him I wanted to live on the island permanently."

"Goodness me," Arra chuckled, "that must have turned his world all topsy turvy. Romilly, he's more resilient than he looks. Could you imagine, a week ago, even bringing up such subjects? He may be unhappy with us—furious, in fact—but he's tolerating our interference into his sacred privacy. That proves he has some flexibility in him."

They were walking toward the well as they spoke, but just as Arra released the bucket to draw up water, they heard a sudden, violent hammering. They looked at each other in bafflement. It must be her father—but what could he be pounding? Arra tilted her head to listen.

"The sound's coming from the other side of the house, near the hut."

Together, they raced around the corner of the house, then ran, panting, toward the falconer's hut. Romilly slowed to a hesitant walk and approached the door, which was firmly barred. Near the corner of the door, a hammer rested on its head, its handle cocked against the stones as if it had been flung there.

Romilly approached the door and ran a hand along the wooden bar. She could see the nail heads, one every few inches. "He's nailed the door closed," she said, dully.

"But why would he do that, Romilly?" Arra asked.

"To seal away his greatest secret."

Arra led her back to the kitchen table and poured out the last of the tea. It was tepid and bitter and the bits of leaf swirling around it in seemed to mirror the disorder of Romilly's thoughts.

"Let's sit down," she said, "while I heat the water for your bath. Take your time with the tale. Your uncle already explained how you came here and about your father's sunstroke and the patching of the *Ingres*. Also, about your kestrel appearing out of nowhere. But beyond that, I don't know anything of what's transpired in you." Arra added some kindling to the fire and swung the kettle over on its arm.

"I can't decide where to begin," Romilly cried, after she had made a half dozen false starts in telling the story of the past few days. Suddenly she had an idea.

"I need to show you something in Aunt's studio, Arra. It's

somehow the center of everything. It will allow you to understand what we've all been through, each of us alone—and together."

When she pulled back the curtains, her aunt greeted the carved doors like old friends, stroking the curve of the swan's wing with fondness.

"Hello, dear creatures! It's good to see you again. I always loved the smell of this place," she said, pulling the doors open and pausing to inhale deeply. The faint linseed smell of the studio and the worn, almost waxy texture of the worktable steadied Romilly too. Romilly described how Robbie had brought her a bronze key, and that Romilly had found the lock it fit in this very room. At Robbie's name, Arra chuckled in delight.

"So, Robbie's back and first thing he does is steal a key, eh! Plucked it right out the lock, I warrant. That's how he got the name, Robbie, you know. He was always filching something."

Arra described how Romilly's aunt had rescued the young bird when he was scarcely fledged into his flight feathers. He had cracked his beak somehow, likely by flying into the windows of the house—they'd found him floundering around in the yard quite pitifully. Her aunt had filled the crack with hard black sealing wax and hand-fed him until the horny surface grew out, "rather like a fingernail," Arra said. Robbie was as attached to her aunt as a baby to its mother.

Before Robbie had brought her the key, Romilly explained, she'd already discovered so much: that Aunt's partner, Digby, whom she'd never even known existed, was also an artist. He had made a mesmerizing collage of a girl and her father at harvest time. "This very one," she said, drawing Arra to the table and handing her the collage. Romilly motioned to Arra to turn it over and showed her Digby's signature. The key, it turned out, fit a cabinet which held a tremendous amount of paper, paper Digby had learned to make.

"Aye, I remember Digby making paper. I used to help him identify likely plant matter for his experiments. But what does paper have to do with your father's secret?" Arra prodded.

"We needed a particularly light yet large leaf of paper because—because..." Romilly looked at Arra in mute appeal. How could she explain? She would have to go back to the beginning, to the moment in the wheatfield when she saw the bright point slit the sky.

"I must back up. Do you remember, Arra, when I came to tell you we were taking the *Ingres* to search for Uncle?"

"Of course, my dear. That was only a few days ago. My brain's not addled."

"Well, the day before that, I had seen something...something unbelievable." Romilly described the slit, how it seemed to heal back together the first time she saw it, but that, the next day, she watched it grow longer and longer, as if some being deliberately traced the horizon with a blade. And how this Being had pushed open the flap so she had glimpsed an enormous thumbnail and felt the gigantic breath like a strong wind against her face. And then, the flap had closed again. She knew her father would think her crazy if she claimed a gigantic Being had appeared from beyond her world. Her father had seemed paralyzed, she realized, unable to initiate a search for his disappeared brother, as if he were resigned to pieces of his life being gradually taken from him. So, she had insisted. She had shamed him into taking this journey. And she had discovered so much more than just her uncle. She had discovered so much about her past, her mother, her future—and she had discovered the vast extent of her father's fear. Because the gigantic figure outside their world *was* Digby, she was certain of it, and he wanted to come home.

"And I know all this because we—Uncle and I—used an enormous sheet of Digby's paper to write a note to the—Being Beyond is what we called him then. And he wrote us his name. But he's not a giant, Arra—it's some sort of trick of the atmosphere that makes him look so. There is a passage to some other world behind the door father nailed shut. He's walled it up with stone. He blames Digby for my mother's death—"

"You are losing me again, Romilly. Slow down! Go back to

the part where your father seemed to soften. Around the time of his sunstroke. What reached him then?"

"I thought it was your tonic, Arra. I'm sure it was at first. But also, it was entering this studio. He gazed around at everything. He recalled taking drawing lessons from my aunt and his dread of the place seemed to fade. He was too weak to climb upstairs, so he let us make a bed for him in here and he slept all afternoon. But before he drifted off, he told me many things about my mother and about his own behavior after she died—it was almost as if he was confessing. Here—" she said, and she reached under the table, where her journal rested in the basket. "As Father slept, I recorded as much as I could about our conversation."

"Romilly, I know that book! Digby taught us to bind books one summer and your mother made that one for herself—but she never had a chance to write in it, it seems."

"When I was about eight years old or so, I found it among her books and noticed it had no writing in it, so I decided to claim it. I didn't know she had made it with her own hands! I was afraid I'd completely forget her—some five-year-olds would, you know. I decided to write down each memory I had of her and any new information I gleaned from you or my uncle—my father never spoke of her. I hid my journal from him, in fact—" here she grew pink with discomfort "—because I was sure he'd take it away from me. I was always afraid to ask him about my mother—the simplest questions seemed to hurt him. I used to steal into her sitting room to look at all her things in secret, because he always kept the door closed and I was sure that if he caught me there, he'd forbid me. Actually, the change started after the *Ingres* ran aground and we had to swim for shore."

"Sometimes a jolt to the head, actual or metaphorical, works wonders," Arra said with a wry smile.

"In any event, after his sunstroke he told me about my mother's death—how he chopped down the holly tree and how I would search the yard for any stray seedling. Here's what he said: 'You were digging at a survivor with a teaspoon, and I jerked you away by the arm, roughly, the only time I've ever laid a hand on you in anger.' I didn't remember this at all. He later admitted that he had loved Digby and admired him, but after mother died, all that love turned to hate. 'I wanted to rip him from the world, I wanted to destroy everything he loved, as I felt he had killed what I loved most. If I could have buried him alive, I would have done it. I wanted him to feel separate— eternally—from everything he cherished. And so, when the villagers set out through the woods with torches to set fire to his house, I was glad. I didn't stop them.' Arra, I think Digby had found a way to pass from world to world. And I think my father discovered the passage and has sealed it up with stones and mortar. I'm not sure if Digby came from that other world, originally, or if he had simply found the passage and travelled to and fro', but one thing I do know: my father wants to ensure that he *never* returns to this island."

Arra stroked Romilly's leg soothingly. For some moments she gazed into her eyes.

"Now do you see why I wish you to use great caution with the emotion of hate? Your father doesn't hate Digby, he still loves him. But he is afraid to love. He has turned his sorrow and fear into anger and hate because these emotions feel active and powerful. You have suffered from this. He's gradually locked away all his softer emotions. It's made him withdraw from you." She squeezed Romilly's leg firmly. "By the by, that holly tree—or rather, its offspring—survives."

"What? How?" Romilly gasped.

"I'm not surprised you don't remember that tree or searching for its babies to save. Your father's actions were so violent and harsh. The mind closes the door on such memories, especially when you're young. But after your father hacked apart that poor, lovely tree, you showed up at my cottage with a tiny seedling in your pinafore pocket, and I told you I would plant it in the woods behind my house. It had been in your pocket some time, so I thought it likely that the root had dried out. But

I'd given you my word. A year later, I saw that the seedling had grown into a sapling. And now it's tall as a house. In fact," Arra continued, with a sly, cagey look, "some of that holly tree is in your father."

Romilly was struck dumb, her mind wheeling through possibilities. "Arra, did you use a tincture of that holly in your tonic?" she asked.

Arra winked. "You know, of course, that different plants have different healing properties. Sometimes they even have symbolic meanings. Your mother loved the holly for its meaning—domestic happiness. That it was green even in winter suggested persistence and lasting beauty. Its thorny leaves signal protection. The holly has long been used as a remedy for fever. In fact, we treated your mother with tincture of holly, but to no avail. The sickness was too powerful. That is why your father punished her favorite tree. But unbeknownst to him, the holly cured his sunstroke. Perhaps his heart knew it was being soothed with domestic happiness. Perhaps that's why his heart softened so."

"But why has it hardened again? Why, after admitting Digby had been his treasured friend, has he now barred him from this world?" Romilly cried.

"Because, dear girl, the hardest work that any heart can do is not to love, or to grieve, but to forgive. You can't make him do this work; you could pry out the nails in that door, but that won't make him face his fears. He must *want* to do that work himself."

Romilly sat, lost in thought, as Arra busied herself with the laundry in the yard. She tried to recall her father's rough grasp of her arm or pulling the holly seedling from her pocket and giving it to Arra. It was no use. The events had vanished. But the consequences and emotions were left behind. Her caution, always, around her father. Her desire to burrow her face into Arra's comforting breast. She could hear Arra singing full-heartedly, then grunting slightly as she bent over the wash board, scrubbing the cloth against its ridges. She had brought with her a bar of soap fragrant with rosemary and lavender whose keen notes made Romilly's nostrils tingle. The largest iron kettle of water was heating on the fire, for Arra had declared her intention to scrub Romilly too. She heard Arra tip the tub and sluice the water onto the grass. And then she saw Arra cross the yard with an armload of garments wrung out tight as sticks. These she untwisted, flapping them sharply to loosen the wrinkles, then arranged over low bushes.

"Well, it was brown as a river after spring rains!" Arra exclaimed as she came in the front door lugging the tin laundry tub. "Now it's your turn, missy. We'll wash you in the studio. You'll have privacy there." She set the tub down and turned briskly with the wooden pails to fetch water from the well. "You take that kettle down, carefully now, and pour out the nice hot water into the tub. I'll be back to temper it with cool."

Romilly wrapped her hand in a thick cloth and carefully unhooked the iron kettle from the pot-arm. Staggering slightly, she carried it into the studio and poured the water out into the tub, standing over it to watch the steam rise off the surface. She was worried about her father. He had not been seen for several hours, and from the look on his face when he had left the breakfast table, he was feeling trapped and resentful, as if he were being driven forcibly down a narrow path. It was all her fault; all was going so well until she had voiced her desire to stay on the island. She was lost in thought, when suddenly she heard her father's voice coming through the open studio window.

"—and thanks to the two of you, now she wants to stay on the island, and she has no idea, no idea what this will cost me, what this will *exact* from me—" and here his voice lowered and grew muffled. She could hear Arra's deliberately softened tones, murmuring with a compassionate cadence, perhaps a question, but couldn't make out the words. Then her father's voice broke out again, "—say he's dead, but I know different…I know he does, why else would I have…don't want to say, I have ways of knowing…especially if he comes back here…take her away from me."

There was a pause, then she heard Arra's voice distinctly: "You make your heart very small when you say such things, foolish man. Can't you see that if you prevent her, or if you give her no choice, she'll always keep you at arm's length?" The voices muffled again, then ceased.

Romilly returned the kettle to the hearth. Her heart was pounding guiltily, as if she had deliberately eavesdropped. Arra bustled in with the full buckets and Romilly trailed her into the studio. Kneeling, Arra poured cool water into the washtub, stirring languidly with one hand.

"Your bath is ready," she said with bland matter of factness.

"I overheard what you said to my father," Romilly confessed.

"And maybe I meant for you to overhear it. Thought you hated secrets, young lady."

"I do. So, perhaps then you'll tell me what he said when your voices got all quiet."

"He said, probably just to get rid of me, that he'd think about what I said. I told him I didn't believe he hated Digby, actually. I told him he had held on to this anger so long, it had begun to define him, but that letting anger go is a choice."

Romilly stepped out of her dress and dipped her foot into the tub. Her skin seemed to drink up the silky comfort of the water. She experienced a sense of novelty, as if this was her first bath. She folded her body into a seated position and lifted the water in both hands to her face. Arra smiled and began to unweave her messy braid, clucking at the "bird's nest" it had become.

"Perhaps we'll find Robbie in here," she groused, and despite her sadness at losing him, Romilly giggled. Arra picked up the cake of soap and rubbed it between her palms, then spread the lather onto Romilly's hair and began to scrub her scalp and pull the suds through to the ends with gentle fingers. Romilly tilted her head back obligingly.

"Arra, you know the boy Micah, don't you?" she asked.

"Aye, about as well as you can know a child. I know all the children because I help to birth them and I treat their ailments, but Micah is a special case because of the burns he received when he was just a little mite—only six years old or so."

"That was around the time my mother died," Romilly remarked sadly. "Why doesn't he live with his own parents? Doesn't he have a family?"

"Well, that's a complicated story. Yes, he has parents. But not ones as, in my opinion, are fit to rear him. I consider Micah the bravest person in our village, you know."

"How so?" Romilly asked, wonderingly. That was a high compliment from Arra. "Does it have to do with his burns?"

"Yes," Arra said, stoutly. "First of all, how they happened. Second, how he endured the healing. Third, how he went on to live his life."

Romilly thought this through. She remembered the way Micah always stepped aside for her and the strange sense, despite being perfect strangers, that they shared a bond.

"Arra," she blurted out, impulsively, "was Micah burned the night the villagers went with torches to set fire to Digby's house?"

"Ehhh!" said Arra, partly in wonder and partly in relief. "So—your father told you of that night. I've gotten all enmeshed and tangled up in what is secret and what is not." She tipped Romilly's head back and trickled a pitcher of water over her hairline and the crown of her head, sending delicious chills down Romilly's neck and arms. "In the spirit of openness, I'll tell you everything I know. But it's a sad tale, a terrible tale. You see, the night the villagers set out with their torches, they took their children with them. I can only guess they wanted their children to witness how those are treated who bring—however innocently—some threat from the outside world. I could have told them Digby's illness was not a risk to the general population. Your mother and aunt only caught it because they insisted on helping tend him. Secluded on this island, at such distance from the village, Digby was no threat. In fact, your mother, who fell ill in the village, would make more sense as a target, but the village decided instead to simply shun you and your father for the rest of your days," she added, indignantly.

Romilly had not considered that Digby was a scapegoat—that the fact that he was driven out might have saved her and her father. Sadness for him and her aunt surged into her heart.

"But to continue. When they arrived at Digby's cottage and Micah saw his father lift the flaming brand and thrust it through a windowpane, he reached out and grasped the torch to prevent him, so horrified was he by the ugliness of the anger and revenge. And the torch set his sleeve on fire and charred that whole side of his body. They carried him to me—he was just a small scrap of a boy—with burns over the entire left side of his torso. I expected him to die that night, but his will was strong. He stayed with me for almost a year and taught me the best ways of treating burns—how to compound soothing salves to reduce inflammation, the importance of cutting away the dying skin to prevent festering and infection. It was a terrible healing. I was often forced to hurt him, but he never complained. At first his scars were livid, running up half his torso, down his left arm, and all the way up to his jaw, but with time they have faded. The last time I examined him they were but a pale and lacy web on that side. He's a beautiful boy to me—courageous and good."

"And he never went back to live with his family?"

"Nay, child! He didn't want to. And they didn't want him either—he reminded them of their reckless and irrational anger. They were likely ashamed of their child showing greater character and compassion. He stayed with me until he was healed and then moved in with the harbormaster, who has treated him well. He became the errand boy for the fishermen, and then the harbormaster put him in charge of the boat livery once he was ten or so. He's in charge of rigging and tending the skiffs and sailboats kept at the docks for rent. A capable boy. In fact—" Arra paused, considering what she was about to say, then shook her head at herself and went on. "I thought about

adopting him myself, as I always wanted children of my own."
Arra was lifting water in a dipper and pouring it over Romilly's
head, holding her chin in one hand to keep her head tilted back.

"Maybe I should have," she mused, "but during that year it
became clear to me that you needed me too. And I was so often
called away, sometimes for whole days and nights. I didn't know
as that would be fair to him." She sleeked back Romilly's hair
and squeezed out the water.

"All done. But let me ask *you* a question. Why all this curiosity
about Micah?" She crawled to the front of the tub and settled
back, gazing into Romilly's face, which turned pink under the
scrutiny.

"The night Uncle and I went to send the note to the Being—I mean, Digby—I looked toward the flat rock where I
had left my mother's scissors and the key. The tide was coming
up and had covered the platform by then, but as I looked out
over the water I saw a boy across the way, standing on the other
side of the flats, thigh deep in water. Of course, he was too far
away for me to see his face. He was wearing a white shirt, which
the moon lit up. He didn't hide from us, but slowly turned and
walked back up into the woods."

"Interesting," Arra said, slowly. "Yes, that must have been
him. As I mentioned, he told me he'd seen you and Uncle on
the tide flats. I brought him here with me once or twice, about
a year after his injury, to check on the cottage and make sure no
harm had come to it after the winter season. And, of course,
he knows the paths in these woods better than anyone but me,
having been so much on his own. Who knows, perhaps of late
he's been staying here and tending the place—he's not been
seen in the village for some weeks. There was a rumor he'd
gone to sea. Though if he had, he would have said goodbye to
me." Arra paused, her face lit with a fond smile. "It's a shame
he doesn't simply come join us here, being a good and handy
lad and all. You would like him."

"That's *exactly* what Uncle said!"

"Of course, his situation in the village has made him very

cautious and reserved. Sometimes sheer loneliness does that." Arra's eyes returned to Romilly's face and rested there, fondly. "You, too, have a reputation for reserve, yet I know you to be a loving and delightful child." She used the edge of a towel to wipe a bit of soap foam off Romilly's chin. "Now you soak in here as long as you like. The sun is hot today. Your dress should be dry in an hour."

After Romilly had scrubbed herself clean and put on her fresh, sun-warmed dress, she felt a surge of hope and inner lightness. Arra had patiently finger-combed her curls, removing all the tangles. She gave in to Arra's touch, its animal comfort. Arra had taken over the cooking and had managed to assemble a fish pie, whose crust was sweating and just beginning to brown around the edges.

"Go on out and take a little walk. And if you see any wild onions, I could use them. Dinner will be served in about an hour. If you run into our menfolk, tell them to wash, comb their fingers through their hair, and dress in their clean clothes before they come to table. I'm going to insist on a little civilization around here." Arra's eyes were crinkling with pleasure at the thought of taming these wild men.

Romilly headed around the house, holding a saucer of minced liver from the large striped bass Arra had filleted for her pie. All morning she'd been sure the kestrel would return, but when she entered the little yard outside the hut, all she saw was a smooth post leaning uselessly against the stone wall—the remains of Mira's perch. She couldn't avoid the truth: Mira was sealed beyond the sky, and the only hope of her return, or Robbie's, was her father breaking down the wall so that Digby could come home. She was sure in her heart that Digby would return Mira and Robbie to her if he could. Lost in thought, she set off down the path toward the overlook, wishing to rinse her fingertips which had become smudged with the fish's dark blood.

She was thinking how odd it was that a place could so quickly become familiar, almost like a beloved face. She walked past the silvery granite bench to gaze out over the water where the

Ingres sat at anchor, her uncle's boat anchored next to her as if on guard. His more robust, muscular, butter-colored boat was like the sun, while the *Ingres*, silvery and delicate, was like the moon. She had a private solar system at the center of her world. As she meandered down the path, she thought how the huckleberry bushes on each side had given their energy to every cell of her body. The island was part of her now. The yellowish clay of the path, that, too, seemed intimately familiar, the silky dust soft to her feet. The scattering of large boulders along the shores—she patted them like warm, ruminant animals as she passed. The tidal currents between the island and the shore braided together and seemed almost to simmer in the middle of the channel.

As she bent to rinse her hand, she noticed a dense school of fingerling menhaden surging toward shore, their frantic backs breaking the surface with a sound like brisk rain. A school of striped bass were driving the bait fish into the channel. She watched the predators slash through the water, their bodies flashing and then submerging, slapping the water with their great tails to drive the bait fish closer together, and closer to shore. Desperate to save themselves, the little fish leapt completely out of the water, scattering against the rocks and falling between like quivering silver coins. Gulls began to circle and cry, the larger ones guttural, the slender, black-capped terns giving piercing squeals like metal scraping metal. They swooped over the shallows to pluck the stranded fingerlings off the rocks, landing all around her as if she were insignificant. Squabbling and stabbing, they held out their wings stiffly to claim more space. Then they lifted off as a group and wheeled away toward the flats, following the roiling trail of the predators. Romilly could still see the school of fingerlings, tightened into a dense brown smudge just under the surface. She knew that, underneath the water, they turned and spiraled as one.

Against the sand, here and there a bright sequin quivered. Now the sandpipers darted in to scour the shore for their dinners.

A voice behind her made her jump. "This is always the way of late summer—so much life in the water. And death." It was her father. He had a small, still fingerling in his palm, shining bright as a shard of mirror. It was hard to believe that it had once been alive. Gently, he set it down on the sand. "Romilly," he began, then paused, his gaze wandering over her face. "Seventeen was our age when your mother and I met," he went on, quietly. He was looking down at the sand, but his gaze was deep in the past. He gave a slight, pained laugh. "Her mother thought she was too young even to go walking with a young man. But a year later, we were partnered. We just knew we were *meant* for each other, knew it was time. And your grandmother knew when she had lost her battles. I don't know if you will ever partner—don't even know if you will be able to partner and have a family, there is such a shortage of young folk in the village now—but you are clearly ready to be on your own—"

"Father—I've given no thought to all that—and don't want to. I just wish to have *friends* and *community* and a place to belong—"

"Let me finish, my daughter. I thought I couldn't bear this place. It reminded me of Digby surviving—when your mother could not. But the truth is, I can stand it, and I can come to visit."

"Father, wait. It's not so simple anymore. I know more than you think I do. I know the reason Digby could teach you about distant parts of the world. He is *from* another world, isn't he? He didn't leave and return by boat. He came and went right from this island, from a kind of passage or tunnel. And he continued to do so—until you blocked the passage—" When Father lifted his hands to interrupt her, she clasped them firmly, interlacing their fingers into fists. "I know it was you who blocked the tunnel with stones so he couldn't return, at least not without a great deal of force, but he wouldn't use force, would he? He's a gentle man, isn't he? So, he appeared to Uncle—and to me— from beyond our sky. The first time was over the horizon at the edge of our wheatfield. Uncle saw him the first time while night-fishing. And then he appeared to us both here, over the split rock. The night of your sunstroke, Uncle and I were able to communicate with him—oh, it doesn't matter how—and he said he wanted to come home. This is *his* home, too, Father—" And here her throat closed, and she couldn't go on.

During her onrush of words, her father had closed his eyes and was slowly shaking his head back and forth while struggling to free his hands. He swayed so she thought he would fall. At the word *home* his eyes started open, and he said, with vehemence, "Romilly, of course I am afraid! His world has taken much from me." He paused and looked out toward the split rock, where the school of striped bass were roiling in the shallows. His next words left her thunderstruck. "But what I cannot survive is driving you away by my refusal to be large-hearted. I am not *sure* I will succeed, but I will try. For you, I will do it. For myself. I will—I will tear down the wall myself. And I will go into that passage—alone—to meet Digby. For private words. Will you grant me that? Will you promise me?" He gently freed his hands from her grasp and held them toward her, palms up, as if to ask her to place her promise there.

But instead of answering, Romilly pushed herself between his arms and burrowed her face in his chest.

12

OPENINGS

"But I'm a healer, for gracious sake," Arra grumbled. "I know all about closings and openings."

Romilly gave her a stern look. "He wants—to dismantle—the wall—himself," she said, stressing the words. "And I promised him."

Her uncle, who had just come up from the beach, smothered a smile, turning his mouth down at the corners. He stood at the end of the kitchen table, filleting a striped bass. He had been working on the cradle during her conversation with her father, and, when the school of stripers moved into the shallows, he cast out a line. But he'd almost lost this fish, he said, spying on the father and daughter instead of setting the hook, distracted when he saw Romilly rush into her father's arms. Delicately, he made a slit down the spine with his knife, then separated the flesh from the needle-like ribs with small flicks of the blade tip. Scales, milky from being exposed to air, sealed to the wooden table like droplets of frozen rain.

"I don't suppose you asked your father to come to the house for his lunch, then, given all these unexpected revelations?" Arra asked anxiously.

"Nay," Romilly replied. "It fled my mind completely."

"Well," said Arra philosophically, "mayhap that's for the best. We have a lot of things to work out, don't we?"

Romilly nodded, torn between fear for her father and relief, even joy. The sensation of her father's embrace lingered, and she realized it was the first time he'd felt fully present during a hug. Usually, he would pull away distractedly, as if she had interrupted some more important plan, patting her awkwardly, or dart away having barely touched her cheek with his lips. She had always blamed herself for her father's rare, stilted caresses. Arra had been right: she had learned to be a reserved and self-sufficient child, both longing for and afraid of touch. The villagers' avoidance of her had caused her to withdraw to protect herself. She had always assumed that her likeness to her mother made her father afraid to indulge in visible fondness for her, lest he lose her too. Now she understood he had never felt worthy of her affection: he had been ashamed. For so much of love, Romilly thought, you are unsure where you stand, unsure of a return. You want to be loved, you want to give your love, you want your love to be accepted—but you feel unworthy or afraid of rejection. Why did it have to be so complicated?

"I understand him wanting to open the passage himself—after all, he sealed it," her uncle said as he freed the filet and set it in a shallow dish. "But it's a much harder job to dismantle a stone wall than to build it in the first place and—"

"Which is why folks should not build walls in the first place, unless absolutely necessary, like a sea wall or a—I can't even think of any others that are *strictly* necessary," Arra broke in, her brows drawn together.

"Sure," her uncle continued, amiably, "but back to the practicalities. To dismantle that wall, he's going to have to chip away enough mortar to remove a stone. Once he does that, once he has an opening, he should progress. But it will be devilishly hard to remove that first stone. And I have no idea how thick the wall is to begin with, or how many layers of stone it involves. He will also need the proper tools—a stone mason's tools, chisels and mauls and whatnot. I've seen nothing of the sort around here."

"Unless—" Romilly began. She fell silent, looking at her hands. When she looked up, her eyes expressed both timidity and determination. "Digby opened the sky with a delicate touch, so finely it sealed again. He harmed nothing, tore nothing apart. Is there no way to do this from our side?"

Her uncle dropped into his chair with a heavy exhale, threw

his head back, and chewed the inside of his cheeks thought-fully. "You are suggesting something magical," he said, finally. "That's not my area of expertise. I am willing to *witness* magic and be quite open minded about it, but I haven't the first clue how to *make* magic."

"Nor I," said Arra stoutly, "but I'm struck by the fact that the wall is not just—nor even primarily—a material wall, but a wall inside your father, Romilly. He's already done the *harder* work of admitting he must dismantle the wall in himself. As far as I have seen, there is magic all around us—and even miracles. Romilly, you are such a miracle yourself—remember, when you were carting all your supplies to your sailboat, when I said you are a *worldwidener?* This is partly what I meant. *You* have worked your way into your father's granite heart like the canniest implement and have convinced him to take down the wall in himself. We just need to find a comparable tool for opening *actual* granite."

Romilly sat thoughtfully, her hands still in her lap. She saw in her mind's eye the cottage walls, the hunks of stone with their scalloped faces. She recalled, over the door, a keystone arch whose wedges must have been fashioned by a mason or a quarrier. "Arra," Romilly breathed intensely, her face lit with intuition. "Who built this cottage?"

"Why, it's been in your mother's family for generations. Your great-grandfather built it for your great-grandmother when they were first partnered. They were new to the village, having lived across the Sound, and before that, in the Old World. He was a stone mason."

Romilly's face lit up. "Well, it's not a 'magic solution,' but if my great-grandfather built this house," Romilly went on, "mustn't his chisels and other tools be here somewhere? Is there perhaps a cellar or an attic here where they would have been stored?"

Her uncle, who had been listening with a pensive face, sud-denly burst forth with animation. "Of course! His tools *must* be here. After all, he lived his whole life on this island." They sat a moment, then abruptly, as one, they all stood. Romilly wiped her palms on her apron. She felt a hopeful nervousness.

"Romilly," Arra said, "it's your intuition. Guide us."

Romilly's mind flew back to the moment when she drew the sheet of Digby's paper from the cabinet and noted its surprising length. Couldn't there be some sort of chamber or alcove beyond the cabinet?

"I have a hunch," Romilly said, and darted out the front door so swiftly that her uncle and Arra had to trot to keep up. She circled the front wall of the house, obscured with ancient rhododendrons, their branches thick as arms. Parting the leaves, she inserted her slim body into the shady tangle, prying apart contorted boughs powdered with pale green lichens.

"What do you see?" she heard Arra call.

She placed her hands flat against the wall and scanned to the right and the left. To her right she thought she saw the wall cut inward, so she sidled that way, the leaves pressing against her back like leathery palms. Yes, sighting along the wall, she saw that it disappeared, that it must cut in perpendicularly to rejoin the wall near the front door. Pressing her way forward, finally she stepped into the angled nook and saw through the dense shade a dark red door, the paint peeling away in curling strips like feathers, exposing pale undersides.

"There's a door, a dark-red door!" she cried.

"Does it open?" she heard her uncle ask, anxiously.

Holding back the leathery leaves with one hand, she felt around for a knob.

"There's no latch, nor knob—why do so few of the doors here have anything to grasp?" Romilly said, her voice rising in her bafflement. She ran her hands again over the encrusted, peeling surface, releasing a rain of shavings that pattered among the leaves, and pried her fingers into the edge where the door sealed inside its frame. Discouraged, she pressed her body full against the door, leaning her forehead against the rough surface as if it could bequeath to her mind its secret. She felt a movement, almost a jiggle, like the settling one feels when stepping into a boat. When she spread her fingers and pushed against the door with more force, she heard, to her surprise, a muffled click—somehow the pressure of her body had released a clasp, and one side of the door sprung open just far enough for her to slip her fingers inside.

"Romilly, are you all right? What's happening back there?" Arra called. "I'm too stout to come after you, girl—give us a report!"

Romilly gave a soft, delighted laugh.

"I've opened it! Somehow the pressure of my body as I leaned against the door sprung open some hasp." Romilly put her nose to the crack and sniffed the air; cool, minerally, it smelled of whitewash and gravel, just like the interior of the falconer's hut.

Romilly heard a rustling and the creak of branches being wrenched aside and saw her uncle's gleeful face, pinked by exertion, his eyes round with wonder and surprise. Over his shoulder, Arra appeared, holding on to her pinned-up braids to shield them from the scraggle of dead twigs that laced the interior of the gigantic rhododendrons. She brought the back of her hand to her mouth and sucked at a scratch, temporarily struck dumb by the sight of Romilly, who was about to thread her slim body through the crack in the door.

"Wait, you foolish child—you haven't even a lantern, you have no way of seeing what's down there! You'll break your neck tripping or falling down the—"

But it was too late. Romilly had disappeared into the opening and the door clicked shut behind her.

13

WORLDWIDENING

Near the far end of the cellar, a bluish light lit up the floor. Ducking her head, she saw two windows, each no bigger than a tea tray. But the narrow stairwell was impossible to sight down, as if it were in fact a shaded well of water. There was a landing at the top, but no way to see where the steps began. Romilly shuffled her bare feet forward, trying to locate the first step. She stood a moment on the brink. Then, testing the gulf with a tiptoe to make sure the first step existed, she began her descent. Gradually, her eyes adjusted to the gloom; she saw that the steps were made of ordinary, thick wooden planks, that the floor of the cellar was packed earth, and that under and between the windows there was a workbench cluttered with a variety of bulky objects. When she brushed her right hand against the stairwell's wall to steady herself, the whitewashed stones left a mineral grit on her fingertips.

She stood on the floor of the cellar, the clay dust silky to her bare feet. She felt like a clumsy giant in this still, secret space, for the ceiling was so low she could reach up and lay the flat of her hand against the floor joists above her. A strange energy seemed to travel up her legs from the ground beneath her, as if her feet were the roots of a tree pulling strength up from the earth. But that didn't make any sense. Nothing could grow in such a dim, dry space. The windowpanes were lined with rivulets of dust after years of rain had splashed against them, making it impossible to see out. Cobwebs had collected the dust and sagged against the glass like small hammocks. A faint light, so faint it looked grainy, dusted the top of a rustic wooden chest. She came forward and touched the iron handles

on each side of the chest tentatively. They were so rough and
pitted with rust, they seemed to tug at her fingerprints. She
reached decisively and grasped the handles. Then, tightening
the muscles of her stomach in anticipation of great weight, she
lifted the chest off the workbench.

But it was light, dismayingly light! It must be empty. A brass
frame centered in the lid held a scrap of yellowed paper, on
which she could see spidery cursive faded to an indistinct color,
like a wine stain persisting on laundered cloth. There wasn't
enough light to make out the word, so she used her fingernails
to tweeze the paper from its metal frame. Bringing it forward
under the window's weak light, she saw a single word centered
in the middle of the paper, written in exquisite cursive with a
fine quill:

Worldwidening

Why, that was what Arra called her—a worldwidener. Her
heart gave a powerful lurch. She slipped the paper into her
apron pocket, then put out her hands to lift the lid of the box.

What she saw confounded her so much that she let the lid
drop back with a clap. How could this be? She grasped the
handles and lifted the chest again. It took no effort. Her breath
began to catch in her chest. She dropped the box as if it had
burned her and wheeled toward the stairs. Then, clear as a bell,
she seemed to hear a voice say, *Stay.* She stood for a moment in
the middle of the cellar, willing her heart to slow its hammering.
What am I frightened of? she thought. *Nothing has hurt me. Nothing
has threatened me.* As she thought these words, the knot of cold
fear in her chest began to loosen and warm, flowing upward
over her shoulders and down her arms. She approached the box
again and slowly lifted the lid, allowing it to fold back and rest
upon its hinges. Inside the box, dimly lit by the granular light,
she caught the gleam of sharpened steel. On the top, there were
chisels of different widths. Beneath them, a blocky iron mallet
with a weathered wooden handle and a tool that tapered like
an enormous nail punch. She reached out a finger to touch the
faceted grip of a chisel. It was real: cool, smooth, and vaguely

oily. But when her fingers curled around it to lift it out, it felt almost weightless, as if it were somehow full of air instead of steel.

She closed the lid softly. Grasping the iron handles, she lifted the box and carried it to the foot of the steps. It was no heavier than an empty basket. As she walked toward the stairs, she was struck by the fact that she could now see each step clearly, as well as the door with its wrought-iron latch. At the top step, she shifted the box to her hip and reached her hand toward the iron plate, which fit her thumb perfectly. The bar lifted and she pushed the door open easily.

As if it were the most ordinary thing in the world, Romilly stepped forward and offered the box to her uncle. "I've found our magic, Uncle." He looked at her quizzically, but reached silently for the chest, grasping the iron handles as she released them. But as the sudden weight sent him staggering forward, the lid swung open, and half the tools tumbled onto the ground. They hit with substantial *thunks*. The iron mallet landed on the top of Romilly's bare foot.

"Romilly, what have we done to you!" Arra cried. She rushed to Romilly's side and crouched there, lifting the mallet off Romilly's foot, circling her ankle with her palm, then feeling along each bone of her foot, all the way to her toes, with care.

"Thanks be to the Great Willingness! Nothing is broken!"

"Arra, how could it hurt me? It weighs next to nothing—like a dry leaf landing on me!"

"Not to me," her uncle grunted. He had settled back on his heels, his face a pale, greenish oval, sick with fear. Arra touched the head of the iron mallet that lay near Romilly's bare foot.

"Arra," Romilly said, "you try—lift the mallet. Is it heavy to you?"

Arra grasped the wooden handle and stood the mallet on its head. Then she lifted it up and dandled it, assessing its weight. "It's not weightless," she replied thoughtfully. "But it's not near so heavy as I thought it'd be. Feels about as heavy as kitchen ladle. See, Uncle, it's light to us. To me, the entire chest feels no heavier than a—a woven thing, like a big nest, and each tool is—airy somehow."

Arra's brow wrinkled.

"Brother," Arra said, "let Romilly hand it to you."

Romilly took hold of the mallet's handle and reached it toward her uncle. As he grasped the head, he gasped. "Eh! it's no heavier with Romilly touching it than a—than a stick of dry kindling!" They passed the mallet between them, then held it together while Romilly placed her palm upon the handle. Her uncle grew uncharacteristically sober.

"Let's take the lot into the kitchen and sort it out," he said. "I'm afraid your father isn't going to have the strength to use these tools, Romilly. Without your help, these are even heavier in my hand than the usual, non-magical variety." He was squatting over the toolbox, picking up the spilled chisels and placing them back in the chest. "Is the door shut?" he asked. But as they looked beyond Romilly, they saw that the door had silently and mysteriously closed without them noticing.

"The strangest thing, Romilly, was that a light seemed to flood up behind you as you opened the door," Arra said.

"I know," said Romilly. "When I descended the steps, it was pitch black at first, but then I noticed thin patches of light on the floor and workbench from two dusty windows."

"But that's not possible!" her uncle interjected. "I walked all around the house to see if there were a window or even a grate, so's we could call to you, or break through in case you needed rescue. The foundation's continuous stone. We were terrified you'd fall down the stairs or trip or not be able to find your way back up in the dark. Not to mention the fact that we had no idea if the door could be opened from the inside."

"The inside of the door had a forged iron latch that fit my thumb perfectly," Romilly explained. "But a light did seem to follow me up the steps."

"Were you frightened, Romilly?" Arra asked. She was laying

out the tools on the table by size, from the smallest chisels and pointing tools, to the broad, stout-shafted chisels, their ends slighted clubbed from being struck by iron.

"I was. At first, I felt as if I couldn't get any air—my throat began to close, and I began to panic. But as I turned to go back up the stairs, I heard a voice inside my head urging me to wait. There really was nothing frightening or even unusual about the cellar. In fact, it felt oddly ordinary."

Her uncle had recovered his jovial spirits. "I admit I was spooked when you let go of the box and the weight of it staggered me, but I guess my tolerance for magic has been built up these last few days! My chief worry is—should we tell your father that these are other than common stonemason's tools?"

"Well, I suspect for him, as for you, they will feel nothing out of the usual. But can you imagine how he'd react should their magic work on him?" Arra said, her eyebrows raised. "Like as not he'd fling himself off the island and swim for the village," she said drolly, her eyes twinkling. "I know this for sure: there's no way we can tell him that Romilly found a secret cellar and appeared in a magical doorway holding an enchanted toolbox with a mystical light behind her." She thought the matter over further in silence as she unbraided her long silvery hair, picked a twig out of it, swiftly re-braided it, and pinned the braids over the top of her head. "No," she said, decisively, "we are going to have to hold our tongues. There's a very good chance these tools will be even heavier for him than for us two," she said, jutting her chin at Romilly's uncle.

"I'm sort of offended, truth be told," her uncle said with mock indignation, "that these tools are like lead to me, being as enlightened as I am." Pleased by his pun, he gave a chortle of laughter.

"Well," Arra objected, "with Romilly's help, they're not leaden."

"Which means," her uncle said, "we should convince him to accept Romilly's help."

"Uncle," Romilly said with firmness. "He'll never let me near him. He said he must open the wall himself. And," she added, "he wants to go alone into the passage. He said he needed to have some words with Digby. And I promised."

"Yes, child," Arra replied. "But what if his heart bursts in the labor of it?"

Just then, Romilly's father came through the door. He stopped short when he saw them huddling together over the kitchen table. Then his eyes wandered over the tools laid out there, his gaze resting finally on the iron mallet. He walked over and touched the wooden handle, then ran his fingers over the blocky iron head. "Where did you find all these?" he asked.

"Romilly found them," her uncle replied serenely. "She had the wisdom to remind us that this cottage was built by a stone mason, and like as not the tools were about somewhere."

They were all relieved that he didn't notice his brother's contraction of the truth. Grasping the mallet, he tilted the tool up on its head. "This is a fine ash wood handle," he said, "good and stout." His eyes scanned the rest of the chisels appraisingly. "These will do," he said. "I suppose Romilly told you of our conversation," he said, looking at Arra and his brother. "I'm sure by now you know of my efforts to keep Digby from ever returning. Well, I am going to break open the wall I built, for Romilly's sake and for my own sake." When he picked up a chisel, Arra exchanged a swift look with Romilly's uncle. Her father appraised the chisel's weight and balance as if it were a sword, then set it in the toolbox. Methodically, he began to set all the tools in the box, beginning with the largest and heaviest and ending with chisels so fine they must have been intended for stone engraving. The musical chink of metal was the only sound in the room. He looked in each of their faces for a second, then clapped the lid shut and heaved the box up by the handles, using his hip and thigh to push the box forward, the veins and tendons in his forearms bulging and corded. He stood there blank-faced.

Arra rose from her chair and folded her arms across her breast.

"Man," she said to him softly, "you never learn. Sit here with us like a civilized being and have your lunch first. If you don't, we will drag you out of that hut in an hour or so and tie you to a chair." On his face, a vague smile passed over like a break in clouds. In a second, he was gone.

"Well," Arra said, gesturing with one hand toward the door, "there goes the proof that you get your magical powers—and your manners—from your mother, not your father, Romilly."

"Here's the key question," her uncle said to Romilly as he swept ashes off the hearth and back into the fireplace. "Why can't Digby simply open the stone wall himself?"

Arra had pulled the fish pie from the grate and was letting it cool in the open doorway while she set the mugs and plates around the table. Romilly, who had felt her remaining energy drain away when her father left with the tools, was reclining on the sofa with a bowl in her lap, picking stems off huckleberries. Arra had brewed more tea, which steamed on a small table next to her. She raised herself up to take a sip, blowing lightly at the steam that collected just above the surface, as if by magic. A memory returned: her mother had once brought her tea and toast when she was sick with a cold. She remembered her mother lightly singing as she sewed near the fireplace—what was it? Something large and white as cream. The sail! Romilly stored this memory in the vault with other memories of her mother.

"He can't open the wall himself," Romilly said, "because he knows my father would have attacked him if he returned by force. And Digby hates force."

"Digby," Arra interjected, "would never even have used the word *hate*. He spoke of hate as an acid that eats away at a person's strength until all that's left is a hollow shell, like a tree whose heart is rotten and is like to fall in the wind."

"Well, if that's the case," her uncle said, "he's coming back to save your father, Romilly, from internal collapse. Don't you think we should come up with a pretext to check on your father, Romilly? Frankly, his strength's not up to this task. As far as I know, he's taken no food this day, and he's been weakened by sunstroke."

Romilly rose and brought the bowl of berries to Arra, who kneaded them into the biscuit dough with deft, circular motions. She turned the dough out on the wooden table and pressed it flat with the pads of her fingers. "First, he'll need to pry out the nails he used to close the door to the hut. Perhaps you could help with that—bring him the crowbar or a hammer. And maybe he'll see that it's in his interest to allow some help."

"Ah, how right you are! I'll fetch the crowbar and offer my help opening the door. He didn't say he'd accept *no* help, at least not to me," her uncle said, thrusting out his chin in mock defiance.

"When you find him, see if you can convince him to let Romilly bring him something to eat. Thinks he hasn't the needs of an ordinary body, that man." She had finished cutting the biscuits and stood at the end of the table pulling the remaining flour into a pile with the edge of her hand, then smoothing it between her fingers meditatively. "It's a sure sign a body doesn't love itself when it won't even take a moment to eat." Rousing herself, she brushed the flour off her hands, then lifted the tin of biscuits and kneeled to place it on the grate above the coals. Then she crossed to the door and felt the underside of the pie pan. "And then come right back, or my pie will be a cold, unsavory lump. You have a body too."

"I don't know why men always have to do everything themselves," Arra grumbled. "You wouldn't see a woman trying to deliver her own baby, unless she had no choice." She cut into the browned dome of the pie and lifted out a piece, pushing it onto a plate with her thumb. "Here, child, we might as well have our own lunch while we're waiting for these impulsive men."

"Arra, Uncle's right: we have to find a way to convince my father to accept my help. Once he starts chiseling, he won't stop unless he succeeds or collapses."

Arra served herself a piece of the fish pie and brought both plates to the sofa. "Child, I almost think we must trick him for his own good. What do you say to that? I think he deserves it." She was still pink-cheeked with indignation that he had refused to sit down with them for lunch.

"I'm not sure," Romilly said. She felt discomfort at the idea of deceiving him, especially now that he'd finally been honest with her.

Arra clarified. "I mean, trick him in the way that I tricked him with the tonic. The legitimate treatment—compounded with his belief in the cure—may save him. What if we let him exhaust himself, then convince him that I've made a tonic that will strengthen him?"

"But how?" Romilly asked, wonderingly.

"You know, Romilly, you are the true tonic. You are what has convinced him to attempt what was unthinkable before. No matter what, you must be ready to spring into action if he becomes exhaus—"

Just then, they heard the distant squeal of nails being pried reluctantly from knotty wood.

"Ah! He must be letting brother help him—that's a good sign. We will do nothing for now. Just keep our ears alert. But if we hear his work falter, we will send you in after him." Arra's eyes narrowed in determination. "I did say we would go in after him and drag him out if he didn't take a break for his poor body's sake. I never promised we wouldn't interfere for his own good. And I think a tonic may help us again—the one I can make and the one that will deliver it: you."

As her uncle finally sat down to lunch, they could hear the dull ringing of steel against stone. Her heart flew to her father in the dark, twinging with every swing and strike of the heavy sledge.

"He was just sitting, cross-legged on the ground, drawing out the chisels and feeling their cutting edges. When I came near, he looked up and said, 'Everyone always said Ingres's grandfather was a miracle worker in stone. Said he could cut stone like butter. It's a lot to live up to.' He seemed discouraged, so I showed him the crowbar and hammer and offered to help him with the door. He took my help, but once the door was open, he gathered the tools back into the chest, lifted the chest to his shoulder and ducked inside. Then he looked back at me over his shoulder in that dark way he's got and said, 'Brother, I must do this myself,' as if he knew we were scheming."

"I've seen women in labor behave that way," Arra said with a chuckle. Her face grew serious. "But when they reach exhaustion, or nothing seems to be progressing, they accept help *most* eagerly." She paused and allowed her smile to return and broaden her shining face. "You know, Romilly, there are significant similarities. It's almost as if your father must labor to birth his better self." She chuckled again. "Think of it—he's even creating an opening in a wall so he can travel down a tunnel into another world!"

Romilly sat up perfectly straight, suddenly alert. "Arra, what herbs do you give to women to strengthen their labor?"

"Why, I compound a tincture of goldenseal, dayflower, milkweed, wild violet, and woodruff—and mint, naturally."

"What if we told my father you had a tonic that would strengthen his muscles and help him open the wall? He accepted your tonic before!" said Romilly with rising excitement.

"You want to give him womb medicine," her uncle summarized drily, looking from one to the other of the women as if they had lost their minds.

"Foolish man," Arra responded with dismissive authority. "Where on this island would I find goldenseal or woodruff." She narrowed her eyes shrewdly. "Now, I did notice dayflowers among the tideline plants near the flats. And milkweed is sure to grow somewhere about, especially at the edges of this yard where the light comes in. But we are speaking metaphorically, aren't we, Romilly? We are just trying to find a pretext to get Romilly's hands into that hut. I suspect that if we say I've made a tonic that will strengthen the contraction of his muscles, he'll take it gladly. In truth," Arra mused, "I can't think why a tonic made of dayflower and milkweed wouldn't help—muscle is muscle, after all. The womb and the heart are the strongest muscles of all."

"So, you are scheming to *trick* him into accepting Romilly's help." Her uncle was smiling broadly now. "*That* I can get behind! Especially when such trickery is based in kindness. But you'll have to hop to it. Two hours is not enough time to prepare a decent tincture. That's about how long I give him before his body wears out."

Romilly felt an uncomfortable influx of guilt and compassion. She wished, indeed, there *were* something in Arra's repertoire of treatments that could strengthen her father. She would vastly prefer he succeed without her help. She must think with all her focus and might. Why had the chest of tools been so light to her? Was it simply that she refused to accept the weight of things? Her father was a man on whom the world seemed to bear down more. But her uncle, who had borne losses like her father's, had a lightness of being even beyond hers. And yet, for him, the chest of tools was all awkward weight. Why did the chest weigh less for Arra? What set Arra and her uncle apart?

As she thought this through, she was rubbing and soothing her instep with the sole of her right foot. Looking down, she noticed how the milky dust brought up from the cellar made her foot glow with a golden pearlescence. Arra had clasped her ankle in the dread that the iron sledge had wounded it. She had followed the bones of her feet all the way to her toes, sure that the weight had fractured them. She had gotten the dust on her hands. Romilly remembered the silky feel of the dust on her feet as she stood before the chest, the powerful energy that seemed to flow up her legs, as is she were rooted. She couldn't prove it, but—

"Arra, hold out your hands!" she cried. Yes, in the creases at the base of her right wrist, the iridescent dust was still apparent. She gripped Arra's hand tightly.

"Arra, we need to put some of the dust from the cellar floor in the tonic!"

"What are you saying, child!" her uncle interjected. "You want to feed your father dirt?"

Arra looked thoughtful. "No need to take that incredulous tone, Felix. There are medical uses for the mineral content of some clays," she responded evenly.

"Uncle, it's not mere dirt. We all noticed that the cellar was infused with some kind of energy—remember the light that came up behind me, whereas all was dim and dead seeming when I first descended the stairs? It was after I rubbed the dust on my feet, as I was doing just now, that I began to feel the energy of the space. It was so frightening, I almost fled! And look—look how unusual it is. It gives off a pearly glow, like the inside of an oyster shell." Romilly held her foot out so Arra and her uncle could inspect it, turning her ankle toward the light.

"Forgive me, Romilly. And you, too, Arra. It's just—your father—my brother—he'll burst his heart open in this project, I'm sure of it. I don't want to lose him too. I am on the brink of wrestling him out of there, tying him to a chair, and smashing down the wall myself." As he spoke, a red flush crept from his cheeks to his forehead where Romilly could see a vein pulsing.

They sat in silence, suddenly aware of the steady, deliberate ring of steel against stone, muted by the distance and the muffling earth. Romilly felt her own hands vibrating with the remorseless shocks.

"Uncle, it's a theory—I can't prove it except by experiment. But after the tools fell to the ground, Arra touched my foot to assure herself I wasn't injured and got some of the dust on her hand. And you did not. And for her the tools were lighter."

Her uncle sat in bewilderment. "I wish we could test this first. But the tools are with your father. Well. What else can we do? It won't hurt him to put some of the dust in the tonic, will it, Arra? So, do we send you back into that cellar, or do you think there's enough dust on your feet for us to work with?"

"We could bathe her feet and give him the bathwater to drink," Arra said, her face lit up with mischief. "And it would serve him right." She continued in a more serious vein. "If it's magic, a touch should do the trick, shouldn't it? I'm reluctant to let you go back down to the cellar just now. All we need is one more unforeseen development."

Romilly was crossing her ankle over her knee to inspect her foot when she heard a rustle in her apron pocket. Why, she had completely forgotten the chest's paper label! She had intended to reinsert it into the frame once she was in better light. She pulled the paper carefully out of her pocket and held it between her fingers, gazing at it.

"What's that you have there, Romilly?" her uncle asked, his face suddenly alert. "Did you find a note down there? Is it Digby again?"

"Nay, Uncle. It's the label from the chest of tools. The light was too dim to read by, so I had to tease it out of the frame and hold it to the window. It says 'Worldwidening.' Arra, that's what you call me—a worldwidener."

"Aye, it's a term I learned from your mother's people. You have the gift of opening hearts and healing all kinds of troubles and conflicts."

Romilly offered the label to her uncle. He grasped it gently, rubbing the paper between thumb and finger, staring at the dim, faded burgundy ink. The paper was a fine-grained, pale golden yellow. He dipped his head to sniff it, then meditatively turned the slip over. On the back, there was more writing, shadow-colored, as if done with water. "Something's written here," he murmured, "but I can barely make it out, the ink's so faded with time."

"What does it say, man?" Arra asked impatiently.

"It says, 'Let the one who washes'—no! 'wishes to widen worlds deserve—' Ach! My eyes!— '*dissolve* this missive.'"

He handed the paper back to Romilly. "Let the one who wishes to widen worlds dissolve this missive," she breathed.

Arra rushed to the corner where the water pail stood and

scooped up a dipperful of water. She hurried back to the table, sloshing and splashing, and set the dipper before Romilly.

"Romilly, try it—lower just the corner of the note in this water."

Romilly suspended the note over the water's surface. As the paper's edge touched the water, it gave the faintest hiss, like a dampened fingers snuffing a candle. The paper melted into the water instantaneously as snow. Whisps of a faint golden hue drifted downward.

"It must be made of the cellar dust!" Romilly cried out, in great excitement.

"There's your magic," her uncle crowed.

After they finished their lunch, Romilly hurried along the path to the tide flats, clutching a handled basket to her chest. She had indeed found milkweed at the edges of the clearing, and cut several stalks whose white, sticky sap made the sides of her fingers cling. She was hunting now for dayflower, one of her favorites, its two small blue petals cupped like a bonnet over the stamens. As a child, she had pretended these sweet-faced, solitary wildlings were her friends, sometimes gathering a small bouquet to keep on her windowsill so that she could enjoy their rare, sky-pure blue. She was sure she'd seen some among the goldenrod and marsh grass, spreading along the ground on jointed stems. They tended to favor sandy soils and didn't mind having their feet in salt water now and again. She climbed down the rocky bank and began to walk along the high-water mark, where the waves had cast up bleached fragments of reed, and where sea lettuce, now a translucent, almost black membrane, covered the stones. There—her eye caught fragments of glassy blue at the roots of the soapwort, whose purse-like, pale pink flowers smelled blandly sweet. Another childhood friend. With her mother's scissors, she carefully snipped off the flowering tips of the dayflower and added them to her basket.

Arra had agreed with her uncle—there was no time or equipment with which to make a tincture, which required a complex distilling process. But she could steep a tisane, into which they could dissolve the magical paper. She would add a few drops of mint oil from her vial to make the mixture palatable, and a bit of the sunstroke tonic for good measure. Her father, battering the wall in the dark, would obviously not have sunstroke. But he could become overheated, and her tonic would help that condition too. Arra's plan was perfectly reasonable—and yet Romilly felt a strange unease, a lethargy, almost, as if she was being rushed toward something she was not yet prepared for. As she hung her basket over her arm and started up the path toward the cottage, she realized that her mind and body were in conflict—her mind urged her to hurry forward, but her feet were lagging and reluctant.

Maybe it was better, she thought, to merely accept direction from the adults around her. What did she know, after all, of charting her own course? When she'd merely had to set a good example for her father, all seemed simpler. But now she'd convinced him to confront the wall he'd built—not just confront it but break it apart. She owed him a similar courage. She felt she was being thrust into unknown territory, lost and alone. But she was not lost, not alone. Arra was there, and Uncle. Beyond that wall, there was a man who had known and loved her mother and her father as well—the open-hearted father she barely remembered. But this was the father her mother had loved, the one they all wanted back. She was part of his return to his true self.

As she turned to climb the steep bank's ladder of roots and rocks, she heard behind her a familiar piping whistle. She turned to see Mira hovering over the sand almost level with her gaze, her tail fanned in a semi-circle, her wings trembling with an oscillating movement to catch the breeze sweeping over the island. Joy leapt in Romilly's heart, and she reached up her wrist to the kestrel, who dove in graceful arcing flight to land upon Romilly's thumb. She stroked the little bird's puffed up, satiny breast, admiring the bright thorn of Mira's beak and the

fathomless pupil, blackberry-dark and shining. Even the barb-
like clutch of Mira's talons filled her with gratitude. Then, out
the corner of her eye, Romilly thought she saw a human figure.

Yes, in the shadow of a white pine, seated on a boulder of
silvery granite tide-stained at the base—the boy. He rose but
didn't come forward. She could see that his dark, large curls
nearly touched his shoulders, and that his eyes also were very
dark. His face was tanned a rich nut brown, except for the scar
along his jaw, down his throat, and along the forearm below
the rolled shirt cuff, which had the milky color of quartz. In
fact, he stood as still as if he were a boy turned to stone. It was
Micah. He was taller than she remembered him, but she had not
seen him for some months.

"What are you gathering?" he called to her, his voice low and
somewhat husky.

"Arra has sent me to look for herbs for a medical tea. I've
found the milkweed and the dayflower."

"What's it for?"

Romilly hesitated. "It's for my father. He is about to under-
take a very difficult labor and he's recovering from sunstroke."

"I see. Well, what else has she asked for? I might know where
it grows."

"She asked me for wild violet, but in my time here, I haven't
seen any."

Micah came forward until he was standing in the sunshine.
"I know of a patch of wild violets in the woods on the side of
the island that overlooks the channel. The flowers have probably passed by, but I can show you where the leaves are—or, if
you'd like, I can gather them for you."

Romilly was silent. She caressed Mira's back, considering.
She felt awkward and clumsy in her words around this boy, as if
the language she needed to use with him was different from the
one with which she spoke to Arra or her uncle.

In the long pause, he examined her face carefully.

"Are you angry with me for knowing the island so well?" he
said. "For knowing things about it you don't know?"

Romilly thought about this. She *did* feel possessive. She didn't want anyone snooping or meddling here. But that somehow didn't apply to him.

"No. The island was untended and unguarded. It would have been easy for someone to mistreat it or damage the cottage. But you haven't. Wasn't it you living here these past weeks, you who neatened the cottage and brought the wood in?" Gradually, she was relaxing, and her words began to come more naturally.

"Yes. I've been coming here ever since I was old enough to explore on my own. Sometimes I would even spend the night since no one wonders that much about my whereabouts. Arra said I could come here if ever I needed to get away from the townsfolks and their stares. I'm past this now, but when I was small, I couldn't bear being looked at. *Not* being looked at was almost worse—feeling the distrust and the guilt. Not my guilt—but their guilt, for treating me like—"

"—an outcast," Romilly blurted out impulsively, then flushed. "I'm sorry, it's just that I know what you mean. To feel the suspicion of other children, who know they shouldn't approach or talk to you, but most probably don't know why and would be afraid to ask their parents," she said, clumsily, but his face brightened.

"Yes. You know. To be that unspoken, unspeakable thing."

Romilly took a few steps toward the boy.

"Did you see us, the other night, under the full moon? Me and my uncle?"

"Yes," Micah said, simply.

"Did you see me send this kestrel toward the sky?"

"Yes."

"Do you know where I was sending her?"

"No, but I saw your sorrow when she didn't come back. So today, when I saw her perched atop the dead white cedar along the shore, I thought that if I whistled to her and she came to me, I would bring her up to you at the cottage, though it's not the right time for me to see you all, it would be too soon—"

"But why?" Romilly asked, bewildered.

"I'd rather not say. But I was very glad when I saw you gathering flowers here alone. I knew then that I could return your kestrel. And now I can help you in some small way, by showing you the violets."

"I wish you would tell me more—you are suggesting there is a right time—?"

"I will tell you, if you tell me the reason you and your uncle rowed a boat out into the middle of the flats past midnight to launch a kestrel toward the moon. And why she didn't come back."

"Maybe you know," Romilly said stubbornly.

"Maybe I suspect. But if you want to keep it secret, that's your right."

Romilly stood in silence for some moments, thinking this through. "But you are *not* a secret to Arra and my uncle, Micah. Both are convinced you were the one caring for the cottage and both wish you'd show yourself and join us there."

At the mention of Arra, a radiant smile lit up his face. "Arra's here too? She saved me, you know. She's the closest thing to a mother I've known these last ten years."

Romilly hesitated, then plunged on. "My mother died, but your mother is alive, yet you also seem not to have a mother."

"A mother is not just the person who bore you. My mother and my father don't want me near them. I'm a reminder."

"Would you forgive them, ever?" Romilly felt herself on the brink of tears and ducked her chin as if looking into Mira's face, but all was a blur.

"I have forgiven them. Sometimes you have to accept that those who should love you are too limited to *really* love, to love, for example, the way Arra does."

"I feared this might be true of my father, but it's not."

"Then you are blessed," Micah said, with simplicity. "Now, should I gather you some violets? It seems to me you should be going back to the cottage. If you like, I can leave them on the stone bench, near the overlook."

"Oh yes!" Romilly cried and watched as Micah promptly sat

back down on the boulder. He rolled each trouser cuff three times, then set off without another word through the shallows.

Romilly clambered up the steep path, her palm hovering protectively over Mira's back. Deep in thought, she startled when the branches parted to reveal her uncle coming toward her. "Ah, there's our beauty! And Mira's back! See—I told you she might find her way. Look at you, with your kestrel and your basket of greenery. You should be in a painting. How I wish for my aunt to come back and take your portrait, just like this." He ducked closer to survey her face and exclaimed, "Why, Romilly, is that worry I see?"

"Just the vestiges, Uncle. I almost lost my courage on the shore, but then Mira came and helped me restore my faith in myself." She was weighing whether to tell him about Micah, when he rushed on, satisfied with her announcement. He seemed strained and anxious, despite his effort at a cheery exterior.

"Doubtless your father's pounding of the wall will be very unsettling to her—not just the noise, but the violence and vibration of it. Birds are very sensitive to energy. We will need to arrange a new perch for her near the cottage. I was just coming to see if you needed help in your foraging, or if I could carry something or—I guess I am a bit anxious, in truth. No sense in denying it." He reached under his cap to scratch the back of his head vigorously as he said this, then resettled his cap with a tug on its brim.

"I am too, Uncle, but I am newly resolved. We just have to move forward."

"Yes, there's been enough stasis this past ten years," her uncle mused. Brightening, he chortled, "And now we are going to see some real ex-stasis!"

"Do you mean ecstasy?" Romilly asked, puzzled.

"Not in the joyful sense, exactly, though perhaps that as well. I mean, we are about to step outside of ourselves, some of us more than others. Your father, for instance, has made a cramped home for himself inside his fears, like a hermit crab in his shell. That home is going to expand exponentially if he breaks the walls down and allows his friend to return. And that's just the start of it."

Her uncle smiled down on her, placing his hand over her fingers to gently extricate the basket handle. He turned and they resumed their way up the path, her uncle cradling the basket in his arms like a baby.

"Do you think Digby knows it's *Father* doing the breaking?"

"That I can't say, child. He must hope so. All he can do is use his intuition, as we must, I warrant. And take quite a bit on faith."

They crested the hill and entered the cottage clearing. Arra was standing on the flagstone landing in front of the cottage, looking anxiously toward the path and giving little stoops and hops, gesturing with her hand to urge them forward faster. The sound of her father's blows against the wall, blocked by the hill and the distance to the shore, were audible again, a slow, muffled heartbeat. Romilly felt her own heart, exerted by the climb, speed up in her chest. Her pulse scrubbed in her eardrums. Her father's blows had become more labored, each one followed by a pause in which Romilly imagined the exhausted arm struggling to lift the leaden maul again. Arra darted toward them in such anxiousness that Mira startled and leapt lightly to Romilly's other shoulder. Romilly reached up to soothe her, stroking her breast.

"Ah, Mira's returned! How wonderful! I am sorry to be so clumsy," Arra said, leaning to peer with appreciation at the graceful dignity of Mira, drawn tall as if offended. "But his hammering stopped for a full fifteen minutes, and I was sure his heart had burst. And now he's back at it again, though you can hear his arm is weary. We must intervene and quickly," she said, grasping the basket and wheeling with it back to the house.

"Give me your kestrel, Romilly. I will make her a new perch on this side of the cottage, where the sound of the blows will be somewhat muffled." Romilly transferred Mira to her hand, then gently deposited her on her uncle's shoulder. Mira trembled her wings as if she meant to return to Romilly, but as her uncle set off for the woods to find a suitable branch, Mira clung to his shoulder tightly.

"Arra," Romilly began tentatively, "I found the milkweed and the dayflower, but I think the wild violet is down the path near the overlook, not on the beach. Shall I run out to fetch some now?"

"Yes, yes, if you can be quick about it. The water is about to boil and ideally all the herbs should be mashed together before steeping," she muttered. Romilly didn't dare to wait, but as she ran out the door, Arra called her back. "While you are out there, pick some wild grape leaves for me—they are growing up the last large ash tree near the overlook. I need large leaves to create some sort of funnel for decanting off the tisane." Relieved that Arra didn't intend to stop her, Romilly turned and flew down the path.

But as she approached the falconer's hut, she stopped short, hesitating. Her heart hung heavy—she could see where the expression 'my heart sank' came from. It seemed to fall through her chest like a stone. Shouldn't she stop? Shouldn't she check on him?

The sun was high above the trees, and she walked toward the hut through a shaft of sunlight. The light was so dazzling she had to look down at her bare feet, which stepped occasionally on a fallen leaf, limp and vivid yellow, the harbinger of fall. She had not noticed until now the way the air had become dry and sharp as a blade, or how the vault of blue sky seemed more distant. She imagined the mist of light she walked through was a field of energy hovering above her skin, helping her detect and avoid harmful presences, the way Mira could detect and flee the damaging vibrations of her father's blows. She was nearing the hut and the ringing blows of steel on stone vibrated through her chest and made her nerves wince.

Outside the open door, she saw a pile of rubble—fist-sized

pieces of stone, some encrusted with mortar—that her father must have moved there to clear space to stand. It looked pitifully meager given the hours he had been at work. She could smell the warm, sweetish scent of stone striking stone. As a child Arra had shown her how, in the dark, you could see the white sparks fly off two quartz cobbles when you struck them together. Showers of sparks must be flying off the chisel in the almost total darkness. Those granite cobbles were so dense and durable that an immeasurable time in the ocean's huge grasp had merely rounded their edges.

Just then, she realized the blows had ceased. She sprang forward, startled, but it was too late; her father was standing in the doorway, just a few feet away, his chest heaving as he struggled to quiet his breathing.

"Arra sent you to check on me, I'll warrant," he gasped. His graying hair was dark with sweat and plastered to his forehead. Sweat and rock dust had mixed into a grime that streaked his thin chest. He had wrapped his palms in strips of cloth, but blisters had oozed through and she could see that his knuckles were scraped raw. One thumbnail was purplish, like the inside of a moon-snail shell.

"No, Father. Of course, she's worried. We all are. But she's sent me to pick some wild violets and fetch some grape leaves at the overlook, so I had no choice but pass by." He nodded but seemed unconvinced. "We've given up on expecting you to take some food, but we're making you a beverage that will give you energy and keep you from overheating and I hope you will accept it. Arra says that prolonged labor in an enclosed space can lead to heat exhaustion."

Her father nodded, whether in acknowledgment or concession, Romilly couldn't tell, but she decided swiftly to act on the latter.

"Once I deliver the leaves and herbs she needs, I will be back in just a few moments with the beverage, Father. Why don't you walk with me to the overlook? It will give you a chance to stretch your back and rest your arms a bit." Her father bit his upper lip in his lower teeth and shook his head, but then, at her imploring look, he dropped his shoulders. Stooping to gather up his shirt, he used it to wipe his brow and neck, then threaded his arms through the sleeves. Romilly took his stiff and awkward arm, feeling it soften slightly as they set off slowly down the path.

"Father, I've agreed not to follow you once you have dismantled the wall, but why not at least allow me to help you breach it? I could hold a lamp for you or help clear the rubble around your feet—surely there's a way for me to help."

"I don't want witnesses," he replied shortly. "Nor distractions. I already feel like a herded animal. You are all so sure you know what's best for me."

"What if we at least gave Uncle a turn at it, Father? How deep did you build that wall? Is it reasonable to expect a single man to smash it apart?"

"I never imagined removing it. I built it a bit at a time, over several years. Once I finished one layer, I started another. I intended it to last lifetimes. I'd say it is at least three feet deep in parts, deeper in others."

"But it can't be, because I heard—" Romilly blurted out.

Her father smiled palely and somewhat grimly at this outburst but said nothing.

"Naturally, it's not reasonable for me to expect to breach the wall on my own. But I'm not a reasonable man, as no doubt you are all aware." Romilly found his self-knowing smile oddly encouraging.

"Even the most unreasonable man would allow his daughter to check on his health throughout the process," she retorted. "For instance, I would like to rebandage your hands before too long." She paused, turning to face him. "Can I see your palms?"

Her father's hands hung stiffly at his side. Slowly, she reached out toward his wrists, lifted them, and turned the palms up for inspection. She felt an animal resistance, like when she needed their cow to move over in the stall and had to lean her entire weight against her flank before she shifted. How had it come to seem that she was his parent, rather than the other way around? She had heard the phrase "wayward child" in the mouths of adults many times before, but why was "wayward parent" not equally common?

"You are a wayward parent," she heard herself murmur as she cradled one hand and leaned over to inspect the scuffed skin over his thumb muscle, the grimy and creased cloth, stained pink over blisters that had clearly ripped open and were oozing fluid. She lay her fingertips gently over his palm and shook her head in exasperation. His hand began to shake, and she realized he was laughing. She looked up wonderingly as he covered his mouth with the back of his other hand, his eyes crinkling with mirth. "Why are you laughing?"

"Because you are such a compound of Arra and your mother—tenderhearted like your mother and bossy like Arra. It's good to have a bit of bullheadedness. Perhaps, in truth, you got that from me." He linked arms with her again and they continued walking until they reached the clearing. While she selected a half a dozen of the largest grape leaves she could find, he wandered past the bench to the head of the bluff and gazed down on the *Ingres*. Their sailboat lay peacefully at anchor, the breeze playing among her rigging lines and making two pulleys chime against each other, sweet in the distance. As Romilly walked toward him, she saw a large bunch of violets lying on the stone bench, the heart-shaped leaves accented by a few flowers. She swiftly picked them up and concealed them among the grape leaves in her gathered apron.

"It's missing," her father said. He gave a grim chuckle.

"What is missing, my father?" Romilly looked out over the water in alarm.

"My brother's boat." He tried to lift his arm to point, but let it fall to his side, a helpless and weary gesture that tugged her heart. He was right: the sunshine-colored boat no longer kept guard over the *Ingres*.

Her father stood, his wounded hands hanging stiffly at his sides. His face bore a haunted look.

"Is my brother at the cottage?"

"Yes. No. That is, he's somewhere in the yard, putting up a new perch. Mira's back. We are concerned the noise of your pounding might unsettle her."

"So, not likely *he's* the one who's taken her."

"No," Romilly groaned. "And he will be devastated at this loss—she's his livelihood." She paused to think. "Perhaps she's merely pulled up her anchor, or somehow slipped her mooring line."

"Nay, Romilly. Your uncle wouldn't make that kind of mistake. Someone's taken her. Might come back for the *Ingres* too. Thieves rarely steal but one unguarded boat."

"I will tell Uncle to stand watch while you are in the hut, Father," Romilly averred firmly. She noticed him clenching and unclenching his fists.

"My hands, they've got a kind of odd tingle in them," he noted. "And my right arm." Romilly's heart leapt—that was the side where she had held his arm, walking together. Could it be from her touch?

"I'm not surprised. It's probably the impact of steel on stone, transferred to your nerves," Romilly said. "Or perhaps it's your blisters, smarting."

They turned back and walked toward the hut. Surreptitiously, Romilly studied his profile. He seemed somber and dull, almost as if he were dreading returning to the labor at hand. As he must be, she thought. When they reached the dark, gaping door, he turned to look at her.

"I will work here another hour and then, when you come with this drink, I will show you my work so far," he said. Romilly beamed at him.

"Really? You'll allow me inside?"

"Just for a moment, to assure yourself I'm still alive. And to have a drink of this fortifying beverage. Arra was quite clever with her tonic earlier." The arch of each ear and the tip of his nose pinkened. "I may have brought the rest of that tonic with me, in case of emergency," he murmured bashfully.

"I'm glad you did. Though I think Arra was hoping to place her newest concoction in the bottle. But no matter. We can use the bottle we brought the spirits in. I'll go tell Uncle about his boat now. Perhaps all our fear is for nothing. Perhaps he moved the boat himself."

ॐ

Back in the cottage, Romilly surveyed the progress. The kettle was steaming on the table next to Arra, who was deftly plucking the leaves off the stems of the milkweed and dayflower. She looked up as Romilly entered, her face flushed with exertion.

"Success?" she asked brightly, lifting her apron to wipe her brow and cheeks. Romilly set the violet foliage and the grape leaves on the table. Arra disentangled the bundle of violets from the grape leaves, which Romilly proceeded to sort and lay flat on the table. "That's quite a lot of violets you managed to pick, young lady," she exclaimed, looking up in astonishment.

"They grew—thickly," Romilly replied.

Arra looked sharply into her face and murmured, "They must have."

"I saw Father," Romilly added quickly, remembering Micah's reluctance to make his presence known. Her face flushed at the uncomfortable mingling of respect, guilt, and conflicting loyalties. But Arra didn't seem to notice.

"How did that happen? Is he worn to a scrap?" she asked, as she pinched off the tenderest leaves and the few scattered blooms and began to mash them in a mortar and pestle. "I do hope," she commented wryly, "this hasn't been used to grind poisonous pigments," as she lifted the heavy stone pestle and let it drop repeatedly until the leaves were a nearly black pulp.

"He's sweaty and grimy and looks tired, and his hands are both blistered and scraped," Romilly explained as she watched Arra scoop the pulp out into her palm and place it in the center of a cheesecloth square. She drew up and twisted the corners together, fashioning them into a knot. Removing the lid from the kettle, she poked the cheesecloth bundle, already stained a vivid green, into the water.

"There," Arra huffed, sitting back on her heels to catch her breath. "That will need a good twenty minutes to fully steep. I want to hear more about your father, Romilly, but first, could you fetch me the tonic?"

"Yes, Arra, but I need to give you some awful news. It concerns Uncle."

Arra stilled and looked keenly into her face. "What—is he safe? Come out with it, girl!"

"No, no, Arra, it's his boat—when Father and I walked out to the overlook, the *Ingres* was safe at anchor, but Uncle's boat was missing."

"Ahhh. You almost stopped my heart, young lady. A boat's just a thing, not a person. Like as not he's simply moved her somewhere. You know how folks fuss about their boats. Boats are like children to them."

"That's possible, Arra, but I doubt it. Uncle's been making Mira a new perch near the house. And before that, he was in the cottage with you."

"Well, girl, fetch me the tonic! And after, go find your uncle so we can sort out this boat mystery."

"I can't. Father took the bottle with him—to fortify himself, he claims. He has great faith in you!"

Arra tut-tutted in exasperation. "How's a body to work professionally here when things keep going missing?" she exclaimed, but her face wore a broad smile.

"Have we ruined the infusion, Arra? Do you think your earlier tonic is necessary for the effectiveness of this one?"

"Absolutely not," Arra replied stoutly. "My concern now is this—what are we to put the new tonic *into*, so that we can deliver it to your father? With that precious paper dissolved in it, you wouldn't want to slosh it along the path in an open mug."

"The spirits," Romilly said, abruptly.

"The what?" Arra cried out.

"Before we set out for this island, my father asked me to gather supplies. One of the things he asked for was spirits, I assume to be used as disinfectant."

"Your father has more sense than I've given him credit for," said Arra, thumping the table with her palm. "That is the perfect thing! Adding the spirits to this infusion will speed the absorption into your father's blood. And then we can place the concoction back in the bottle and transport it to him! But that will be the last step. First, it must brew. And you will need to find your uncle and tell him about his boat. And then, bring him back here with you, missy. Don't you go disappearing too!"

~

Romilly stood on the doorstep and scanned the yard. There he was, near the giant lilac tree. He had Mira on his shoulder and was just tamping with his boot sole around the base of a straight, silvery-barked pole made of a young tree.

"There you go, Mira—try that out for size." He transferred the kestrel to the horizontal branch of driftwood that was pegged to the top. The kestrel gripped the silvery, suede-soft branch with her jet-black talons. Romilly stepped up to the new perch and together they appraised it.

"Uncle, what a beautiful perch—even better than her old one," she began. Then she put out her hand gently and touched his arm. "Uncle, I have some news—don't worry, we are all safe and sound, but—just now I came back from the overlook. Your boat—" she paused and took a deep breath "—is missing. We were hoping perhaps you had moved it yourself?"

"Missing?" her uncle enquired, pushing against the pole to make sure it was firmly seated in the ground.

"Yes, Uncle." He tilted his head and looked up at the sky, considering. "Uncle, do you understand what I'm saying? Did you move your boat to the other side of the island? If not, we are afraid someone stole your boat."

"Stole it?" Her uncle looked startled. "No, no one would do such a thing. Borrowed it, maybe."

"Uncle, be serious! If someone took your boat, they might very well come back for the *Ingres*. Father wouldn't survive that—"

"Yes, Romilly, he would. He has survived much worse."

"Uncle, you're teasing me! Why are you so unconcerned?"

"Why are you so *concerned*?" her uncle retorted. "After all, we're not marooned here. We can easily walk back to the village if need be." He narrowed his eyes. "What do *you* think has happened to my boat?"

"I think—I think Micah may have taken it."

"Taken it? Stolen it?" Romilly looked at him uncertainly. "Nay, Romilly. I know that lad."

"I—I met him, Uncle. He's the one who brought Mira back to me. I met him on the shore where I was gathering the dayflower."

"Eh, you met! So, I take it he's the person who had been tending the cottage. What did you think of him?"

"Yes, he admitted he was the caretaker, Uncle. I liked him, I liked him—but he was very strange and stubborn in some ways. And secretive, which I didn't like at all. He seems to know why we're here but won't admit it. When I asked him why he was hiding from us, he said it wasn't time to reveal himself."

"Well. Nothing in all you say could make me think he would steal from me. I prefer to consider this a case of borrowing. He's a good sailor too. Grew up to it." Her uncle bent down and pulled up a tall blade of grass, inserting it in his mouth and chewing reflectively. "So, I will wait to see what turns up," he concluded.

Romilly linked her arm in his. "You are the most open-hearted person I know," she said. "Or the most innocent—or both."

"You sound like Arra!"

"Speaking of Arra, she sent me out here to bring you back to the cottage. She's ready to decant the tisane."

"She's a clever one, that Arra," he said, as they walked arm and arm to the cottage.

Her uncle regarded the bottle of spirits mournfully as Arra twisted out the cork. "Well," her uncle said, with a sly half-smile, "we may not need *all* the spirits for this remedy. Perhaps we could save a few measures with which to toast our inevitable success?"

Arra rolled her eyes. "Brother, you are incorrigible. I suppose you will also propose we declare this an annual holiday?"

"Not a bad idea, that," her uncle replied, rubbing his hands together. "I am ready for some vigorous new traditions! Preferably ones involving dancing!"

Arra set to work. Draping a length of cheesecloth over a bowl, she poured the steeping liquid out, straining the pulp from it. Then, doubling up a clean swath of cheesecloth, she filtered the tisane back into the kettle. With a reproachful look at Romilly's uncle, she poured half the spirits into a mug, reserving them for the hoped-for celebration.

"I am almost ready to add the tisane to the bottle, Romilly. I just need to make some sort of funnel out of the grape leaves. Now. Tell us more about how you found your father."

"Well, he appeared in the doorway while I was passing by the hut. He refused help again, but I persuaded him to walk with me to the overlook. He's driven and rather grim, as usual. And suspicious of us," Romilly explained as she watched Arra snip the stems off the grape leaves, layer several into a fan, then twist and coil them into a cone. Arra inserted the narrow opening into the spirit bottle, then stepped back to regard her work with a critical eye.

"Driven and stubborn, but oddly reasonable at the same time," Romilly ruminated. "He even made a little joke about being *un*reasonable," Romilly explained.

"Eh!" her uncle interjected. "That reminds me of how he used to be—he had a gift for gentle sarcasm, especially toward himself."

"My, he's developing self-awareness in leaps and bounds. Hold the cone like this, my dear," Arra instructed Romilly, cupping her palms about the leaf-cone to hold it together. She had transferred the beverage into the tea kettle and now began to decant it slowly into the funnel.

"I know these leaves are waterproof, but I hope they are

also rigid enough. Also, that the tisane isn't too hot. Tell me if it starts to burn you! If it's too hot, it'll turn these leaves to slime before we can get all the mixture into the bottle," Arra fretted.

"It feels warm, but not hot," Romilly reassured her. "Have you dissolved the paper in it yet?" she asked, anxiously. She didn't want to miss that part.

Arra pretended to be shocked. "Place the magic ingredient into the potion without the presence of our good fairy? Fie!" she said, smiling broadly.

For safekeeping, she had placed the delicate rectangle of paper in the pouch she had used to bring them tea, what seemed like ages ago. She withdrew this now from her apron pocket and carefully picked open the drawstring.

"Here," she said, holding the pouch toward Romilly. "My hands are shaking. And this is your moment, Romilly. Your hands should be the ones that complete the magic." Romilly extended her palms and Arra placed the pouch gently upon them. It was so light, Romilly was afraid the pouch was empty, but when she peeked inside, she could see the pale golden, slightly wavy edge. With her thumb and finger, she withdrew the paper, noticing again the pale burgundy cursive, so fine it seemed to have been written with a crow quill.

"Worldwidening," she whispered.

She would need to scroll the paper into a tube so it would fit through the mouth of the bottle. She lay the small rectangle down on the wooden table and began to lift the short end. But as soon as the paper began to flex, the end dissolved into a pile of golden crumbs. Romilly gasped, staring at the pearly dust in consternation. Arra patted her shoulder.

"That's all right, daughter. Maybe rather than scrolling it, you should tear it into tiny bits. We can brush up the dust—the paper would have dissolved in the infusion anyway."

Romilly held the paper down to tear off the top corner, feeling an odd, simultaneous fragility and resilience.

"I can't! It's like tearing skin!"

She made one more attempt to scroll the paper, but it was

clear that every time the paper flexed, it began to return to dust.

"Well," said her uncle, "this isn't a disaster. It's just a bit messy. We need something to collect the dust." He went to the pantry and rummaged about.

"Where are you off too, man?" Arra grumbled in impatience.

Her uncle returned holding a piece of translucent paper—he had torn off a corner of the letter to Digby. "We can use this paper to capture the dust," he explained, "and to direct it into the bottle." He folded the paper and creased it firmly with a thumbnail.

Romilly set the remainder of the label on the translucent surface of the paper and rolled it up from the short end, as best she could. She was afraid to pick up the crumbling scroll, so she picked up the paper like an upside-down tent, shaking the scroll and all the loose powder into the center.

"Are you ready?" her uncle asked, his eyes sparkling with anticipation, the fingers of both hands interlaced beneath his chin.

Carefully, Romilly raised the paper and, jostling it slightly, persuaded the scroll to slide through the mouth of the bottle. Almost instantly the scroll was eaten away by the liquid, disappearing like snow on water. The powder, which had begun to clump and cling in the moisture of the kitchen, dropped atop the murky green liquid and settled there a moment. Tiny hillocks, rocking lightly, darkened as they drew the fluid up. Then they heard the faintest hiss as the dust melted into the infusion and was gone.

Yet something persisted. At first, Romilly thought that she was seeing her own lashes as she squinted down the bottle's neck at the water's surface.

"Look! Look atop the water," Romilly cried.

They all leaned in, taking turns to peer through the warping glass at the surface, upon which some minute filaments seemed to float on little islands.

Romilly pulled the bottle back toward her and looked down the neck of it. Atop the water she could see that the pale bur-

gundy filaments were letters floating upon remnants of undis-
solved paper, as if the ink were holding it together.

"What is it, Romilly, what do you see?" Arra half-whispered,
breathless with impatience.

"I see a word, formed by the letters that haven't yet dissolved."

"What word?" Arra and her uncle cried out simultaneously.

Romilly peered into the bottle as the delicate letters shifted,
drew closer. She lifted her face and looked at them with blank
uncertainty.

"The word is *girl.*"

Sitting at the table in her aunt's studio with the bottled tisane
beside her, Romilly reached for her mother's journal. She
rubbed her palm along the waxy, ivory vellum, fingering the
spine embossed in gold with stylized lilies. If she should ever
have a girl, a daughter, she thought, she would name her Lily.
That name hovered inside of hers like a promise. But what had
it meant, the word on the water? Was it a sign that she was the
key to opening the wall? Was it simply a reminder to be a child,
yet? Or was it mere chance? She opened the book and began
to write.

*I must wait another quarter of an hour before going to my father, as
I promised.*

*I sit in Aunt's studio, thinking through the morning's events. Why the
tiny scroll didn't dissolve all at once, why four letters rested like tiny islands
on the surface, why those letters happened to spell out 'girl.' Is this part of
the magic of this place? And why, when I told Arra and Uncle this word,
did they look swiftly at each other?*

*Even with the windows closed, I can hear steel on stone, the metallic
ring. I feel the shock of the impact through my father's arm. As the sledge
hangs from his arm, I feel its weight. Then the labor of lifting the sledge
back over his head. I'm eager to enter that darkness, my father's darkness,
and end this.*

I want to meet Digby, who taught my mother to make this book. I know now that her hands didn't just touch this book, they formed it, folded and cut the pages, sewed them in, wrapped the vellum, gilded it. Mother, guide me now. Mother, could you also be waiting beyond the wall?

She lifted her eyes from the page and gazed, without focus, at the expanse of table in front of it. Her eyes came to rest on the collage, perfect emblem of her world, the daughter cradling the soft body of her kitten, facing the viewer, but oblivious to the world around her; the father gazing down, away from the daughter, reaching toward the gathered sheaf of corn. She shifted her eyes to encompass the butterfly, the page in which this world reposed. So delicate: each antenna was a mere thread of paper. What was a butterfly? It was the culmination of a life-cycle. It was fragile, yet immensely strong. It must be handled gently. Romilly remembered pursuing butterflies through a field of Queen Anne's Lace as a very young child, how, capturing one between her cupped palms, she had run exultant to the adults to show her prize. One of them leant down to her and cradled her hands in his, opening them gently to show her how the butterfly, floundering inside, had tattered the rims of its wings and powdered her palm with feathers so fine, they looked like a pearly dust. Like the dust on her feet, like the dust the magical paper was formed of. Who had this person been? Could this have been Digby?

She was lost in thought, when now was the time to act. Her father needed her, and she needed—all of him, not the pre-occupied father, the one who pent up his rage and bitterness and sorrow within a brittle shell. That shell had deprived her of his full and open love. And it had created reserve in her, too, a sense of never trusting and never being safe. Abruptly she stood and grasped the bottle's neck in her hand, then lifted it and held it to her chest, aware of its lingering warmth. She would go to him now. She was ready.

Just then, her uncle opened the studio door a crack and thrust his head inside. His hair stood on end, as if he had been plowing his fingers through it in his anxiety. He opened and closed his mouth, then looked at her a moment, abashed.

"I'm sorry," he said, "but Arra and I can scarcely stand the suspense any longer."

"I know, Uncle. I've been gathering my thoughts. But I'm ready."

She walked toward him steadily, holding the bottle to her chest in both arms.

He swung the door open for her, revealing Arra's tall, firm form. Her sun-burnished face gazed proudly at her.

"You are as brave a daughter as your mother *ever* could have hoped for," she said, as she stepped forward. She reached out both hands to disentangle a few curls, running her fingers through to the tips of Romilly's hair, then cupped her face in her roughened palms.

"Your color's good, like a wild rose. Your eyes are clear. I'd say you are ready." Romilly nodded wordlessly and nestled a moment into Arra's chest. Her uncle placed his arms around the two of them, resting his chin atop Romilly's head. They stood, taking comfort in each other's breathing, until the spell was broken by a sudden quiet—the pounding, which had somehow become part of the island's soundscape, the great, steady heartbeat of the island itself, had ceased. They pulled back from their embrace and looked at each other with anxious intensity.

"He needs you now—go to him," Arra said. "We will follow and wait outside the hut."

"Just a moment!" her uncle cried. Crossing to the hearth, he picked up a small lantern of pierced tin, already lit. "Take this but walk carefully with it. I had some trouble getting the wick to draw."

Romilly grasped the lantern and, taking one last look at their faces, set off down the path toward the falconer's hut.

The door of the hut was a dark, mouthlike hole, and eerily silent. Romilly stood in the doorway, her left arm cradling the bottle, her right hand extending the lantern into the dimness, scattering pinpricks of light like golden stars upon the shelves. She swung the lantern left, toward the narrow stone corridor. She was afraid to call out, afraid her father wouldn't answer. She inched down the passageway, hearing nothing but the sound of her own breathing. Summoning courage, she called out, her voice startlingly loud in the close space.

"Father, I'm here."

She heard her name uttered low and saw, at the end of the passage, her father sitting upon the floor with his knees drawn up. His head leaned wearily back against the stone.

"Father, are you all right? Father, I've brought you the drink."

She crouched next to him and lifted the lantern up to see his face. By its dappled light she saw he was smiling faintly.

"I'm sure I'll breach it soon. Just going to rest a minute and have that drink you promised me. It's been going easier since our walk this morning. I've made good progress."

Romilly stood again and held the lantern high. At chest height, she could see a crater about six inches deep and two feet in diameter in the back wall. Even in lantern light, the broken edges of the stones glittered with compressed crystals. Her heart sank. What was he thinking, *almost through*? It would take days of such labor to open the wall. At her feet, there was a pile of rubble, pale with dust and smelling faintly of burnt sugar. The chisels in the open box of tools were also covered in a ghostly layer of fine dust. She set down the lantern by her feet and turned to her father again.

"Father, I want you to drink this down, as much of it as you can." She uncorked the bottle and handed it to him. As he reached for it, she saw that the rags bandaging his hands were dark with fresh blood. She bent over, grasped her apron hem, and lifted it to her mouth. With her teeth, she ripped a strip from the bottom of the garment. Her father watched her without comment, then tipped the bottle to his lips, his eyes on her face as he drank. She could see him grimace at first, but then he began to down the contents with slow, smooth swallows. He stopped to take a deep, sighing breath. "Tastes both salty and faintly sweet," he murmured. "And spiritous," he noted, smiling wanly.

"Yes, Arra added some seawater for salt and the spirits we brought with the medical supplies."

"I didn't realize how thirsty I was," he said, then tipped the bottle again, finishing the contents in one long draught. Romilly leaned her back against the rough wall and inched down it, folding her legs until she sat next to her father, comforted by the abrasive solidity of the stone. Taking the bottle from his hand, she turned his palm upward and began to untie the bandages which were warm and limp with blood. His blisters had burst and torn. He winced from the sting as she exposed his ripped palm to the air.

"I thought I had toughened my palms by now from years of plowing and scything," he said, chagrined. "But I guess each new kind of labor tests the body in its own way."

Romilly wrapped his palm round and round with the cloth strip from her apron, tying the ends firmly. Pivoting to face him, she reached for the other hand, and he gave it meekly. This hand, which had held the chisel in place, was not so badly blistered, but the thumbnail had now turned completely black. As she rebandaged his hand, she scolded herself. She had no plan in case the tisane failed to enact its world-widening magic. She couldn't very well wrestle the sledgehammer out of his grip. And she knew he needed to strike the blow that broke the wall down forever.

"Why are you frowning, my daughter?" he asked. She started, coming back to him, unaware that her consternation showed on her face. She ducked her head to peer at the bandage, feeling around for the ends of the cloth strip, tying them together. She gave the knot a final tug, then looked up into his face.

"Just trying to make out the ends of the bandage. The light's so weak." Just then, as if on cue, the lamp sputtered, flared up briefly, then went out.

14

THE PASSAGE HOME

Romilly gasped, but her father gave a low rolling chuckle.

"Back into darkness," he noted drily. "It's a good thing I don't need light for such monotonous labor." She heard him pivot onto his knees, then push himself to standing.

Romilly sat silently, struggling to hone her vision, feeling almost as if her eye muscles were gripping down upon the darkness. The faint light from the passageway was enough to make his bulk visible, but only so long as she looked slightly to the side. When she looked at his form directly, he dissolved and melted into the blackness. She heard him stoop and feel about on the ground, evidently seeking the sledgehammer.

"Father, let me go back to the house and relight the lantern," she urged.

"Nay, daughter. It's time to begin again. You were only to deliver the beverage, which I have drunk. You should go on back to the cottage, or Arra will worry about you too."

"But how can you hit the head of the chisel in pitch blackness," she wondered aloud.

"Well, as you and my thumb know, I missed a time or two, but repetition has made me expert. Here—if it'll reassure you, I'll show you how I manage."

This was her chance. If, when his arm was back, she could touch the helve of the sledgehammer—just to be sure the magic worked… Romilly concentrated, focusing her vision on the swarm of darker darkness that was her father. She saw, in slow motion, a bit of her father's darkness break off and flow backward. That must be his arm. Shifting forward softly, she reached out and touched the end of the wooden helve lightly, letting her arm move forward with the completion of the stroke. As the iron head of the sledge impacted the steel chisel, an arc of sparks lit for a fraction of a second the stone face, then suddenly her father was pitching forward. She heard the sledge clatter upon the rubble. He gave a soft gasp, and she heard him feeling about the wall where the chisel entered it.

"It's turned to sand!" he cried out. "The chisel's buried all the way to the hilt!" Romilly could hear a soft shushing sound of sand falling to the ground as his fingers dug around the chisel's shaft. "How on earth—" he panted out, his breath rasping as his throat tightened in anxiety.

"We need to leave, Romilly, this could be something evil, it could be a possession of some sort. The walls could fall in, we could be trapped!" he continued, in rising panic.

Romilly gently took hold of his arm. "Father, nothing is collapsing. The wall you built to seal the passage has simply softened, somehow. This is a good thing. You'll have much less trouble opening the passage now—and isn't that what you want?" she asked. Romilly couldn't see her father, but she could hear and feel his breathing calm slightly.

"I was expecting it to take many hours, if not days. I'm not sure I'm ready, is all. There's so much you don't know. Once the passage is opened, our lives will be changed forever, daughter. There'll be no going back to the way things were before."

"That's already true, Father," Romilly said, matter of factly. "And I'm ready for the new. For the relief of it. Aren't you?" She listened to his breathing in the dark. She could just see the moist glimmer of his eyes—the whites like faint stars in the night sky; he seemed to be looking searchingly at her. Then he turned back to the wall. Silently, he reached out and touched the chisel's shaft, then grasped it. Romilly could hear him rotating the chisel in widening circles to carve out more sand. He pulled out the tool and began to dig out sand from the hole he had made.

"I will continue," he said. "But first, daughter, you must leave as you promised. I must do this alone—I must have a chance to speak to—the one behind all this."

"I'll leave you, then, but I will be waiting right outside the hut when you are ready." Just then, they heard a raucous, jubilant cry from beyond the wall, *Gaw, gaaaaaw*! And then, confidingly, as if he had inserted his beak to croon into an ear, Robbie drawled out a word—

"It's Robbie, Father!" Romilly cried out. "But what's he saying?" She moved closer to the wall, feeling around with her fingers until she found the hole left by the chisel. At her touch, spurts of sand poured out, and she heard a scrabbling friction. It was Robbie, worming and squirming through a passage just wide enough for his body. She felt his crisply feathered head and the smooth beak emerge into her palm, hot as a polished beach stone.

"Holly!" he announced triumphantly.

Her father lurched backward.

"Holly! Holly! Holly!" Robbie repeated gleefully as Romilly grasped his body and tugged him from the wall. He scrabbled up her arm and, in a moment, had tucked his sandy body under the curtain of her hair, croaking once more, but softly in consideration for her nearby ear. "Holly." Romilly couldn't speak for smiling as she stroked the sand from his back. She felt oddly calm. The worlds were coming together—she felt sure of it now. Her touch had assured this.

"Father, I am going to take Robbie outside and give him to Arra and Uncle, who"—she fumbled slightly— "are waiting outside the hut, actually." In the darkness her face felt hot.

"Go to the cottage, daughter, all of you," her father said with surprising calm. "I'll join you as soon as I can."

"Might I at least wait outside the hut, Father?"

"Nay, child. You must be patient with me a bit longer. If you do as I say, I promise I will emerge with—"

He didn't finish. Romilly put her hand out and felt for his upper arm. She stroked it twice, then turned and felt her way out of the passage, toward the light.

ॐ

"This is really entirely too much like labor," Arra grumbled as the three walked slowly back to the cottage, "except if it were the birth of a baby, I'd be attending and not hobbled up in all this suspense." Robbie, after his outbursts in the hut, was uncharacteristically quiet, but it was a gloating, smug silence, Romilly felt. As soon as she reached the door of the hut, Robbie had flown with a long low swoop to her uncle's shoulder, accepting her uncle's playful wagging of his beak with the delight of a puppy. He hunched his back to spar with the affectionate hand, then tossed his head and fluffed his feathers around his neck and breast until they stood up like crisp, soot-black shells. Romilly described how she heard him caw, how he had squirmed his way through the sand-clogged tunnel.

"And he was saying the oddest thing! He kept crying out, *Holly!* quite triumphantly. Do you think this has to do with the beverage you made, Arra, the first one? Could it be that both tonics were necessary?"

"There's no saying," Arra said, smiling at her excitement.

"But whether it's my touch on the sledge that dissolved the stone to sand, or my father's drinking of the infusion, I simply have no idea," Romilly concluded.

"Like as not it's both," her uncle opined, as he scratched the side of Robbie's throat with a forefinger.

"But if it's not, if it was my touch that turned the stone to sand, it's possible that Father will be laboring for some time," Romilly said, sadly. "He wouldn't permit me to stay, nor even to wait outside the hut. He practically made me promise we'd go back to the cottage, the three of us."

"But," her uncle said slyly, "did he say you must go *inside* the cottage?"

Romilly smiled. "No, Uncle, he did not. What are you up to?"

They had neared the front door to the cottage, but her uncle barred her from entering, putting up his palm to stay her. Arra trailed him quizzically inside. In a few moments he returned carrying a chair, which he carried to the edge of the yard, just where the path to the hut began. Romilly retraced her steps and took a seat. From this vantage point, though a few delicate low-hanging branches of young birches intervened, she could see the dark cavity of the hut's doorway clearly. Arra came up alongside her and handed her a mug of tea.

"I found wild chamomile near the well and made a tea that will soothe your nerves," she explained. Romilly accepted it gratefully. She had not realized how exhausted she was from the morning's events. Her knees felt weak, and her eyes longed to close, as if she were a toddler needing a nap. We can be toddlers all our lives, she thought, overwhelmed by the complex and challenging work of growing. Perhaps her father felt this too. She took several sips of the fragrant tea, which tasted of lovely things: green apples, fresh grass, and lemon verbena.

"Drink a little more," Arra urged, "and then you can lean against my side and close your eyes for a while. We'll keep watch, won't we, Felix?"

Romilly obediently drank her tea down, then leaned her head into Arra's warm and comforting side, soothed by the roughened palm stroking along her hair. As she closed her eyes, she wondered a moment at Arra's recent use of her uncle's first name. She had always called him brother, like the rest of the village.

"I will take care of you," Romilly was murmuring. She surfaced from her dream to see Arra smiling down on her. Romilly looked at her hand and realized she was holding on to Arra's pointer finger, as if she were a little girl.

"You were kicking your feet as if you were swimming," Arra said, "and then you reached for my finger."

"How long was I sleeping?" Romilly asked, pressing her fingers to her eyes.

"No more than a quarter of an hour—and probably less," said Arra. "Your uncle's gone to fix us more tea."

"I was having a dream," she said, "but so real, so clear, it was if I had been dropped into another life."

She was back in the woods between her home and Arra's cottage, she explained, looking for the holly tree that had grown from the seedling she had saved. But instead of being a sapling, the holly had grown to enormous size, the trunk the width of a small room—but this would take hundreds and hundreds of years, she remembers thinking. She notices a latch in the trunk, a door of some sort, and she pulls it open and steps onto a floor as clear and cold as ice. Under the ice, she sees a contorted tangle of what look to be bare branches, but she realizes they must be roots. They almost precisely mirror the spreading branches of a tree's rounded canopy. Then she feels the floor softening and dissolving into warm water that she slides beneath, alert but unafraid. She is somehow able to breathe the water in and out, just like air. She dives down under the tangled roots, where, in the very center, she sees a baby, a newborn infant. She realizes the roots are no longer rough and hard, but pliant and pulsing. The baby's thick hair drifts in the water, a dark halo. Its eyes are open, black, and looking right into hers. When she reaches out a forefinger to touch the baby's palm, the infant's fingers instantly wrap around and grasp her finger with surprising strength. A fierce protectiveness fills her, and she thinks, *I will take care of you.*

"So that's what you were saying when you woke up," Arra exclaimed. "It's a good dream, a hopeful dream," she mused, "perhaps even a prophetic dream," she added quietly.

"Why do you say that?" Romilly asked wonderingly. "Do you know what it means?"

"It doesn't matter if *I* know. What do *you* think of the dream?" Arra asked.

"Perhaps it means two worlds are coming together. In the dream I was able to move into another world, another element entirely, without fear. But what did the baby mean? Is that *me?* The holly was my mother's favorite tree—and I was literally inside the holly. Perhaps she is still joined to me somehow, the way the infant was joined to the tree?"

Abruptly she sat up straighter. "Holly! That's what Robbie was saying when he emerged from the wall." Arra narrowed her eyes, then smiled down at her brightly, but without comment. Romilly noticed her ducking a bit to look down the path at the black opening to the hut. She realized that all was quiet.

"I no longer hear the pounding," Romilly said, her heart lurching in her chest.

"Yes," Arra said, and sucked her front teeth. "While you were sleeping the thudding went on, duller than before, more of a digging or scraping sound. But just before you waked, all went silent." Arra plucked out the hairpins from the top of her head and her two braids fell over her shoulders. Leaning her head to the side, pins in her mouth, she raked her fingers through the braids to undo them, then swiftly and neatly re-braided them tight again, crossed them over the top of her head, and pinned them secure. It all took less than a minute, but Romilly knew this meant Arra was thinking through something important.

"What?" she asked her.

Arra pressed her palms together and held their edges to her lips.

"Your father has gone through to meet Digby."

"How do you know?" Romilly asked wonderingly.

"Because in your dream, the floor of ice softened as you entered the other side. And because of the infant."

"What has the infant to do with Digby?"

"The infant is a very profound symbol of beginning. But also, it was Digby who named you when you were born."

"So, the infant *is* me."

"Among things, possibly, yes," Arra replied evasively.

"But why would Digby have named me?"

"Well, it's not so simple as that. Your mother wanted to keep with the tradition of her family and link your name to an ancestor of the female line. Digby believed this ancestor should be Yllimor, because Yllimor was a great healer. He thought this name portended well for your future. Perhaps he suspected even then that great healing would be needed. At any rate, your mother and father agreed."

Romilly looked down the path with a soft gaze. She remembered finding the portrait of Yllimor in her mother's book, with the kestrel on her shoulder, wearing the rose-embroidered white gauntlet. It was really, she thought to herself, that girl who had started this entire journey, remembering the girl's eyes, the complex blue-green-gray of deep water. Her mother's words came back to her: *An artist is a healer. An artist makes whole.* Could not a healer also be an artist of a kind? With sorrow she thought of Digby forsaking his home, unable to heal the chasm opened by her mother's death.

"You can live out your entire life with an unhealed wound," she whispered. Tears brimmed in her eyes, blurring the path.

"Yes, my love. Or," Arra whispered back, "you can have the courage to forgive. Look, my dear. Look in the doorway."

Romilly stood so swiftly, the tears dropped out of her eyes. She saw, in the dark opening, like a white birch lit up in a dark forest, a slim figure. Slowly it drew forward, then rested a palm against the doorjamb. She caught a glimpse of bare, suntanned legs, and, above the white dress—but it was not white, she saw now, but palest yellow, like a rising moon—dark curls held off her face by a wide green ribbon. The girl stepped out of the doorway.

"Arra," she burst out, "who—" Arra held up a hand gently. "Hush—just watch."

The little girl stepped forward and looked over her shoulder expectantly. Emerging into the doorway, a second figure set down a bulging leather satchel and placed on his head the straw hat he was carrying. She could see, despite the shadow of the hat, that his hair was fine, seagull white, and very straight, gathered into a loose queue at the back of his head. He bent to retrieve his satchel and stood a moment, looking down the path uncertainly, then stepped forward next to the girl, who reached for his other hand.

"You should go out to them now," Arra urged gently. Romilly looked at her in wild uncertainty, then stepped forward onto the path. But just then, a streak and flutter passed by her left side, so close she felt the wind of it—it was Mira, flying to Digby and hovering before him, until he set down the satchel. She came to rest on his forearm. His face brightened as if lit from within by a candle. The girl clapped her hands together in delight and leaned toward Mira, evidently murmuring to her. Romilly stood, uncertain the pair had even noticed her yet. Behind her, she heard her uncle's step on the gravel in the yard, then Robbie croaking in brash excitement: *Holly, Holly, Holly!* The girl looked out toward the call, running forward a few steps. But then, as she saw the group of strangers, she instinctively backed close to Digby's side again. And then Robbie launched himself, landing with a flourish a few feet in front of the girl, hunching his back and bobbing his head, evidently urging her forward.

"Look at that," her uncle mused, "a bird coaxing a human!"

And he was. He circled behind her and inserted his beak between her ankles.

"Looks like, if he had a shoulder, he would brace it against her and press her onward. That Robbie!" her uncle exclaimed, gloating on Robbie's behalf.

He had succeeded in dislodging her. She reached for Digby's hand and they slowly advanced, Robbie leading the way, his tail wagging officiously, like the mayor of a village of two.

Arra reached forward and squeezed Romilly's hand.

"Go forward and meet them, my dear."

"Please tell me, Arra, who is this little girl? Why is she here? And where is my father?" Romilly asked, stunned by the sudden fear that perhaps her father had changed places with Digby and would not return.

"He will come out in his own time, my child. He has much to absorb, perhaps even more than you."

She felt the truth of this. She stepped forward toward the pair. Since they had emerged from the doorway, the sky had clouded over; the gentle light through the green leaf canopy

made the girl's dress a buttery hue. She could see that Digby
relied on the girl. Not that he leaned on her, exactly, but that
she reminded him to keep his attention to the path, to watch for
roots and stones, to keep moving one foot after the next. He
was frailer than she had imagined, yet she could see that his face
was less furrowed than her father's. It was peaceful and smooth.
His gaze roved over the scene ahead with open gladness, as of a
traveler who has reached the end of a toilsome journey. When
she was about ten feet from him, he stopped short, removed his
hat by the crown and held it to his breast while he took a deep
and searching look at her face.

"You are so very like your mother," he said, his voice inflect-
ed with a slight accent she had never heard before, the words
emerging as if under some pressure, as if he were overcoming
a stammer. He extended his hand to her and she came forward
to take it, noticing, as she grasped it, traces of ink in the creases
of his knuckles. This close, she could see that his eyes seemed
to look both inward and outward, as if he was simultaneously
watching his memories. There was a dust of auburn whiskers
on his cheeks. His hair, she saw, was not entirely white, but
shaded gradually to a faded, driftwood tan toward the ends.
When he saw her looking at his hair, he mentioned, almost as
an afterthought, "I haven't cut my hair in ten years—since I left
this island." She nodded once.

"I think it's beautiful," she murmured.

"I love it too," said the girl, who leaned into Digby's side
almost protectively.

Romilly looked to the girl, who appeared to be eight or nine
years old. Her eyes, she saw, were such a deep brown you could
barely make out the pupil, almost as dark as Mira's. Her hair,
curly as Romilly's own, could be called black, though Romilly
could see even in the gentle light a dark red hue like that in mahogany wood. Across her nose and cheeks there was a bloom
of coppery freckles. She reached out her hand to the girl, who
touched her fingertips uncertainly, then grasped her hand in a
tight grip.

"So! This, at last, is Romilly. And I, as you know, am Digby. And this," he declared, "is Holly, dear Ingres's child. My god-daughter and—your sister."

"You are the infant!" Romilly gasped. Then, somehow, the child's wiry arms were about her neck, and they dropped to the ground, clinging to each other.

15

DIGBY

Digby led the way into the cottage. Romilly's uncle, as if he had predicted the morning's events down to the last minute, was just setting their tea on the table. He looked up as Digby entered and—as if Digby were in the habit of joining them for lunch—called out to him in simple pleasure.

"Good to see you, old friend." The two men locked eyes and some wordless message of gratitude and deep friendliness passed between them. Then Digby advanced, reaching for her uncle's hand, clasping it, and then grasping his forearm.

"Felix," he said, "your name is apt." Romilly looked questioningly at Arra.

"Felix," she explained, "comes from the root meaning 'happy, lucky, successful.'"

"Though in this case," Digby gently interrupted, "I chiefly mean we are lucky to have *him.*"

As this exchange was happening, Holly, just like Romilly had done when first entering the cottage, was wandering from object to object with avid curiosity. She stopped before the drawing of Romilly's aunt, who, Romilly realized with a start, was Holly's foster mother.

"Look, Digby, look how young and beautiful Aunt is here! Of course, she is *even* more beautiful now," she said, without a trace of shyness. "I have heard so much about this place, I had already pictured it in my mind," she continued, picking up the tiny clay mink that had so captured Romilly's attention when she had first seen it. She held it in the palm of her hand tenderly.

Digby looked at the interior with satisfaction and evident

comfort. Every object, Romilly realized with a start, had its origin in *his* life, was literally made by him and held memories shaped by him and her aunt. And here she had been thinking of this place as an expression of *her*. She was encountering complicated emotions, too, watching Holly rearrange the clay animals. She was a very careful child, so Romilly wasn't afraid she would damage them; but she recognized with a start that watching Holly was like watching herself, as if she had split off from herself. For so long she had been the focus of attention—or object of inattention—but now there was another child in the house. She felt her small world stretch to expand more than she had ever imagined.

A sister. She had been careful never even to allow herself to wish for a friend, and now she had a sister, the way her father had a brother. Her children, if she ever had them, would have an aunt. She stepped up next to Holly in front of the mantel and linked fingers with her. As if Holly had read her mind, she whispered, "You are also just as I pictured you. I knew about you, but you knew nothing about me."

Romilly smiled. "That may be true, but somehow you are also exactly as I always pictured you," she whispered back.

Digby was looking at the broken panes over the embroidered sofa.

"Ah!" he caught his breath softly. "I have the glass in my satchel to repair that window. I will set to that immediately after our tea."

"But how did you know?" Romilly asked, wonderingly.

"Because your aunt, my partner, has been here recently, my dear. She wished to know if the cottage were fit for habitation before she willed it to you. It has been sadly neglected these past years."

"Let us all sit down to lunch, shall we?" her uncle roused them.

Just then, Romilly heard a high, sweet, distant note. She listened intently, trying to determine its source: was it a bird, or wind rubbing two boughs together in the canopy? No—

nothing in nature made that sound. The note came again, lower, richer, quavering like a dove's call. And then it dipped still further, cascading like water into a melody so sweet and mysterious, Romilly thought of moonlit forest glades. She shot a pained, questioning look at the adults around the table. Arra and her uncle sat placidly eating, while Digby, looking down at his plate, simply said, "Ah, good."

Romilly stood abruptly, then rushed out of the cottage to the edge of the yard. Walking up the path slowly, his head and shoulders dappled in sunlight, was her father, his neck cocked and his elbow sweeping the bow smoothly across the strings of a violin. When he caught sight of her, he held her gaze as he stepped forward. His hands, she could tell, were sore and stiff, but he played the tune sweetly all the same, drawing out the ending and allowing the final note to linger until he reached her. He lowered the bow and held the violin carefully to his breast, like a baby.

"Whatever you have to say to me, daughter, I will accept," he finally said, "as you have every right to blame me for the solitude of your life."

"I'm not angry, Father. I am bewildered and lost and—torn between joy and confusion. Everything I thought I knew has shifted. Every time I think I have come to the bottom of your secrets, a trap door opens, and I descend even further. How could I not know that my mother had a child before—" Her throat closed, and she was unable to finish her question.

"Holly was born the morning of your mother's last day. Were it not for Arra, like as not the child would also have died, your mother was so weakened and her breathing so shallow. It was your mother who made me promise to send the infant away—so that she wouldn't sicken, but also, because she knew the townspeople would blame our family for the disease, that there would be no one willing to give their milk to her. I wanted to send you away, too, to protect you. But she knew I would need a purpose. She knew I could not survive without—you." His voice broke. "I meant to bring our child back when she was weaned. Somehow, I lost my way, Romilly, and my grief became almost my entire world. Let's go inside, my dearest. At lunch, I wish us to lay the past plain, finally and forever." He caressed her cheek with the tips of his fingers. "No more secrets."

It would be impossible, with Uncle in fine fettle and Arra similarly jolly, for supper to have been a serious affair. Uncle had made a fish chowder, using the tender inner stalk of cattails in place of potatoes and wild onions as a garnish, which gave the broth a garlicky intensity. He had persuaded Arra, Romilly's father, and Digby to partake of a small measure of spirits, and Digby's nose and cheeks bore spots of pink from the exertion of laughing. Romilly suspected that life had offered him little joy recently.

"I haven't had such a lively supper in recent memory," he said, looking appreciatively at the company. Holly was standing between him and her father, her arm around Digby's neck, her other hand lightly on her father's shoulder. It was a start to overcoming the distance between them.

"I am here," Digby continued, "in part because of my memory. It is beginning—I am not sure I should say 'to fail,' since saying so implies there is nothing of value to the experience. It's beginning to blend times together somewhat. I feel the need to delve down into familiar things, to come back to my happiest moments. I feel I should like to spend my remaining years making art near what is dearest and closest—this land and those who make it a sanctuary."

"You forget that this land also harbors the village folk," Arra broke in with indignation, "who were hateful to you years ago, when you returned here a desperately sick man."

"No, my dear, they were not cruel. They were not hateful. They were terrified, then ashamed of themselves."

"That's true of me," Romilly's father said resolutely. "I watched the villagers pass my house, two by two with pitch torches held high, and I did nothing, when I could have warned you. Instead, I blamed and raged. And Ingres, far from blaming Digby, entrusted her newborn to him."

"Yes, she was deathly afraid that the fever and cough would seize the baby if she remained here," Arra said. "Digby, having survived, was immune. But you, Herald, were not, and what's more, you had spent your every minute by the sickbed."

"Why," Romilly asked, uncertainly, "do I have no memory of my mother's pregnancy?"

"I think you do," Arra replied, "though perhaps not at the conscious level. Remember, child, how you kept seeking seedling hollies? You knew something was missing, that something vulnerable needed to be protected."

"We did not speak of the pregnancy, Romilly," her father added, "because your mother had endured some losses. She desperately wanted more children, but after your birth, she lost two pregnancies—one at five months, and one at sixth months. Her sadness didn't prevent her from wishing for another child. She accepted that life has both beauty and pain. Like the holly itself, whose beauty is balanced by a thorn. Perhaps that's the real reason she gave her infant girl this name."

Romilly had the strange sense of something stopped short, some relationship that never grew. Not only was her one living sister hidden from her, but she could have had two additional siblings. Was this part of the reason her world had seemed so lonely, so diminished? She did not, she realized, feel that torment anymore. This day, a great knot of anger and foreboding seemed to have melted into insignificance.

"It's a great mystery why so many women in the village still have trouble," Arra added somberly, "carrying a child to term."

"Or are unable to conceive a child at all," her uncle said, his face momentarily clouded. His sparkling eyes dimmed in memory. He sat in uncharacteristic silence, adjusting his plate, knife, and fork meticulously, then crossing his forearms on the table. "It's as if some poison ran through our air, or our water, or through our very soil. It's not," he said, "just the great anger of the last ten years, though of course that is most toxic." He paused again, brooding, then burst out, "What if the village folk still blame Digby for the sickness? What will happen when the village learns that not only Digby, but Ingres's and Herald's child, this exquisite Holly—" he reached over and sleeked his hand down her forearm "—have returned?"

"Holly will be treated no differently than Romilly. Though the townspeople have inflicted the silent treatment, which is a disgrace to them, there is no danger that Holly's arrival will cause violence," Arra said stoutly. "Digby is another matter," she continued. "Digby, we will need to introduce you carefully, or else we may see torches again." At this, Holly looked at her godfather, her eyes enormous with worry.

"Will they come again, Digby, and burn our houses down?" she asked.

"Nay, child, nay," Digby murmured. "Most of the folks who burned down our home have moved away or have suffered too much themselves to venture further harm on others. Besides, I don't plan to leave this island." He looked at Romilly entreatingly. "So long as Romilly permits me to stay."

"This home belongs to all of us," Romilly said, rising and circling round to Digby and her father. She clasped her little sister around the waist.

"Well, Felix and I will visit with the greatest enjoyment, but we are going back to the village now that you have a housemate, Romilly. I am the only healer they have, and the villagers need me for general medical care."

"But, Uncle, you said you wished to stay on the island," Romilly said, her consternation visible on her face.

"Well, as regards to that—" said Uncle, a beam of delight restored to his face, "we have another announcement." Arra and he looked to each other smilingly. In the long pause, the rest of the company shot questioning glances at each other. Their confusion turned to joy as they watched Arra place her palm on Uncle's hand.

"We have discovered that our long admiration for each other has deepened into love during our time on this island," Uncle said.

"We wish to be partnered and to join our lives together in the village," Arra continued.

"I keep thinking, 'a partnering, what fun,' and then realizing it will be *my* partnering!" her uncle said, rubbing his palms together.

"And we wish the ceremony to happen here, on the island, in a month's time," Arra continued.

"But what will happen to your house, Arra?" Romilly blurted out, then blushed. "Oh, Uncle, don't think I'm not overjoyed for you, but Arra's house has been my second home!"

"I will keep my own house for my work and consultations and join Felix in the evenings in our shared home, where you, of course, will always be welcome," Arra said, smiling broadly.

"A *partnering*," Digby sighed, contentedly. He lifted the bottle of spirits and poured a few drops into his mug, then passed the bottle to Romilly's father. "May I offer a toast?" he asked. "And a vision?" The company nodded in unison.

"Holly will be the flower-bearer. Romilly will be the ring-bearer. There will be no need of an officiant—Arra and Felix will write and propose their own vows. Herald will be the musician. And I will prepare the invitations. For we must have celebrants. We *will*," he stressed mildly. "The villagers' respect for Arra and Felix will temper their suspicious natures regarding strangers. And we'll revive the Summer Festival just before the ninthmonth solstice begins!"

The evening passed serenely. Romilly's father played the violin in front of the fire, and Holly and Romilly sat close by him. Arra had replaced the bandages made of Romilly's apron strips with proper bandages, and despite his blisters, his fingers moved nimbly over the fingerboard. Tunes seemed to scroll out of his brain, and he played on and on. When his fingertips grew sore from the friction of the strings, he shook them out and blew on them, laughing ruefully. Digby, Arra, and Felix challenged him with requests and assessed each song as a potential dance tune. Arra and Felix stood to dance a few numbers by firelight, their steps still light. As they circled each other, palm to palm, the fire's glow took the past ten years from their faces.

For Romilly, this father who played the violin so beautifully was as much a stranger to her as he was to Holly, yet some part of her remembered. It was as if her uncle's stories of their youth—the festivals, the dances—had come to life. Her father had been as remote and inexpressive as the dusty violin above the cupboard, neglected, no, abandoned. She had felt safe hiding her journal there, sure he would never look. But now his heart had opened and was as expressive as the instrument he held. The delicate pod of wood glowed lustrously rich in the firelight.

Her journal! She would give it to Holly to read. That way, Holly would know everything about her mother that Romilly had been able to glean. Already she knew Holly was quite a reader, for Digby's satchel bulged with the child's favorite books. No, she reflected—they would read it together, starting tomorrow. It would help Romilly draw closer to Holly, binding them together in their family history. Holly was the closest relation she had in the world, the nearest and dearest blood. What if she had never known of her, as if she were one of her mother's lost babes? Her mother probably didn't realize what a risk she'd taken, sending Holly away to save her from starving. But perhaps she did. Perhaps she knew there was a chance her partner might never face his rage at Digby or his grief for her. Might never forgive. But in the end, she had showed great faith that he would bring her three beloveds back together.

With a start, Romilly realized her mother bound father and daughters together through their names. Yes, she must have predicted a great healing. For she was named after one of the great healers in her mother's line. Her father's name, Herald, meant a portent of a future event. Holly's name, binding home and happiness, was the perfect name for her sister. Suddenly the pieces came together: by naming her baby Holly, her mother had combined their names—Herald's and Romilly's—into one.

Just as everyone was beginning to say goodnight, the clouds which had gathered steadily since the afternoon gave a protracted, muttering rumble and they heard a scatter of droplets in the tree canopy. Gradually, the sound intensified, and they noticed a low drumming undernote as the rain pelted the roof.

"Rain!" Arra exclaimed. "The first we've had in all our time here. *That's* what I've been missing. A good drenching rain will do us all much good!"

"Uncle," Romilly perked up, "do you know how many days we've been on the island?" Her uncle lifted the lantern and approached the hearth's dying embers. He scrutinized the stone to the side of the fire.

"It's seven days that I've been here—three for you! I scratched a charcoal mark for each day that passed."

"Doesn't each day seem a year?" Romilly asked, puzzled by the way time sped up or slowed down, as if it were a tune played by some cosmic hand.

"Yes," said Digby, "and yet the years I've been away suddenly seem merely moments!"

Romilly drifted to sleep to the patter of light rain and her sister's quiet breathing. In the morning, hot sun on her face through the window woke her. Holly's pallet was already empty, the blanket bunched up at the foot of it. Romilly's eyes came into focus on the bundle of clothing Holly was using as a pillow, where a long, wavy hair was caught. She pulled it out and stretched it between her fingers. In a shaft of sunlight, it shimmered like the finest violin string. She could see that Holly's hair was not brown like hers, but the deepest imaginable red, a red so rich that it almost appeared black.

The cottage was silent—she had slept late. She sat up, stretched her arms overhead, then looked out the window for

the sun, which had already cleared the tree canopy. It must be
midmorning. The sky was a delicate blue, but she knew that by
midday it would deepen to mussel shell. She leaned upon the
windowsill and looked out over the clearing. The leaves, worn
out and pale just yesterday, had been revived by the rain and
appeared crisp and strong still, a glassy, vibrant green. Perhaps
it had been her own exhaustion that had made them seem so
limp and passive.

Arra was not in the kitchen, but a teapot wrapped in a cloth
waited for her, alongside a huckleberry biscuit and a bowl of
wineberries. She felt the teapot with her hand—still warm—
then noticed a gentle cough. The door to the studio was open
a crack; when she peered in, she saw Digby seated at the worktable, his head bent over a scattering of engravings. Romilly
stole up beside him and looked down at the images: in one,
a fisherman hauled a net bulging with fish over the lip of his
boat. Another page featured three different kinds of swallow-
tail butterflies, the patterns in their wings rendered in exacting
detail.

"Pull up a chair, child. I am considering what images to use
for the collage of Arra and your uncle."

"For the invitation?" Romilly enquired.

"Nay, just as a partnering gift. I've no means here to replicate
such art. Even the invitation shall have to be handwritten. Were
I still *there*, I would have use of my printing press. You have a
fine hand—perhaps you would like to be my scribe?"

"How do you know my hand is fine?"

"Because, dear girl, you provided a specimen in the note you
sent to me, not more than a few days past."

"Of course! But those letters were gigantic. We thought,"
she said, meekly, "that you might be an omnipotent being, then.
We called you the Being Beyond." Digby laughed.

"I would settle for being merely potent. My powers are quite
limited and becoming more so all the time. For the rest of my
time on this earth, I wish simply to make art. To that end, what
images should we join to symbolize the sharing in store for

Arra and your uncle? What seems fitting as the frame—a fish?
A butterfly? Some other animal?"

"Nay, Digby, I think—a tree. Arra is rooted like that, to the
earth. Also, she knows the powers and uses of the plant world
like her own hands. But Uncle, on the other hand, is more of a
sea-being—so I think inside the tree's frame you should place
a sailboat, perhaps *this* one with the full moon rising beyond it.
Yes—the way it was when he first glimpsed you opening our
world."

"It shall be done," Digby said, gravely.

"But—" Romilly, began, then faltered. "May I ask some
questions?"

"Of course. I'll answer anything you ask, if I can. What is it
you wish to know?"

"You don't come from my world, do you? How is it you've
been able to come back and forth?"

"*That* I'm not sure I can answer. I seem to have been part
of two worlds since my earliest memories. I was often severely
beaten in school for telling 'fancies,' the master called them. Or
set in the corner in a dunce's cap. You know, I wrote with my
left hand and often mixed up my letters, getting them backward
and upside down as like as not. For some reason, that, too,
was a terrible crime. After I was forced to write with my right
hand, I ended up with such a stammer, I ceased for some time
to speak at all. My stammer is always much improved in this
world."

"I had thought, well—feared," Romilly went on timidly,
"when I saw you open the horizon over our field, that my world
wasn't real, that the gigantic being I was seeing had made everything I know and set it in motion. That I was just this being's
dream, in effect."

"I haven't made your world any more than you've made
mine, Romilly. When I was exiled from this place, I almost died.
I felt as if my heart had been torn from my chest. If it hadn't
been for my partner, your aunt, I would have despaired, but she
encouraged me to continue to steal back through the passage.

And she would meet me here on the island once a month at the waxing of the full moon, risking Holly's life and her own by sailing across the Sound. Then she would sail me back across the Sound to our home there in the dead of night, so none would see. I was terrified for her—sailing that stretch of sea all by herself. Micah—do you know him?"

Romilly, who listened with held breath, her heart racing at the strangeness of it all, simply nodded, so Digby continued.

"Micah befriended us, though he was no more than ten years old at the time. He helped us. You see, I was petrified your aunt and the child would perish in the crossing—she wasn't an experienced sailor. He arranged with your aunt to sail me across the Sound each time I emerged on the island, so I could spend a few precious days with your aunt and Holly. And then he would come for me and sail me back to this island so I could return through the passage. I would always have to leave before the moon waned three quarters bright, when the passage closed—I have no idea why. That was always the way."

He paused and laid both hands gently atop the image of the ship, which seemed about to sail through the rising moon as through a brilliant tunnel.

"Then, one night about two years back as I was crossing through, I met your father in the passage. He had been watching the comings and goings, you see. He had seen your aunt's boat anchored off the island. He had made a very close inspection of the island, the cottage, the falconer's hut—and had entered the passage to see where it led. When he met me, he was so enraged he reached for my throat—I thought he would choke me then and there, and perhaps he meant to. He accused me of coming to infect you and take you away from him, the way I had done to Ingres. The next time I attempted to cross, the passage was sealed with stones. I didn't have the strength to force my way. Even if I had, how could I? Your father had lost almost everything. If I hoped to see my loved ones and my home again, I would need to find sympathetic witnesses who could persuade your father and soften his heart."

"But how did you know, the night you appeared over the split rock, that you had found—what did you say?—sympathetic witnesses?"

"Well, the night I appeared to your uncle near the full moon, he was night fishing. I recognized his boat. We always saw eye to eye, as it were. As for you, when you sent up the note, I could not mistake the paper. Your mother helped me make it, and we put, you see, some trimmings of your baby hair in it. Did you not notice, when you looked up close, some small auburn fibers? We named that paper 'Romilly,' after you. And in addition, Robbie, whom I had sent into your world, would not stop crying, *Yllimor, Yllimor, Yllimor*, when he returned to me through the flap. Who else could you be? And who had a better chance of teaching Herald to forgive? My greatest fear has been that *you* would not forgive me for your mother's death. And yet, as soon as you sent the note, my fear melted away."

Romilly leaned in and kissed his cheek.

"Kisses too?" Digby said under his breath, his face pinkening with emotion.

"Digby, do you know of the cellar here, where I found the stone mason's tools?"

"Of course, child."

"There was a label of gold-colored paper affixed to the box of tools, a label that read *Worldwidening*. On the reverse were instructions to dissolve the paper and drink the solution if you want to widen worlds. Did you make that paper? Did you put it there? Do you know what was in it?"

"Ah. Yes, that is one of my favorite papers, made on a whim. I did put it there—it was one of a few intuitive steps I took before I was forced to leave the island, hoping it would find sympathy. Did you notice, when it dissolved, how the ink was suspended on the surface of the water, like little island-letters?"

Romilly nodded vigorously. "Yes! The letters spelled out *girl.*"

"Ah! Did they now," Digby exclaimed, then chuckled in pleasure. "Then the plan worked better than ever I hoped."

"Is the paper magic?" Romilly breathed.

"Of course, child. But the whole world is magic."

"Be serious, Digby! Can you tell me what the paper was made of?" Romilly tried to keep the note of pleading out of her voice, but failed.

"Child. That paper had two very secret and rare ingredients called hope and love. The rest of it was made of nothing but the very finest sugar—and, of course, some gelatin to hold it all together."

Romilly frowned in concentration. "We thought the dust of the floor was the magic. That the paper was made of this dust. That the magic had gotten into *me*. But you're saying that the paper is not what softened the wall."

"No, my love. But you *are* part of the magic. Love and hope—and sympathy—have the power to soften and transform. Evidently, when Micah could no longer bear the stares and coldness of the townsfolks, he would stay a few days at a time at the cottage. When your father sealed the wall, the lad Micah observed him at work, trundling barrows of stone into the hut. As I told you, Micah was in the know. Perhaps one day he'll tell you how he caught me emerging from the passage the first time, years ago—I can tell you, it was all I could do to persuade him not to use it himself, so shunned and lonely did he feel. He wished to—to begin again, though that sounds redundant. I knew his despair. But back to the story at hand. As soon as your father left the island, Micah went into the hut and dug out the still soft mortar and replaced the inner layer of stones with beach sand. Your father would return every few months to check the wall and add a layer of stone. But Micah was watching for him. Each time, the lad would undo your father's work, preserving just a veneer of stones. That is why your father's chisel sank into the wall like that. Once your father breached the exterior layer, the way, of course, was easy."

"I thought the wall had turned to sand at my touch," Romilly said, ducking her head. Her eyes were filling, making Digby's stout walking boots swell larger and larger, magnified through her tears. Digby reached out gently and lifted her chin.

"Romilly, in every way that matters, that's exactly what happened. Don't be ashamed of magical thinking. As I said, nearly everything in the world is magic." He raised her apron and carefully blotted the inner corners of her eyes. "You aren't going to drown my butterflies, are you?" he chided gently. Romilly smiled at him and reached a finger to trace the scalloping outline of the insect, its lower wing extending into the white sea of paper like a narrow black peninsula.

"Digby, if you stay here forever now, will you teach me to make art too? To be an artist?"

"Child, no need—you already are. We are just not sure of your medium. You could turn out, in fact, to be a poet or a healer. You bring to mind John Keats, who once wrote 'a poet is a sage, a humanist, a healer to mankind.'"

"A humanist," Romilly breathed. That, she thought, would be a fine thing to be.

"It will be a great joy to acquaint you with his work. My dear, you'll discover your path—you just need to *be*."

A cry of excitement shifted the mood of the room. Holly was dancing and leaping outside the tall windows, beckoning with hand gestures, her dress plastered along her body as if she had just emerged from the water. Her face was lit up with joy.

Romilly kissed Digby again on his cheek by way of parting and pushed up the window sash.

"We were bailing rainwater out of the *Ingres* and— Oh, you must come quickly, you must see how beautiful—" Holly grasped her hands and tried to tug her out the window.

Romilly laughed as she struggled to disentangle her hands.

"Wait, Holly, wait! We cannot just abandon Digby here—he must see this wonder too!" But Digby, still seated at his table, waved them on.

"I think I know what the wonder is—run along! I will make my way to the overlook presently," he said, settling his straw hat atop his flaxen hair.

Holly met Romilly at the door and yanked her along the flagstones, gripping her fingers so fiercely they ached. Finally, Romilly freed herself and they skipped along the path, past the falconer's hut, unbalancing the startled Mira who had been preening her feathers sedately in the sunshine. At the lookout, they rushed to the edge and gazed out over the water.

Her uncle and Arra were at the water's edge, seated on a flat-topped boulder, while her father was standing on the deck of the *Ingres*, one arm encircling the mast, the bailer still held in his other hand. Rounding the island was a familiar boat, the color of marigolds. A boy with a wreath of dark curls sat at the tiller, playing out the rope to slacken the mainsail as they entered the channel. Romilly made out a slim figure in a white dress, one arm around the mast, waving a scarlet headscarf with her other hand. Her hair streamed out behind like a rippling silver and auburn cape.

"It's Aunt," Holly cried, then scampered down the steep path to the shore. Romilly watched Micah uncleat the main-sail rope completely so that the canvas luffed passively in the wind. The sail curled around the stately form of her aunt, then lowered obediently into a pillowy mound at her feet. The boat glided toward the *Ingres* until the bows almost kissed, then the boats came alongside each other. Romilly's father reached for her aunt, and they clasped hands. Then they raised them high in greeting first to Arra, Felix, and Holly on the shore, and then to Romilly, and last, to Digby, who just then came around the front of the stone bench and stood there at Romilly's side, doffing his hat to his beloved.

16

MICAH

Romilly and Holly took a seat in the dory—Holly in the bow, Romilly in the stern—and Micah gave a great heave to set the small craft afloat. Coarse sand scrubbed the underside of the boat. Then there was silence and a sensation of being loosed from gravity. He walked the boat out into knee-deep water, then deftly stepped in. The craft barely rocked as he poled them out deeper with a single oar, then settled down on the seat. He threaded the oarlocks into position and began to row with leisurely strokes toward a gap in the low branches between two massive pines, where the path back to the village began. It was early morning and the water lay flat calm and brimming.

Holly held a fine mesh net in one hand and a tin pail on her lap—her constant companions these past days. She was absentmindedly singing the chorus of a song over and over, timing her notes to Micah's strokes, the low notes accompanying the crisp lapping of the water against the boat's sides, and the high notes surging with each pulse of forward movement. *Gypsy rover came over the hill, and down the valley so shady, He whistled and he sang till the green woods rang, and he won the heart of a lady...* Whenever she saw the water dimple, she dipped the net into the water and raised it expectantly, pausing her song to scan the fine netting for hatchling fry. Micah absently began to whistle her tune under his breath as he rowed, occasionally looking over his shoulder to make sure the bow was pointing in the right direction. They were rowing toward the path on the far shore, where Micah had stood to watch Romilly and her uncle send the gigantic note spiraling through the sky and out the great flap of the heavens.

Although much she had initially believed to be magic had been rationally explained, Romilly still could not understand that moment, mysterious as death or birth, when the moon seemed to fall toward them, when its light went out and the stars surged in brightness. She had thought then that Digby was an omnipotent being, an enormity. Perhaps, in fact, we are all enormities, she thought, watching Holly dip the net to release a tiny, large-eyed hatchling into her pail. She felt suddenly the largeness of her heart. She would live in a way that embodied this largeness. She would cease living as some sort of shadow on the village's conscience. She refused to participate in the vanishing of herself.

They had been sent on a mission to deliver the partnering invitations to the townsfolk. Romilly held them safely on her lap in Digby's leather valise. Her uncle had fitted it with straps so that Micah could wear it like a rucksack during the five-mile walk into the village.

Whom they should send as ambassadors had been the subject of a vigorous familial debate. At first, Arra thought she and Uncle should be the ones to deliver the news together—after all, they were the ones who had resolutely insisted on carrying on their public life and social connections after Ingres's death and Digby's exile. Romilly recalled her uncle's habitually cheerful greetings to each and all whenever she accompanied him to the fishmonger in the market, where he sold his catch. He had refused to submit to the shunning of the townsfolk, unlike her father, who had seemed to shrink into himself. What strength her uncle had showed. Over time her uncle had prevailed with a few of them, such as the harbormaster and two or three of the older fishermen who had known her family in the bygone days. But even they associated with him somewhat furtively— except for the harbormaster, whom Micah knew well, having lived with him since childhood. It was her aunt's idea to solicit the harbormaster's help—he acted for the village as the general postmaster.

"Nay," Digby had said. "Send the children. Partnerings are

symbols of hope and beginnings, and children are too. And if the townspeople see the bond between Romilly and her new-found sister, between Micah and these two girls whose lives were also drastically altered by anger and fear, they will think of their children and all they hope for them. Send the children." He had helped them write a succinct script: Digby was back and planned to live out his final years on the island; he had returned Holly, Ingres's child, to Herald and Romilly; Felix and Arra planned to partner in ninthmonth; there would be a festival on the island as in the olden times, and all were welcome.

"But what if no one comes?" Romilly had asked, twisting her fingers anxiously.

"Well," said Digby, "so be it!"

"Yes," said Arra stoutly, "so be it! We don't need the village to create a festival. We can have a festival of—" Arra counted noses "—seven." She blinked a moment. "Seven! Imagine seven folks together at the same time under the same roof! That's practically a city!" They all laughed roundly at that, and their plotting and planning turned into a lively debate over what to name their city.

She gazed at Micah. The past few days had melted away the awkwardness she had felt around him. Now it seemed as if she had always known him. She realized that the strangeness had mostly been the inexplicable certainty that he—somehow, some day—would become an intimate part of her life. As he turned to look over his shoulder at the shoreline, she observed a vein in his tanned throat pulsing, and the edge of a scar, the silvery, pink-tinged white of rose quartz. She was considering what animal best represented his spirit, but she couldn't think of anything warm, rounded, and steady enough. He could be a horse, she supposed, but he had a sort of otherworldly quality about him as well, as if he lived in some other element than the earth and air. He could be a whale, but that seemed too large. He wasn't quite lively and gregarious enough to be a seal, but he could, she reflected, be a sort of self-possessed, reliable dolphin. She was so engrossed in her thoughts, she didn't notice that he had turned back around and was now watching her face, his eyes lit by a slight sparkle, a smile curling his lip.

"Why are you staring at me, Romilly?" he asked. Her eyes came into focus on his face.

"I was sort of looking into you, not at you. I was trying to decide what animal you would be—what reflects your spirit."

"Maybe I'm not an animal at all—maybe I'm a tree."

"No, you wander too much for that. I think you are a sort of wise dolphin."

"I like that. I've always loved to watch dolphins—and they often come up out of the water and smile at me, as if they want to say something."

Holly, who was listening, broke in. "Micah is a rock, actually. A thin layer-y one, such as they used to make windows with." Romilly and Micah began to laugh at this. Holly was hurt. "It's true—Digby said so. He taught me the rocks."

"Mica, the mineral, is spelled differently," Romilly explained, "though indeed it sounds the same."

"Perhaps she's right, though, Romilly. Arra would attest that I shed many layers as a child."

"Then you're a snake that sheds its skin," Holly burst out.

"I am just Micah, just a human," he retorted peaceably. Romilly lifted her chin to smile at him. She had the sudden feeling that happiness was a small boat—when you managed to balance your blessings and your sufferings, you experienced a sudden sense of grace and lightness. A movement caught her eye, just beyond the bow—two pewter-bright, lithe forms were cutting through the water, weaving together and apart, their pale sides flashing as their bodies tilted and arced.

"Look!" she barely had time to cry before she heard Holly's laugh of delight. The dolphins had joined together at the bow. Raising their smiling faces, they clicked and squealed at Holly, before submerging to circle the dory. Micah, who had stopped rowing and whose eyes were lit with a soft smile, gently dipped the oars in and began to row dreamily toward shore while the dolphins wreathed them, arcing and diving, sometimes surfacing at the bow to whistle and chirp at Holly, as if they wished to gently shepherd and nudge the boat forward. Romilly remembered the grim sail to the island, what seemed like eons ago, when the dolphin rode the bow wave and turned its knowing, kind, delighted eye to her as if urging her forward. The girl who watched that dolphin seemed entirely different from the one who faced the difficult task before them now. Not different—it was as if she had found room to grow into the human being she had been meant, all along, to be. Micah was smiling at her—why, around him, did she feel this immense delight in the present moment, this confidence that whatever courage or strength she needed was already within her?

"Yes, Micah," she said, her heart swelling, "you are most definitely a dolphin!"

ACKNOWLEDGMENTS

Most of my poems begin after an encounter with an image. This is true of my novel *The Collagist* as well. This novel began when I visited the artist John Digby and saw his collages firsthand. Profoundly conservationist, Digby's collages bring together and preserve nineteenth century engraved images of butterflies, birds, and landscapes. I spent three days in his personal archive examining nearly every collage Digby ever made during his long career, much of it unframed and stored in flat files. I was drawn into these sheltered and private realms that united the animal and the human, the tiny and the enormous, and which made me feel like a giant spying benignly into another world. I wrote an essay about John's work, published it, yet still these images haunted me in the best possible way. During the pandemic lockdown, when we all seemed sealed inside our solitary worlds, I found myself imagining what sort of girl might live in a Digby collage; moreover, I began imagining her befriending the collagist, and the image of a cottage on an island coalesced in my mind. I sat down at my desk—my own little island—and started to write, unsure where the story was going but delighted with each day's discoveries. I owe an enormous debt of gratitude to John Digby, who passed away in the fall of 2022. When the creations of a fellow artist unfailingly unlock the wellspring of our own making, I count this a gift from the universe. John Digby's collage work has always opened worlds for me. I would like to publicly express my deep gratitude to John and Joan Digby for generously allowing me access to John's personal archive, welcoming me into their home, and supporting my work in every way imaginable.

A second source is the place I call home. A place can be a first love. This story attempts to capture and pay homage to the shorelines of my childhood, to the birds, fish, boulders, beaches, tides, trees, and native plants of the Poquetanuck cove estuary and the greater Long Island Sound, where I grew up crabbing, clamming, boating, and mucking about with nets. Many of my characters are influenced by the elders of my childhood (like Romilly's father and uncle, my paternal grandfather was one of nine children) who lived on and farmed the land around my home. This novel preserves many fragments of story gleaned from my family's own "bygone days."

I'm grateful to my family, who invisibly populate this story. To my sisters, Julia and Liza, the manuscript's earliest readers and first champions, and to my brother Steve for being my muck-about partner on the Cove. We were, in many ways, a village of four, growing up. To my father, Art Holmberg, my biological and botanical fact-checker; always, for all of us, you have been a sun-warmed boulder to lean against, and the joyful father-figure Felix has his origin in you. To my daughters, Ava and Lily Minu-Sepehr: you have been my greatest gift, and my passionate hope for you is that you will remain open-hearted in this wonder and wounder of a world. And to Aria Minu-Sepehr, their father, who taught me so many dimensions of the human heart.

To Jaynie Royal and the Fitzroy Books community, profuse thanks for shepherding this book and this newborn fiction writer through the unfamiliar terrain of novel publishing. You are the model of the kind of community-making that editors and publishers can foster.